Praise for The Witch's Coin

"Essential reading if you want to be ⎯⎯⎯⎯⎯⎯⎯ in every area of your life. A comprehensive, engaging, and helpful book, full of valuable insights and helpful advice … Quite simply, the best book available on prosperity magic."

—Richard Webster, author of *Success Secrets*

"Most important of all, the magic worker learns here how to begin the process from within, for this is the true source of magic."

—Ann Moura, author of the Green Magic series

"Penczak at his best! Christopher clearly outlines the steps you need—spiritual, magical, and mundane—to uncover your inner potential for real prosperity."

—M. R. Sellars, author of the Rowan Gant Investigation series

Praise for The Witch's Shield, *the first book in the series*

"This is a wise, helpful book for beginners and intermediate students of the craft."

—*Publishers Weekly*

"An ethical guide to using spiritual enlightenment even in difficult or threatening situations. Packed with insights on the nature of good and evil."

—*Midwest Book Review*

"A thorough, well-written, exceptionally astute book on psychic hygiene and self-defense."

—*NewWitch*

WITCH'S THE COIN

ABOUT THE AUTHOR

Christopher Penczak is an award-winning author, teacher, and healing practitioner. Beginning his spiritual journey in the tradition of modern witchcraft and Earth-based religions, he has studied extensively with witches, mystics, shamans, and healers in a variety of traditions from across the globe to synthesize his own practice of magick and healing. He is an ordained minister, herbalist, flower-essence consultant, and certified Reiki Master (Teacher) in the Usui-Tibetan and Shamballa traditions. Christopher has been involved with the Gifts of Grace Foundation and is a faculty member of the North Eastern Institute of Whole Health, both in New Hampshire. He is the author of many books, including *Ascension Magick*, *Magick of Reiki*, *Spirit Allies*, *The Mystic Foundation*, *Instant Magick*, and *The Inner Temple of Witchcraft*. Christopher is also a co-founder of the Temple of Witchcraft tradition and religious organization. For more information, visit www.christopherpenczak.com.

CHRISTOPHER PENCZAK

WITCH'S THE

COIN

PROSPERITY AND MONEY MAGICK

Llewellyn Publications

Woodbury, Minnesota

First Edition
Second Printing, 2010

Book design and format by Donna Burch
Cover design by Kevin R. Brown
Interior illustrations by the Llewellyn Art department
Llewellyn is a registered trademark of Llewellyn Worldwide, Ltd.

Tarot cards from the *Universal Tarot* by Roberto de Angelis © 2000 by Lo Scarabeo and reprinted with permission from Lo Scarabeo

Chart wheel on page 105 was produced by the Kepler program by permission of Cosmic Patterns Software, Inc. (www.AstroSoftware.com)

Library of Congress Cataloging-in-Publication Data
Penczak, Christopher.
  The witch's coin : prosperity and money magick / Christopher Penczak.—1st ed.
    p. cm.
  Includes bibliographical references and index.
  ISBN 978-0-7387-1587-2
  1. Finance, Personal—Miscellanea. 2. Magic. I. Title.
  BF1623.F55P46 2009
  133.4'3—dc22
                                                                      2009022784

Llewellyn Worldwide does not participate in, endorse, or have any authority or responsibility concerning private business transactions between our authors and the public.

All mail addressed to the author is forwarded but the publisher cannot, unless specifically instructed by the author, give out an address or phone number.

Any Internet references contained in this work are current at publication time, but the publisher cannot guarantee that a specific location will continue to be maintained. Please refer to the publisher's website for links to authors' websites and other sources.

The author and publisher of this book are not responsible in any manner whatsoever for any injury that may occur through following the instructions contained herein. The herbal combinations in this book are not recommended as a substitute for proper medical care, and they are not for commercial use or profit. New herbal recipes should always be taken in small amounts to allow the body to adjust and to test for possible allergic reactions.

Llewellyn Publications
A Division of Llewellyn Worldwide, Ltd.
2143 Woodale Drive, Dept. 978-0-7387-1587-2
Woodbury, Minnesota 55125-2989, U.S.A.
www.llewellyn.com

Printed in the United States of America

OTHER BOOKS BY CHRISTOPHER PENCZAK

City Magick: Urban Rituals, Spells and Shamanism
(Samuel Weiser, 2001)

Spirit Allies: Meet Your Team from the Other Side
(Samuel Weiser, 2002)

The Inner Temple of Witchcraft: Magick, Meditation and Psychic Development
(Llewellyn Publications, 2002)

The Inner Temple of Witchcraft Meditation CD Companion
(Llewellyn Publications, 2002)

Gay Witchcraft: Empowering the Tribe
(Samuel Weiser, 2003)

The Outer Temple of Witchcraft: Circles, Spells and Rituals
(Llewellyn Publications, 2004)

The Outer Temple of Witchcraft Meditation CD Companion
(Llewellyn Publications, 2004)

The Witch's Shield
(Llewellyn Publications, 2004)

Magick of Reiki
(Llewellyn Publications, 2004)

Sons of the Goddess
(Llewellyn Publications, 2005)

The Temple of Shamanic Witchcraft: Shadows, Spirits and the Healing Journey
(Llewellyn Publications, 2005)

The Temple of Shamanic Witchcraft Meditation CD Companion
(Llewellyn Publications, 2005)

Instant Magick
(Llewellyn Publications, 2005)

The Mystic Foundation
(Llewellyn Publications, 2006)

Ascension Magick
(Llewellyn Publications, 2007)

The Temple of High Witchcraft: Ceremonies, Spheres and the Witches' Qabalah
(Llewellyn Publications, 2007)

The Temple of High Witchcraft Meditation CD Companion
(Llewellyn Publications, 2007)

The Living Temple of Witchcraft, Volume One: The Descent of the Goddess
(Llewellyn Publications, 2008)

The Living Temple of Witchcraft, Volume One, Meditation CD Companion
(Llewellyn Publications, 2008)

The Living Temple of Witchcraft, Volume Two: The Journey of the God
(Llewellyn Publications, 2009)

The Living Temple of Witchcraft, Volume Two, Meditation CD Companion
(Llewellyn Publications, 2009)

FORTHCOMING RELEASES BY CHRISTOPHER PENCZAK

The Witch's Heart
The Key to the Temple of Witchcraft

CONTENTS

LIST OF TABLES AND FIGURES

Tables

Figures

LIST OF EXERCISES

A special thanks to all the people who shared their ideas, philosophies, spells, and feedback with me, including Carla Ingeborg, Adam Sartwell, Steve Kenson, Rosalie and Ronald Penczak, Leandra Walker, Alixaendreia, Bonnie Kraft, Lisa Dubbels, Patricia Monaghan, Judika Illes, Trish Telesco, and Dorothy Morrison.

INTRODUCTION

In today's busy world, most of us are focused on how we earn a living, to pay our expenses and survive in the day-to-day world. When I look around, I see many of my friends and family members locked into a cycle of working to live, confronted with the next big financial hurdle, rather than living to work and truly enjoying every moment of their day. Work is something to endure in order to get enough money to enjoy life on the weekends and nights off. But the proportion of work to the time we have off to enjoy what we've earned is out of balance, and even when we do have time off, we spend it recovering from the exhaustion of work. Because of this imbalance, everybody is looking for the magick secret to getting rich quick with little or no effort. So many of us believe that the get-rich-quick scheme—like the legendary Fountain of Youth or the lost city of Shangri-La—is a reality, even though we have very little evidence of it. Still, we each believe we could be the one to find it.

When you make yourself publicly known as a witch, people will think you know the secrets to everything. They will think back on fairytale fables and myths, of turning lead into gold, granting wishes, and using crystal balls, and they will immediately ask you for some winning lottery numbers. If anybody has the secret to getting rich, it must be the witches.

If it were really that easy, most witches would have won the lottery by now. Although I know a few who can boast some successful lottery magick, as a people, we are not known for our lottery winnings. Traditionally, witches are said to know how to conjure spirits who know where treasure is buried, or simply to divine where riches are hidden. As with the lottery, I don't know many witches who have dug up treasure chests, so perhaps these ideas have a metaphoric meaning for us today.

As witches, we are known for understanding the cycles of the Earth, and the manifestations of energy in the physical world. All the things we value—from modern paper money to precious metals, gems, and even cattle, grain, and produce—stem from the same life force of the Earth interacting with the heavens. If we know how to bend and shape the flow of the life force with our magick, then our magick should also include the ability to manifest prosperity. Most importantly, if our wisdom is based on the cycles and seasons, then we know about the flow of prosperity, of resources, in and out, and can be prepared to move with those flows rather than against them. But it takes a special witch to apply these magickal principles to everyday life. In seeking to separate ourselves from the rat race of modern society, we dissociate our spiritual traditions from our work and money, but these are actually some of the most important areas in which to apply our spirituality.

You might expect a witch who is writing a book on "money magick" to be rich. In fact, you might even require it! If so, it's my duty to inform you that I am not a multimillionaire, or even a millionaire. Despite having several successful metaphysical books, I do not have the material wealth that some would suspect. Witchcraft books and classes have a very limited audience when compared to mainstream literature. Yet, I am rich. I am lacking nothing that I want, materially or otherwise.

If I truly want something, I have the resources to get it. I have a job and schedule I love, with time to work and the flexibility for myself and my family. I have a purpose and feel strongly about my purpose. I do work a lot, but it is work I enjoy. I am secure in my life financially, but more importantly I see the security as coming from divinity and my magickal relationship with divinity. To me, those qualities are riches. I am prosperous on any level I could desire, and I know my prosperity is growing and flourishing as I continue my path. Do I want to be a millionaire? If it serves my purpose to go on to the next step of my life's adventure, yes, but I know a specific dollar amount does not bring happiness or satisfaction. Despite my bank account being of normal size, I feel confident in sharing with you the magickal wisdom of how you can be "rich" too, at many different levels.

The Witch's Coin is a manual for the practical application of the witch's wisdom to how we earn, use, and even think about money. It looks beyond the first desire to accumulate money and toward the underlying patterns we have regarding resources, prosperity, and success. Through our magickal principles, we can tap into the "secret" and "hidden" resources within and around us, to manifest the life we desire, in balance and harmony. We can step out of the high-pressure race to succeed and define our own quest for success, enjoying every step, every adventure along the way. That is the power of prosperity.

CHAPTER 1

THE SECRET OF
TRUE PROSPERITY

Historically, witches are generally not associated with wealth, but with the rural poor. Yet the wise ones and cunning folk who knew the ways of magick didn't seem to be wanting for anything, because they did know a secret. Many modern witches and pagans today seem to be emulating the poor aspects of our spiritual ancestors, rural or otherwise, but lack the same satisfaction, living in a culture that promotes the get-rich rat race all around them. Life is not as simple as it was in the time before modern industrialization and worldwide telecommunication. While the old ways of witchcraft do work, these are not the old times from which they sprang; we have to try to draw upon the wisdom of the old ways as we find new ways to apply them.

In the old ways, the true wisdom was from life satisfaction. Prosperity is quite literally the growing of the green and gold crops in the land. If you had enough to eat, a roof over your head, and a sense of purpose in life—a vocation—then you had everything you could possibly need. Life is hard, and to a certain extent hard work is expected. Yet the agrarian life also has a time of rest, a time to be fallow (like the land), and a time to relax, unwind, and enjoy. A pagan blessing on this topic comes in the form of four letter *F*s, FFFF, standing for Flags, Flax, Fodder, and Frigg. These four "necessities" stood for everything you could need.

Flags are not pieces of cloth, but the flagstones used to build a good foundation for your home, so that you have a roof over your head. Flags represent a solid home, sturdy in the winter and able to protect you and shelter you from all inclement weather. *Flax* stands for flaxen thread, and specifically for good, comfortable clothes. *Fodder* is exactly what it sounds like—food. Traditionally it was food both for the family and for the animals you raised. Lastly, *Frigg* is named for the northern goddess Frigg, also known as Frigga, who is found in the Norse pantheon. She is the goddess of the home, wife to Odin, and also a goddess popularly thought to share associations with Freya, a goddess of sexuality and the fertility of the land. In this fourfold blessing, Frigg generally means good love, sex, and a happy home.

When you think about it, what more do you need to be happy? The wisdom of the old ways was in satisfying those basic desires. They still hold true today. All we really need to be successful is to have the resources to have a nice home, good clothes, good food, and a happy home. Yet the modern standards we've created for these four benchmarks have grown beyond our reasonable means of fulfillment. In many ways, we are like a swarm of insects devouring everything in our path. But eventually, a devouring caterpillar has to become a butterfly, at which point the whole cycle of consumption is broken and a new perspective can be found.

The wisdom of witchcraft does have a secret regarding prosperity. The secret is in living with satisfaction in your life. We know that you can have anything you want if you are clear in your intention and have sufficient power. The more you do magick, the clearer your intentions become, and you get to the true roots of what you want, of what makes you happy, healthy, and vibrant. You begin to distinguish between what you really want, what your soul wants, and what you think you want because society tells you that you want it. Those who continue to consume, seemingly getting what they want, yet not being happy with it, aren't truly getting what they want. They are satisfying momentary wants, not the true desire of the soul.

Those who live in accord with their soul can have use of anything. It is said that "an initiate owns nothing, yet has use of everything." The British author and occultist Dion Fortune popularized this timeless teaching. It simply means that an initiate of the mysteries knows that all possessions are transitory. They are simply tangible manifestations of energy on the physical plane. Those who know the mysteries of the great ages know how to manipulate energy to create whatever they need, recognizing that those manifestations are finite and not the ultimate goal. Resources are just a means to an end. What do you want to do with them? If initiates are not attached to some material possession, and do not feel they "need" it, they can have anything, and use anything they want.

Just because society sets a standard and you desire it, there is nothing evil or wrong with that desire, as long as you are clear and unattached in that desire. New cars, big homes, vacations, and big investments are not good or bad by themselves. Strangely, we have one of the few religions that theologically doesn't have any problem with money or material goods. Most witches believe in the sacredness of the physical world, where all things are sacred. Pleasure in the body, in the home, through sensuality and luxury are wonderful things, and considered sacred. If you want to put the energy into any goal, you can make it happen, as long as it's aligned with your will, your purpose in life. The secret is the paradox of simultaneously being focused on your goal, putting all the necessary energy into manifesting it, but not being attached to the outcome. It's the mix of will and surrender.

Strangely, though, we don't always truly know our will, even as witches. While other religions renounce the material world theologically, they often gather the most riches and worldly power. While we don't shun the benefits and powers of the material world, as a re-emerging tradition, we have to readjust our understanding of the world and all that it has to offer. While we seek out the spiritual mysteries, we also have to understand that mastering the material world, the physical life, is part of the mysteries.

As a witch, I learned that the secret to a happy life is balance. We don't seek out riches just for the sake of having riches. There is no point to accumulating wealth with no intention regarding its use. On the opposite side, we don't seek to renounce the world and take vows of poverty. Poverty is unnecessary, unless you have a desire to be poor. Happiness is somewhere in the middle, where we have what we need and want, but don't become consumed with quests on either extreme.

Witches look for the end result of their magick. What do you really want? Many people hear about the power of magick and think they would do magick to win the lottery, to get lots of money. But why? Why do they want the money? Many people do money spells, but they really don't want money, they want something specific. When people come to me wanting to manifest money, we talk about what the goal is behind the quest for money. They often want money for a vacation, for a new car, or for a new home. When we get beyond the material possessions, the constant theme is that they want money to be secure. They don't want to worry about money, to worry about a job and all the problems that come with a job. They want the freedom to pursue the things that make them happy. They want the freedom to do whatever they want, whenever they want. Don't we all?

The magickal initiate knows that you have that freedom already. We all do. We might have self-imposed responsibilities, but if they are self-imposed, we can remove them. I can hear what you are thinking already: *It's not that easy. I have to pay my bills. I have to support my kids. I have to put gas in my car. I have to, I have to, I have to ...* And yes, if you signed up for those responsibilities, perhaps you do. Yet, if you created the responsibilities, or agreed to them in some fashion, you can create a way to fulfill them in a manner where you are both secure and free. Or you can release them and find a new set of responsibilities more appropriate to you. It all depends on where you find the source of your security and freedom. Many people all over the world lead wonderful, magickal lives of freedom and security while paying their bills, support-

Figure 1: Imagery from the Devil Card

ing their kids, and putting gas in their car. They simply know the secret of true prosperity.

In the major arcana of the tarot, a pictorial form of the mysteries that pertains to all religions and traditions, one card sums up this mystery: the Devil. Like our worldly responsibilities, the Devil scares us. Although many believe him to be a personification of evil, in the tarot he represents a wise lesson. Although you might be afraid of the image, witches have a saying: "Where there is fear, there is power." When we look at what we are afraid of, we can unlock great resources of strength.

In the traditional forms of the Devil card, such as those in the Rider-Waite deck, you will find the fearsome Devil, horned and monstrous, sitting on a pillar with two slave figures chained to it, one male and one female (fig. 1). He holds fire over them and makes strange and frightening signs, keeping the two figures captive. Or does he? The Devil's lesson is twofold, but you only see one side of its message when you are stuck thinking you "have to" do anything. What seems like a monstrous tormentor at first is shown to later be nothing of the kind. He is not holding the chains. The chains themselves are in wide loops, like dangling necklaces, around the two enslaved figures. They could take them off at any time, if they so choose. The light the Devil holds shows them the way out. The gesture he makes is the same one as the Hierophant, the religious teacher found in an earlier card. The pillar he resides on, to which the figures are chained, is the double cubic altar of the macrocosm (the heavens) and the microcosm (the Earth). Although the chains are tied to the upper cube of the macrocosm, in this context the inverted pentagram above the Devil's head doesn't mean Satanism as popularly thought. It actually represents the rulership of the material four points of the microcosm—earth, air, fire, and water—over spirit, rather than spirit and the macrocosm of the heavens ruling and guiding the powers of the world. The natural order is inverted, and if you do not choose to make it upright, you will be forever bound.

Most people look at the card and figure that they are one of the two figures bound by the Devil. A witch or magician looks at the Devil card and knows that we are the ones who are free, holding the torch. To embrace the Devil card is to know that you are like the black sheep of the family. You are the stubborn and rebellious goat, going against the grain, but staying true to your own heart and will. Astrologically, this card is ruled by the zodiac sign of Capricorn, meaning that it shares its energy and attributes with Capricorn. Capricorn is a very responsible sign, executing its duties and obligations for the self and for others. The highest manifestation of Capricorn is being in a position of leadership and authority, acting as a pioneer or trailblazer for others, and ultimately getting to do the work your way. The authority of the Devil comes from spirit. The Devil teaches us how to work with the experience of the inverted pentagram, for he has already reversed it. His connection is to the deepest levels of spirit, and through this connection he is free and has true purpose.

Those who don't understand that their ultimate security and freedom comes from their spiritual connection to the ever-abundant universe are those who live outside of balance. They seek to find their security and freedom in the material world. They seek to amass and hoard wealth. They seek to gorge themselves on whatever is available, keeping it all. They seek abundance.

Energetically, abundance is very different from prosperity. Abundance simply means a lot of something. Spells, magick, and affirmations that ask for abundance, and don't specify what kind, often get mixed results, because you simply get a lot of something. You can have an abundance of misfortune, of ill health, or of stress. Abundance doesn't mean money. Abundance certainly doesn't mean the FFFF blessings. Abundant money doesn't bring happiness, health, or a sense of purpose, though it makes some things easier. When you don't have money, it's easy to think it's the solution to all your problems, but without a greater framework for its use, money can bring as many problems as it solves.

Prosperity is more than abundance, and less. Prosperity is different from money. To be prosperous means you are healthily growing. To prosper means you are thriving. You are flourishing. This means your entire life, not just your bank account. The image of prosperity we have as pagans goes back to the flourishing land, filled with green and gold grains, providing crops, feeding the herd and the people. Things are growing. The world is turning. All are blessed by the gods as the tides of life come in and provide sustenance.

When you are simply abundant, even with money, you can become stagnant. There is no flow. There is no growth. There are no tides to life. The many people who say they want millions of dollars don't really know what they would do with it after the obvious, such as pay off debt, buy a house, buy nice things, travel, and take care of some friends and family. They have no vision to sustain their abundance nor a higher purpose for having it. They don't know how to flow with the cycles of creation, and that is why they say they want millions, but they are usually struggling financially and personally with a lack of direction, success, and fulfillment.

Those who are truly successful, abundant millionaires often have some passion, drive, or desire, a purpose, that helped them become millionaires. Although most are not considered magicians by the occult community and would not consider themselves magicians or witches, they use many of the same principles for success that we will be discussing in this book, even if they use less ritualized and less esoteric forms. Magick comes in many forms, and there are many covert master magicians who are so covert that they don't even know they are magicians.

In the mythic tales of paganism, prosperity and abundance are symbolized by some powerful images that also resonate with our modern ideas of prosperity. Abundance is mythically portrayed as the hoard of treasure. Anyone familiar with fantasy myths and role-playing games, as well as real-life burial tomb excavations, would be familiar with the treasure hoard.

I first came across it in the fantasy tales of European dragons, sleeping deeply in their lairs, right on top of the treasure hoard of gold, gems, and precious jewelry. Usually the dragons were portrayed as the villains, hoarding wealth for no apparent purpose and terrorizing the villages around them. Dragons were associated with evil and demonic forces that needed to be vanquished by noble and holy knights. We see such a tale in the story of St. George. If we look to earlier images of dragons and serpents, and see the alignment of the dragon force in pre-Christian traditions with the land and the elements, we have a different idea about dragons and their hoard of treasure.

In the East, the lines of life force, of chi energy, that flow across the landscape are called dragon lines. They may or may not be the same thing as what Western occultists call ley lines, the paths of energy that connect sacred sites. Ley lines are described as the life-force meridian lines for the planet Earth. Just as our physical bodies have subtle lines of force that can be manipulated to heal with the arts of acupuncture and acupressure, the Earth has a similar system of lines. Both terms, *dragon lines* and *ley lines*, describe a geomantic phenomenon, but experts debate as to whether they are describing the same phenomenon. In the East, the art of feng shui, roughly meaning "wind and water," is used to manipulate the flow of energy lines, big and small, to promote health and bring blessings and prosperity to an individual home or business, or to an entire community. The placement of the entryways, objects, and color schemes attracts the flow of healthy energy and combats harmful or toxic energy.

In the West, dragons and serpents have been associated with feminine or earthly wisdom and power. The medieval dragon image is seen as an amalgam of all of the traditional four elements—breathing fire, flying through the air, digging a tunnel or cavern in the Earth, and being able to swim in water. Modern witches see dragons as guardian spirits for the land and sacred sites, as well as wise, otherworldly beings. The dragon spirits are the guardians of the land, the elements, and the flow of life force. They are not literally hoarding treasure as the old myths portray, but they are guarding the flow of life force, and often blocking the accumulation of power and wealth to those who are not in alignment with the land. They bring scarcity and fear to those who are imbalanced with the tellurian power of the land and gods. But dragons are also beloved by people, even after the Christian era of demonizing them. We still flock to their images in mythology and even in modern magick, for deep within us we also know that a relationship with them is a key to magick, to flowing with the power of nature and the gods.

The human guardian of such abundance, who can aid the flow of abundance to create true prosperity, is the sacred king. Although we can debate the veracity of the sacred king mythos in literal history—as historians will argue about the true nature of the tribal chief or king in various lands and times—the image adopted and romanticized by modern pagans and popularized by both our esoteric and fantasy literature is of the king as consort of the land goddess. The relationship between the sacred king and the land is embodied by the fertility of the Earth. When the king is in right relationship with his people and the land, there is fertility. When the relationship is out of balance or toxic, the fertility disappears and the people suffer. The sacred king or an elected representative is sacrificed, or some other ritual is performed, to restore the balance to the relationship and return prosperity to the land and people.

Our most famous sacred king mythos is the Arthurian cycle, with King Arthur and the Round Table. While there is not much evidence to say that Arthur was truly a king, or even an actual living person (though he was probably based on some historical chieftain), in the myth cycle he is the son of Uther Pendragon. *Pendragon* means "dragon's head" or "head dragon," referring to Uther's role as warrior chief, yet linking him to our dragon imagery as guardian of the land. The entire tale is one of the relationship with the king, the land goddess embodied by the queen, and the people. Like the pharaohs of ancient Egypt, this line of kings is really a line of priest-kings, not just political or tribal rulers, but this fine point is usually lost in most of the myth's renditions. Priest-kings must mediate the divine energy between (a) the Otherworld and the gods and (b) the people and the fertility of the land. Some British occult traditions teach that this line of kings and king-making comes from the fabled land of Atlantis.

The entire tale of King Arthur is about his relationship with different facets of the Goddess and her blessings or banes. The stone that holds the first sword, which he withdraws to become king, is the stone of sovereignty, the stone of Mother Earth. Elemental earth is a feminine element. Arthur also receives the sword Excalibur from the Lady of the Lake, the sorcerer goddess of the water element, another feminine power. He is married to the bright goddess, embodied by Gwenevere, and is antagonized by the dark and wild goddess, embodied by Morgan Le Fey. His wife, Queen Gwenevere, is usually portrayed as unfaithful, and she has a relationship with his best knight, Lancelot, his brightest champion, and as a result, the fellowship of the Round Table—the trust of this group of knights with the king and people—is broken. But it is really Arthur's relationship with the Goddess, through Gwenevere, that is damaged. The result is the Wasteland. The land withers, and the quest for the Holy Grail, the sacred healing chalice, begins, for only finding this goddess power will restore the relationship between the people and the land. The king figure of the Holy Grail quest is the wounded Fisher King, who guards the grail itself. Although he is seen as a separate figure from Arthur in this tale, an older king, mythically all kings are one king, and his wounded groin or thigh is linked to Arthur's emotional wounds.

While Arthur is the most famous sacred king and guardian of the land and its fertility, other European king figures, in myth and in history, have their own hoards of treasures, charms, and weapons. Many of these kings are buried with their treasure hoards. The sacred metals are the gifts of the Earth Mother. The hoards themselves, and the ways in which the kings manage them, are representative of the tribes' "luck" or personal power. We might call it mana or life force today. Those with strong power and blessings grow strong and wise. Those who do not honor the gifts and offer appropriate sacrifices and blessings to the gods do not prosper.

When one of these kings gave out a part of the hoard to a tribesman, that tribesman then had both additional honor and additional duties and responsibilities in order to live up to that gift. The king also had his duties as the monarch, as keeper of the hoard. As a whole, the tribe receives gifts from the abundant Earth and must live up to its responsibilities in relationship with the Earth and all of its gods. Pieces of treasure flow in and out of the king's hoard, being the terrestrial vessel of the tribe's power, the physical manifestation of its blessings. While there is always a base amount, the specific pieces can be used and returned, depending on who needs what and how they reciprocate their duty to the tribe and gods.

The secret of true prosperity is finding our security through our connection with the divine, with the spiritual world. To the witch, the physical world—the Earth, the land, and plants—is the manifestation of the spiritual world in the physical dimension. We believe that the land and all living things, all of nature, is divine and sacred. The intangible light of the Sun and stars becomes the green of the land, a tangible form of energy. All our prosperity is based on this principle—even our modern stock market with green cash and gold reserves. Like the cycles of day and night and the tides of the seasons, prosperity is a flow of powers. The divine controls the flow of all things, including water, weather, and even wealth. There are harvests and there are famines, but those who are wise enough to listen, to feel, and to trust will know what to do to take advantage of the boons and ride out the lean times. Wealth is divine, just like the tides, the harvest, and the cycles of birth and death. To the witch, everything is divine. When we start treating wealth as something divine, something originating with the gods, and when we learn to flow with it and trust in the relationship we have with the divine, then we are open to this magickal secret.

CHAPTER 2

PROSPERITY CONSCIOUSNESS

Once we understand that prosperity is an energy, we can learn to bend and flow with that energy to create the changes we desire. The first "tool" for any witch is the mind; it is the key to unlocking the gifts of magick. In initial magickal training, we learn to alter our consciousness, to get into a ritual or meditative state. Sometimes we do it through repetitive visualization techniques, such as countdowns, or through repeated words and rituals. Each technique acts as a trigger to alter our consciousness, and in this altered state of consciousness, what we focus upon can become our reality. We can both receive extrasensory information and send out our intention to manifest a new reality. Altering consciousness is the key to both receiving and sending energy.

Prosperity is not only an energy, but also a state of consciousness. For witches, perspective is everything, and we specifically enter an altered state of consciousness in order to have a different perspective, to become a walker between the worlds, so that we can see the greater possibilities and work with forces that most people around us do not see. Without that unique magickal perspective, we would not be able to perform our craft very well. The more we live a magickal life, and use magick in everyday situations, the more we hone a unique perspective, a type of altered state, that stays with us throughout the day, rather than only being available during ritual or meditation. When we work prosperity magick, we learn to cultivate a state of prosperity consciousness. We cultivate a fairly unique point of view, and through living that point of view, we create the life we desire.

Although there's a lot of gray between these two extremes, we can generally choose to see the world as either a hostile and dangerous place, or as a beautiful and abundant land. We can live as if it is a world with limited resources where we have to protect ourselves and our "own" from scarcity, or a world with unlimited resources when we approach it through an effort of cooperation and community. Prosperity consciousness is usually considered the second of the two extremes, but there are a lot of midpoints between the two.

Someone embodying prosperity consciousness knows that both extremes are true, and all the midpoints in between are also true. How can this be? How can two totally divergent views both be right? In magick we learn the power of paradox as well as the power of perspective. Understanding paradox is another key to the mysteries of magick.

As a skeptical person, I would think the first perspective is quite true. The world does appear hostile and violent, from the behavior of animals in the forest and jungle to the actions of people. We only have so much land, water, metal, wood, and food. As the world population grows, the demand on our resources grows, and we will reach a point, if we haven't already, when we cannot sustain this demand. Then the world will become even more difficult than it already is, with conflicts between the "haves" and "have nots."

As an optimistic person, I see the wonder of the world, and the universe. I see the connections between all things, even when they seem unrelated. I see how the cures to many diseases are found in plants prevalently growing in the geographic location where those diseases first sprang up. I see the animals and plants not worrying about tomorrow, and not only surviving, but often thriving, as they have no choice but to live in the moment. I see the basic goodness of people and how they will often take care of each other. I live at a more comfortable economic status than my parents did, with greater resources, knowledge, and education, and I know that the next generation will have even more available.

Yet with all my optimism, it doesn't negate the skeptic's view of finite material resources. How can the world be ever abundant if we can physically run out of the things we want and need? From the viewpoint of prosperity consciousness, spiritual connection is the key. Much of what we think we need is simply what we want. And what we want, as a personal self, as the ego self, is often different from what the soul wants. Our desire to consume and hoard comes from the ego, not necessarily from the soul. The soul wants just the right amount of resources to fulfill its purpose. If everybody were in alignment with their soul's purpose, they would give up the resources they don't need, making them available for others. The space in their lives from what they have given up would attract the things they need in order to fulfill their purpose.

The abundance of the world is not rooted in the planet's ability to continually make more of our finite resources. They are finite. The abundance comes in our relationship, to keep the flow of "wealth" by releasing what doesn't serve, so that energy can be put to better use elsewhere. Prosperity is having what you need to grow and prosper. Prosperity consciousness is aligning with your soul to create the best life you could dream up. This shifting of goods, services, items, and ultimately energy embodies the ultimate form of recycling for our resources. It's a radical idea to be in alignment with your soul, but it's the only source of true prosperity on all levels.

The mind plays some interesting "tricks" on us, by giving us choices in perception. We can develop more than one "mind," or at least more than one point of view. We can develop a mind of skepticism. This can be helpful to truly understand, so as not to be naïve or gullible, but when it turns on itself, ceasing to be a tool and becoming what some call the "negative" mind, it creates scarcity consciousness or poverty consciousness.

We can develop an optimistic mind. This is helpful for developing prosperity consciousness. The way you look at the world is the way the

world looks back at you. If you behave as if the world is always dangerous and as if its resources are scarce, that is how you will perceive it.
If you behave as if the world is abundant and pleasurable, then that is
how you will perceive it. At times, the optimistic mind can become too
optimistic, ignoring any gloomy information and drowning out other
reasonable "voices" within you.

We must develop the neutral mind, the practical mind, that can contain both points of view as possibilities and operate from the divine perspective of our soul. Sometimes it's called the higher mind, or the perspective of the higher self, as it is impersonal. It is impersonal in the sense
that it is not ruled by fear or pleasure, but by what the soul's will and
needs are at the time. The neutral mind knows that poverty consciousness and prosperity consciousness are not two separate things, but two
sides of the same coin. The neutral mind harnesses the flow of energy to
get rid of what you don't need and manifest the life your soul wants.

To attain a sense of prosperity consciousness, we must change our
minds and develop a view of life in which the world is ever abundant if
we know how to work with its cycles and seasons of energy. Magick, of
course, requires not only wistful daydreams of wealth and happiness, but
following up our intentions with real-world action to make our dreams
come true. However, if you cannot first attain that state of consciousness
where prosperity is possible, the actions you take will be much less effective because your total being will not be in alignment with your actions.
The biggest obstacle we have in achieving a sense of prosperity consciousness is in changing our minds.

Yes, it seems simple. You can simply decide to change your mind, to
think a different way, but in application, changing your mind is a very
hard thing to do. Our minds are sometimes described as being like great
computer storage banks. All our past thoughts, ideas, and experiences
get "recorded" and become a part of our minds' programming. This
programming is often subconscious, beneath the surface of our everyday, aware thoughts, but it still influences us.

The ideas presented in this book, as magickal wisdom, are not the
norm. Modern Western culture has very different ideas about money
and career, and those ideas dominate our collective psyche. Most of us

are not raised in a pagan household, so we are not exposed to pagan ideas at a young age. We are more likely "programmed" with the dominant culture's ideas about finance and money, thereby limiting our possibilities. We have difficulty shifting our consciousness, because everything we've learned up to this point does not support the concept of an ever-abundant universe where we are fulfilling our souls' will. To successfully change your mind regarding prosperity, you must examine your perception, beliefs, and knowledge of prosperity, and consciously decide which of these programs you wish to keep, because they serve your own conscious goals, and which of these programs you should delete, because they work against you. While it would be nice to simply push a button to accept or delete specific programs and be done, we are truly not computers, even though the analogy can serve us at times.

To accept something, we must encourage it, reinforce it, and believe that it is true. We must water and feed it like a plant in the garden, giving it plenty of our attention and energy. With such attention, it will grow strong and deep, and it will become a core part of who we are in this lifetime, this Earthwalk.

To delete a program, we must get to its root, where it first began. We must understand the root, and "dig up" the root, but we must also examine the circumstances it came from. What was the seed? Why is it here? We can simply allow the unwanted program to starve and wither by not giving it attention and reinforcement. Once we become conscious of it and get to the root, we "heal" it, or rather, we heal our relationship with the forces it represents. Everybody does this differently. Some cast it out entirely, and look at the unwanted forces as enemies. Others, myself included, thank the unwanted program for bringing this lesson to my attention, and once the lesson is over, I release it and dismiss it from my consciousness, and therefore my life. I don't forget it, but I remember it by focusing on the lesson, the healing and correcting, and feed the correct program, rather than dwell on the unwanted one.

To understand what programs you already have, start by asking yourself some questions regarding your beliefs and experiences with finances and career. I suggest keeping a prosperity journal to answer these questions, or if you keep a Book of Shadows–style journal or any other diary, you can use that book to record your answers. Actually taking the time to write out your answers, and seeing them on a page, helps bring them to your full consciousness. When we just quickly think about them when skimming a book, it's easy to let uncomfortable thoughts and feelings submerge again in our consciousness and not be healed. If you belong to a magickal group, such as a coven, circle, or lodge, include that group in either your friends or family category, depending on the level of closeness you have to it.

- How do you feel about money? Do you think of it as "good," "bad," or something else?

- Do you have "enough" money? How do you define "enough"? Can you meet your financial requirements—your bills, debts, and living expenses? Do you have resources for enjoyment and entertainment?

- Do you plan in advance with your money? Do you have a budget? Do you have a retirement or investment plan?

- Are you in debt? If so, for what reason? Were the debts foreseen and planned for, or unforeseen? If you have been in debt for a period of time, has your overall debt amount changed, and if so, has it decreased or increased?

- If you have had, or currently have, financial problems, when did they first occur? Was anything else significant occurring in your life at that time? How was your health? How were your primary relationships with friends and family? How was your spiritual life?

- What is your perceived economic position in life? What words would you use to describe your position? How do those words make you feel about yourself?

- What is the perceived economic position of your family, including your parents, siblings, and spouse, if applicable? Again, what words would you use to describe their position? How do those words make you feel about your family?

- What is the perceived economic position of your friends and acquaintances? Again, what words would you use to describe their position, and how do these words make you feel about your friends?

- Is there a difference between your economic position and the position of those around you? Do you feel your position is more or less favorable? Why do you think there is a difference?

- Do you feel you "deserve" what you have? Is that a "good" or "bad" thing for you?

- When you receive a large sum of money, expectedly or unexpectedly, what do you do with it? Are you likely to save it? Do you budget it? Do you spend it immediately with no thoughts to the future? Are you so frugal with your saving that you deny yourself things you want and could afford?

- What do you think and feel about your job? Do you generally like or dislike it? Is it something you want to do, or do you feel that you "have" to do it? If you have to do it, why? Is your job a career, or simply something you do?

- Growing up, what did your parent(s) or other primary care providers do for work? What were their attitudes toward their work? What were your attitudes toward their work at the time? What are your attitudes toward their work now, looking back as an adult?

- Are you thankful for your job? Why or why not?

- Do you feel there is a higher purpose to your job? If so, in fulfilling that higher purpose, how do you feel—joyful, stressed, unhappy?

- As a child, what did you dream of doing with your life? Are you doing it? If not, when and how did the dream change?

- If you could do anything for a job, what would be your dream job? If you are not living your dream job, are you working toward it? If you are not working toward it, why not?

- Are you ready to change your economic status? How would your life change? You cannot make such a change without affecting every other part of your life. How would your relationships with family, friends, lovers, co-workers, and casual acquaintances change? Do you want to change these parts of your life? Are you ready for them to change in ways you do not expect?

- If you are not "rich," what do you think the biggest impediment to you being rich is? Examine your first gut-instinct answer. Does it have anything to do with other people or circumstances? Does it have anything to do with anyone or anything else besides yourself? Are you blaming someone or something else for your lack of riches? If so, this blaming of people and things you perceive as outside of yourself is probably one of the biggest blocks you have to developing riches.

These questions are aimed at helping you heal your relationship with money and the methods by which you can generate money—namely, your work in the world. There are no right or wrong answers, but if the questions were hard or uncomfortable to answer, then you probably have work to do in healing your relationship with money. We don't often think of the term *healing* in regard to money, but our relationship with money and career can be fundamentally unhealthy, and until this relationship is addressed, we cannot move forward with the goals and dreams of our lives.

ARCHETYPES OF SUCCESS, STRUGGLE, AND FAILURE

We all identify with archetypes. Sometimes it's a conscious identification, but most of the time it's unconscious. Ritualists, including witches and magicians, have learned to consciously tap into these powers through the magickal persona. Assuming a magickal persona for the ritual taps into a momentum of power that makes the ritual easier. Actors can also consciously tap into this archetypal power, consciously or unconsciously, depending on their method. Discovering your archetypes—and in particular for this work, your archetypes in relationship to prosperity—is an important step to make sure you are heading in the right direction.

The following archetypes relate to the themes of finance. Do you see yourself in any of them? Perhaps you identified with one in your younger days. Does any of this identification still linger? Perhaps you aspire to another archetype? Which one strikes a cord within you, for good or ill?

Poor Student

The Poor Student is the archetype for students who feel that just because they are students, financial success is beyond them, as if the status of "student" prevents them from success. Many people who identify with this archetype are eternal students, never starting a career. They simply take class after class, even earning degrees, but never putting them to use in the world or finding a greater purpose for their education. The Poor Student archetype can be transformed into the Successful Mentor/Teacher archetype. If you so love education that you never want to stop learning, you can facilitate the process of learning by helping others learn and passing on information as you continue your own education and research.

Starving Artist

The Starving Artist archetype is for creative individuals who believe they must suffer to learn, to make great art. Many look to the lives of famous artists, musicians, authors, and poets and feel the path to greatness is through poverty, pain, addictions, and madness. The desire to make great art supersedes their desire to be happy and balanced. Great art often comes from imbalance, and we come from a culture of imbalance. Our art often reflects this imbalance. If we seek a culture of harmony and balance, our artist can and will show us a better way. The Starving Artist archetype can be transformed into the Successful Artist.

Drowning Victim ·

The Drowning Victim doesn't refer to water, but to debt. Many people live in a cycle of debt in which they feel they are continually drowning. They cannot get their head above water, and they continue to sink deeper and deeper. Many resign themselves to the fact they are drowning and don't change their lifestyle or seek outside help to reorganize their finances.

Spendthrift

Those who have the Spendthrift archetype are similar to the Drowning Victim, in the sense that they outspend what they earn and live beyond their means. They are not necessarily in the dire situation the Drowning Victim is in, but if they continue on the path, they can easily turn into that archetype. Spendthrifts often are unconscious of their financial situation, and they simply follow a pattern of spending they have observed in friends or family, until it dawns on them that they cannot sustain such a lifestyle at this time.

Free Spirit

The Free Spirit is the bohemian archetype, floating from situation to situation, living arrangement to living arrangement, without much thought or worry about the future. Free Spirits earn what they need to support themselves in any given situation, but often through unusual and transitory circumstances. They are usually creative in their pursuits and find others of like mind to support their lifestyle in small communities. The only problem with the Free Spirit archetype is that it is unconscious of each step. With more awareness of purpose and will, the Free Spirit can be transformed into an Adventurer or Spiritual Warrior archetype, capable of moving from situation to situation consciously as its spiritual awareness dictates, rather than the winds of change.

Gambler

The Gambler is the archetype for those who take risks with their finances, either for the thrill of a game of chance or through inherent instability of their lives. The Gambler can be the traditional gambler playing, or perhaps addicted to, games of chance and skill, believing that soon the next win will come and everything will be set. Successful Gamblers know when to quit while they are ahead, but it is easy for a successful Gambler to become an addicted Gambler. The Gambler can be the one who has new "schemes" and inventions for making quick cash. The Gambler can be transformed into a Trickster archetype, one who doesn't follow the preordained paths and takes chances, but does so with a higher divine purpose, rather than simply on the whims of chance. The Trickster is not attached to the games or their results, but he or she can move in and out of a situation, rather than becoming addicted and stuck in the game.

Miser

The Miser is one who accumulates wealth, but never with a reason in mind, other than security. Misers collect to collect, but they do not use their wealth to enjoy the world and all that it has to offer. Seeking security in a large bank account, the Miser will lessen the potential quality of life, living from a contracted point of view, even when the resources are available.

Prostitute

The Prostitute archetype is meant in the modern concept of the prostitute, not the sacred priestesses of the ancient goddesses. In our day, prostitutes are usually individuals who sell themselves, or sell out from their ideals, to survive and make a living. Those who give themselves away for financial reward are living the Prostitute archetype. Often it has nothing to do with sex. Those who live a falsehood to have financial reward or security, rather than be themselves, would qualify. The Prostitute archetype can be transformed into the Sacred Prostitute, an archetype identifying those who offer themselves to others in service to divinity.

Merchant

The Merchant is one who makes a living by selling products. The archetype is not inherently good or bad for an individual, but the nature of the archetype depends upon how that person feels about what is being sold. If you feel that a product is of high quality, and has a use, you can sell it with integrity, and then the Merchant is a powerful archetype for you. If you feel that a product is harmful or of poor quality, the Merchant archetype devolves into aspects of the Prostitute, as you will be selling out for your own security.

Servant

The Servant archetype identifies those who put their abilities toward serving the public. It can include all public and social services, as well as commercial service. Spiritual service, including ministry, is part of the Servant archetype. The health and balance of the Servant archetype depends on who and how one is serving. When the service is done well, the Servant is a highly rewarding archetype. If it is not what you want to do, but what you feel you've been forced into because economically there are always a lot of low-level service positions, the archetype becomes toxic—the archetype of the Slave. Many of us are wage slaves in our own mind, but unlike actual slaves, we have the power to walk away if we truly want. The Servant archetype can be elevated to Divine Servant, even when serving the public in a "low" position if we look at every person we serve as an aspect of the divine, embodying the power of the gods.

Trader

The Trader archetype identifies those who make their living from trading, bartering, or exchanging goods, much like our modern stock brokers and bonds dealers. The Trader, like the Merchant and Servant archetypes, can be helpful if you enjoy what you are trading and it has a higher purpose in your perspective, but it can be toxic if you feel that whatever is being traded is toxic.

Builder

The Builder or Craftsman archetype pertains to those who make their living from crafting their own product and selling or trading it. On one level this applies to anybody in any manufacturing industry, but the Builder's highest expression is found in the Divine Craftsman archetypes and forge gods, such as Hephaestus, Vulcan, Goibhniu, Bridget, and Tubal Cain. The making of something useful out of raw materials is a sacred art. Many Craftsmen are highly skilled artisans. Others are filling positions where little skill is involved, but the act of creation is always sacred.

Ruler ·

The Ruler archetype includes people who direct, manage, and lead others. Their skill and talent for earning their way in the world is through guiding others and holding the vision of the big picture, while others fulfill the details. Rulers can be visionary and inspiring, but they can also be micromanaging. On the divine level, the Ruler is associated with the divine kings and queens, the divine emperors and empresses, guiding their people, but they are also ultimately responsible for the success and failure of their people.

Patron

The Patron or Philanthropist archetype pertains to those who have amassed or inherited financial resources and applied those resources to finance and aid others, usually in the arts, sciences, or humanitarian sectors of the community. The Patron on the highest level believes deeply in the institutions financed while on the lower level, the Patron is offering financial support for perceived respectability or out of guilt for having such vast resources.

Magickal practitioners have a far wider range of mythic archetypes in their personal lives and practices. We often identify with the wise old woman and cunning man, the wizard, the sacrificed god, the sacred harlot, the scribe, the healer, the traveler, and the temptress. The archetypes listed here are simply for our relationship with prosperity.

Once we identify the archetype(s) we are working with, we must determine if we want to continue on this path, and fully evoke the archetypal power in forging a new self-image, or banish this force and select another power. Change is the essence of magick, and it is the stumbling block for most people seeking magickal success. Most people fear change, even if the change moves them closer to what they say they want. Many people both want and fear success, because to be successful means their lives will change. For many who come to me for help with prosperity, they initially find it easier to complain about what they don't have, and their complaints give them a certain solace and something to do, rather than actually taking action to make concrete changes.

Some of these patterns are more likely to bring you success, health, wealth, and happiness than others. Some are a struggle, but you can manifest whatever you desire. If you enjoy a challenge and struggle, one of these may be your archetype. Other archetypes may represent surefire plans for misery and failure. People who are not successful financially are often living one of these difficult archetypes. Until you know it, you cannot change it. We'll explore techniques to change how you see yourself, and how the world sees you, as we explore the chakras.

CHAKRAS AND PROSPERITY

Many witches work with the Eastern lore of chakras to understand their healing journey. A chakra is a spiritual organ, processing energy, much as our physical organs process food and waste. We have seven of these spiritual organs, aligned from the base of the spine to the crown of the head, described as spinning wheels or spinning vortices of light. In modern lore, they are depicted with the colors of the rainbow, with red at the base of the spine and either white or violet at the crown. Each chakra processes a particular level of consciousness, acting like an electrical transformer, moving life energy up or down through seven levels of complexity. They range from the simplest levels of basic survival to spiritual enlightenment. When we want to change our "mind," or really any aspect of ourselves, we are moving energy through these centers. When we have energetic blocks in the "circuitry" of these centers, we cannot easily change our consciousness, and even when we do, the changes distort our true intention. Our subconscious patterns are the blocks found in the chakras.

Knowing how to work with the chakras directly helps us work with these energetic blocks directly. While talk therapy can do great things, working with energy can facilitate healing on a much quicker and deeper level than talk therapy alone. While talking is a technique to process and transform energy over time by changing the mind's thoughts and beliefs about something, bringing new realizations, magick is the art and science of transforming energy through ritual, visualization, and the inherent energy of natural substances. It can bypass many of the stubborn aspects of the mind by working with the energy directly. Talk therapy with energy work is a great combination for stubborn blocks and deep healing.

Root

The root chakra is located at the base of the spine, or at the perineum point, between the sexual organs and the anus. If you are sitting cross-legged on the ground, it is generally in the area that is touching the ground, "rooting" you to the physical world, though many Western magick traditions look at the root chakra as being between the feet, because most Western ritual is done standing up rather than in a sitting yogic position. The root's energy does extend down through the feet, to connect us to the Earth. While the chakras can have multiple elemental associations—because each chakra, even the "simple" ones, have very complex energies—the strongest element for the root is earth. As earth deals with physical aspects of life, including food, shelter, and money, the root chakra is a great first place to look when considering your relationship with finances.

The root's level of consciousness deals with survival. If we are not surviving, we don't have to worry about any of the more "advanced" levels of consciousness embodied by the remaining six chakras. Food, shelter, and our resources are the means by which we survive in the physical world. Those who feel disconnected from physical life—usually because they either feel it's too difficult or have a notion of spirituality that holds the false program that the physical world is evil or shameful—have the most difficult time with money at this level. If you don't feel like you deserve to be in the world, your consciousness makes it harder to be in the world. If you feel like you are at war with the world, with your physical existence in the world, your consciousness gives you an epic struggle to play out your own internal war. If you believe that life is basically enjoyable, you'll find your needs met and enjoy everything you have and everything you do.

There are many people in the world, such as those in the Third World, who are occupied with the root level of consciousness; they are focused on pure survival, because they live in extreme conditions of poverty and malnutrition. Focusing on the belief that the world is an enjoyable and prosperous place does not necessarily transform their conditions. Yet many people who live in poverty also live with great enjoyment of life. Many members of my own family were poor immigrants when they came to the United States, but they enjoyed everything they had. My mother didn't realize her family was "poor" until much later, when her schoolmates had to point it out to her. Until that time, it wasn't a concept for her, and she enjoyed her life and family, and learned a way of looking at the world that allowed her to continue to enjoy everything through the ups and downs. Likewise, there are many people surrounded by relative abundance, but they approach life with contracted consciousness at the root, and they do not enjoy any of it.

Since the root is about survival, it is the most physical of the chakras, the most likely to motivate physical work. Those with contracted root consciousness don't enjoy anything and don't want to do anything about it, while others with overactive root energy will want to do too much. They will equate work with survival and think all of their time must be focused on work. There is an old saying: "Work to live, don't live to work." It means that you must enjoy your life, and your job is only a part of it. Your whole life should not be dedicated to work. While I do believe in working at a fulfilling job that is in harmony with your soul, even still, you must realize that life is more than any one job, no matter how fulfilling it is. Prosperity includes family, friends, health, and relaxation. Overactive root consciousness promotes a "live to work" mentality that many people in the modern world have. I know I had it. We spend much of our lives planning out career options and getting ahead, not enjoying the moment. We enter a drone mentality for larger companies that promise to provide financial security and health benefits, so we do anything to keep and get ahead in these jobs, not looking at the larger cost.

Our modern culture, influenced by the dominant philosophical and religious paradigms, keeps to the "Protestant work ethic" far more than one would believe. We even have the saying, "Idle hands are the Devil's playground," implying that if you are not working hard, there is greater opportunity for evil or harm. If you are not working, you will get yourself into trouble. As modern pagans, we have to look at our cultural programs and realize that while such insidious sentiments have made their way into our culture, we don't have to accept them. I work because I am fulfilling my True Will, doing whatever my soul calls for in any given time. I've done my spiritual work to have a better idea of my soul, but I don't work out of fear of getting into trouble, or because religiously I have to. It's practical. I want to survive. I want to thrive. I want certain things in my life, with work as the means to those ends, but relaxation, sensuality, and play should be a part of my wants as well.

In an effort to feel safe and secure in the world, we accumulate stuff. We acquire lots of things, often unconsciously, as status symbols to show to ourselves and others that we are "making it." It's fine if we really want it, but we tend to keep things far longer than we are going to use them, and they eventually end up collecting dust. Our hoarding mentality loses sight of the king's hoard, or dragon hoard, where objects were given out to the community in an effort of exchange and mutual responsibility to the tribe. Today we think that if we give away a possession, we have lost something precious. Who knows when we will need it back? Yet the more spiritually attuned cultures encourage people to get rid of the clutter and live simply.

In some Native American traditions, there is a concept of a possession not really being a possession, as objects each have their own spirit, and that spirit has its own journey, leaving people and finding new ones. This concept led to the European's term "Indian giving," as the natives did not understand why the Europeans would not pass on the items, and they asked for them back so the items could continue their journeys, rather than get stuck.

Those well versed in the magick of the root chakra as well as the magick of prosperity will encourage you to have a flow to your life. You must release that which no longer serves your highest good, thereby releasing its accumulated energy in your life, to make room for new blessing and gifts. Those who tightly hold on to life, never taking a chance and thinking that this brings security, will eventually discover that they are living an unfulfilled life. Those who are open to the flow of the universe usually receive what they need, and they realize that what they need and what they might want in any given moment can be two different things. New witches start their magickal practice doing waxing Moon magick to accumulate all the things they want. Wiser, more experienced witches find as much value, if not more, in waning Moon magick, banishing unwanted forces to make room for blessings they might not yet have dreamed of.

• EXERCISE I: TRUE HOME CLEANSING

Everything has an energy, including all of your accumulated possessions. If you want to receive prosperity, let go of all the things you do not need. Give back to the abundant universe, and by making room in your life, the universe will give back to you. Clean your home or office from top to bottom, getting rid of the things you no longer need or use. If you are holding on to something questionable, ask yourself if you are holding on to it because you fear giving it up, even though you don't use it, or if you honestly believe you will—not might—use it in the future. Then make your final decision accordingly. You might have an exception to one category of possession, but don't have more than one. As an author, I rarely get rid of occult books, as I do a lot of research, so that is my big exception, but if you don't get rid of books, music, videos, and clothing, you are missing the point.

Get rid of anything you no longer need, and make room in your life, physically and energetically. If you can sell items, or better yet, give them away to charitable venues, do so. If the material can be recycled, recycle it. Throw it in the garbage only if there is no other option. Part of this exercise is realizing that just because you don't need something, it doesn't mean someone else cannot benefit from it. Likewise, when you make room, you can receive something someone else no longer needs, and our "possessions" continue their journey.

After this physical purge, complete this exercise with a spiritual cleansing of your home. Once all the unwanted possessions are out, smudge your home with purifying incense, such as a mix of frankincense and myrrh or sage. Anoint or spray the door frames with a floral water such as rose water or lavender water. Perform any other protection magick or cleansing you feel is needed.

Belly

The second chakra is known as the belly chakra, spleen chakra, or sacral chakra, and it is generally described as being either at the naval or a few finger widths above or beneath the navel. The second level of consciousness reflects our ability to go beyond our basic needs for physical survival and speaks to our ability to trust. The belly is where we learn to trust ourselves, reach out and trust each other, and eventually trust the divine.

The belly chakra is associated with water, the element of emotions. While the root is primarily a physical center, dealing with the physical world, the belly chakra deals with the intimacy of the emotional world. Although it is not as specifically linked with prosperity magick as the root, the belly holds a key teaching that is often at the heart of failed prosperity magick—mistrust.

Many people do not take chances in life because they do not have a strong relationship with the divine, however they choose to "see" the divine. Relationship with the divine, through the natural world and the spirit world, is a key teaching for any magickal person, but particularly for witches. The belly chakra teaches us how to have relationships.

Our first emotional relationship is with ourselves. We cannot have a relationship with anyone or anything else until we have a connection to ourselves. An often-quoted ancient phrase comes from the Temple of Delphi in Greece: "Know thyself." Mystics today see it as a guiding principle. We must learn our own motivations and desires. We must learn what makes us happy and what leaves us unhappy. We must learn what our larger goals and dreams are, and how to best approach them. Many people fail at any prosperity working because they fail to ask themselves, "What do I really, really want?" Only by knowing yourself can you approach what to do next.

Then we must learn how to relate to others around us, starting with family and friends. The pagan concept of prosperity, the king's hoard, was community wealth, showing us that we cannot always act in a vacuum. Our success is interconnected with the success of those in our immediate surroundings. In fact, modern metaphysics stresses the idea of "win-win" relationships, as opposed to "win-lose" relationships, in which you have to beat someone else to get what you want and the other person loses what he or she wants. In a true sense of abundance, we can all have what we want, within reason, if we know what we "really" want. "Know thyself" becomes a foundation for knowing others.

As magicians, we learn to build a relationship with the world around us, both immanently in the sacred land and spirits of nature, and in the transcendent world, the divine that is ever present but not visibly seen. We build a relationship with the divine and invisible forces, with intangible powers we now call "energy" and "intention," and through this relationship, we change our reality. Although we are also likely to mistrust ourselves and our own sense of motivation for magick—as well as the people around us, because we don't come from a time and place where community is stressed—much of our mistrust comes from our lack of confidence in our relationship with these intangible forces. Some strictly look at them as divine powers, gods, and goddesses. Others think of them as spirits and angels. Still others simply think of the invisible powers as the "universe." But when you live in a time when magick is not the default reality, it is easy to mistrust and have your fear overwhelm your chance of success.

Mistrust is a contractive energy, and most prosperity magick is based on the concept of expansion. One must start with a sense of spiritual bounty and abundance, even if that is not the physical reality, and the magick expands that feeling, your optimistic point of view, to create it as a tangible reality. When you are insecure with life at the root, and filled with mistrust in the belly, as well as any of the contractive forces of the next five chakras, particularly the fears associated with the solar plexus, you are more likely to be operating in scarcity consciousness.

Some of the blessings of the "negative" mind, or contracted point of view, are good for us, because they help us judge when there is not enough and when to be frugal and prudent with our resources. However, rooting our consciousness in the negative mind rather than the neutral or abundant mind creates a full-time perspective of scarcity or poverty, even when that is not our reality. When you are rooted in poverty consciousness, it is very hard to access your magickal ability, or to trust in your relationships with yourself, others, and the universe. The contracted viewpoint limits your ability to reach out to this wider network, and it restricts your ability to communicate your needs to the universe and see the wider range of possibilities.

The neutral mind is the balanced, detached perspective, but if you are going to err on one side or the other, the continual "positive" view of eternal abundance is much more helpful than the "negative" mind in making prosperity a reality. We can prevent ourselves from living in scarcity consciousness by learning a greater sense of trust in ourselves, in others, and in the divine powers. Ideally, the balanced, neutral mind is the best choice.

A great way to develop trust is through reflecting upon the success, blessings, and prosperity we already have in our lives. We enter into scarcity consciousness when we think we don't have anything, and we become desperate to protect and conserve what we already have. We enter prosperity consciousness when our worldview expands. When we see what we already have, and reflect on other tough times that ultimately turned out all right in the end, we are able to feel more secure and expand our consciousness to trust ourselves, others, and the universe.

EXERCISE 2: THANKFULNESS JOURNAL

Every day, for at least one month, write down or type in a journal five things you are thankful for in your life. The five daily items can be anything at all that you are truly thankful for having. They do not have to be strictly financial things. You can be thankful for the people in your life, your current situations, a good meal—anything at all. But everything you have received is a part of the abundant flow of the universe, and by seeing the blessings that are already in your life, you will recognize new blessings as they come to you.

Once you have completed a month of journaling, decide for yourself if you want to continue this exercise. I highly recommend doing it for at least six months, if not a year, to truly change your outlook on life. I still often start my own journal entries with the five things that I am thankful for that day. You can later make it a weekly ritual, instead of a daily one, if that works better for you. Occultists Taylor Ellwood and Lupa write their thankfulness lists on Thursday, the day of prosperity. It's a simple but life-altering exercise, and it will prepare the way for greater success in prosperity magick.

If you perform a daily altar devotional or daily prayers, you can make thankfulness a part of your daily ritual regime. But if you've never done a thankfulness journal, and you feel like your prosperity is lacking, the very act of writing out your blessings, and being able to see them, is very powerful. It also gives you a useful tool to use and look back upon when times are difficult and you don't feel very blessed.

Solar Plexus

The third chakra is the solar plexus, which is found at a nerve cluster located above the navel but slightly below the diaphragm muscle. The solar plexus is our engine of fire, where we digest our food, and it rules the stomach, liver, and pancreas, and generates energy so that we can perform our tasks for the day. While the root reflects our ability to survive and the belly reflects our ability to trust, the solar plexus engages our drive to accomplish, take action, and do things that go beyond survival.

The solar plexus rules our sense of self, our ego. Ego plays a strong role in our success and failure. Although many spiritual traditions speak of destroying the ego, their harsh language really refers to transcending the ego, to know that you are more than your ego self and have a higher spiritual nature. Many people get trapped in their ego persona and don't realize that they are more than what they do and accomplish. But without an ego, we can't accomplish much. Most of us have to develop a healthy ego to transcend. Our problems are found in the fact that we are still stuck on just survival and trust, and haven't developed an ego, healthy or otherwise.

Those with strong egos, who feel that they are successful and deserve success, usually are successful. They take actions that bring them success. Those who don't have a strong ego, who feel timid and undeserving, often don't get what they want. You might know yourself well enough to know what you want, but if you don't also feel like you deserve it, or that it's within your power to accomplish it, you will rarely get it.

Ego is a force, just like any other. When healthy and balanced, it is a great tool to help you achieve success in whatever you do. But as with any other force, when the ego is out of balance within you, you can suffer. You can have too much or too little ego. The trick is to have just enough and to be able to transcend it, to stop identifying with it and see the ego as just another tool, like a ritual tool on your altar or a tool in your garage. It helps you, but it's not you.

When the ego is too low and insufficiently developed, you are also low on vital energy and power. The contraction of the solar plexus is much like the contractive power of the root and belly, restricting the flow of life force, and thereby prosperity and blessings, to you. The key indicators of low solar plexus energy, of low self-esteem, are fear and anger. When we feel that we are not in control, that we cannot accomplish what we want, we also feel unprotected. We don't have any control, so other forces and people who do have control over us can hurt us. When we don't want to admit to our fear, and flare up the power in the solar plexus, we express our fear as anger, believing the anger will protect us.

Fear and anger are not necessarily bad things. Fear can be appropriate, to inform us when we are in danger. Anger can be righteous, to help us draw a boundary when we are incapable of doing so intellectually. Yet to live in a state of fear or anger is to invite the contracted consciousness of scarcity to dominate our lives. Most people who are living in fear and anger do not enjoy life and its blessings very much. Some are overtly successful, even without the enjoyment, because they are seeking wealth in an effort to compensate for low self-esteem. While they may have money, they do not have happiness, and that usually stems from knowing what makes them happy but not acting upon it, because they do not trust that it will work, or because they fear they will not have control over their lives.

When the ego is overly developed, it seeks to control you and your life. Your higher self gives the ego this important job in order to get things done, but the overdeveloped ego starts to think it's running the show, no longer acknowledging the existence of any higher part of you. Most people in our world hold a psychological or secular view of the self, believing the personal mind-emotion center is the true self. "I think, therefore I am," said the philosopher René Descartes, yet to the mystic and witch, this is untrue. Thinking, and the ego, are tools of the true self, but the true self is beyond just thinking. When the ego is overly developed, we forget about community support and think that we are the only ones who can possibly get something done, and we must get it done now. We become so goal driven that we lose track of the overall picture of our lives, and in turn focus on accomplishing our "goals." While this looks like success on the outside, if we are not healthy and happy, it is not necessarily true success.

The overdeveloped ego presents a second challenge that is becoming more prevalent in our modern world: the entitlement complex. When the ego is too strong, we don't see the natural flow of give and take in the universe, and we not only believe that we, and our ego, deserve whatever we want, but we expect that it should come to us with little effort on our part. While we as witches believe that we can have anything we want, we also believe that as divine beings, we can "deserve" it, for we have no spiritual doctrine, such as the Christian concept of sin, that would put us in a state of not deserving something.

Our doctrine does tell us of the cycles of life, of waxing and waning, of light and dark. While the universe is abundant, there is also the struggle for life. Plants are challenged to take root, to grow, to bear fruit. Some seeds fall in fertile soil, and some do not. It is not the divine right of the seed to fall in fertile soil, it is the wheel of fate that turns. Animals are challenged to be born, to graze or hunt. Not all have the same level of skill for survival. Some live, some die, and the wheel of fate turns.

People, too, are challenged. We are not entitled to have everything we want. We are not entitled to optimal conditions. There is no good or evil to it, just the circumstances of our lives. Nature is both bountiful and dangerous. When we think we are entitled to something, we stop working. All we are entitled to is our chance at life, whatever it is, how long or how short, how healthy or how sick. All things are relative. In a time and place where the life expectancy is age thirty, reaching forty-five is considered a long life. In an age where the life expectancy is eighty, forty-five seems like a short life. But a life of eighty years filled with pain and problems seems too long. In the end, all we are entitled to when we are born is a life, and what happens in that life is a mixture of our actions and what some would call fate or karma. The difference between plants, animals, and people is that people can learn to move the strings of fate and do magick, becoming one with the gods.

In the comic-book story *The Sandman*, by the truly magickal author Neil Gaiman, one character, Death, tells the soul of an almost immortal being named Bernie, who dies unexpectedly in a construction accident, "You lived what anybody gets, Bernie. You got a lifetime. No more. No less. You got a lifetime."[1] That is all we are guaranteed, and we must make the most of it. At death, it is the body and the lower energies, such as the astral body, where the ego is anchored, that die. Like everything else, they break down. The immortal parts of us continue onward, yet they are not tied to the ego, so they have no fear of death. The ego is the part of us that fears loss, fears lack of control, fears time running out, and fears death. It is the part of us that tries to forget these facts of life, leaving them unacknowledged while seeking entitlement. Only through developing the ego so it can be a helpful tool, and transcending the ego so we do not get stuck in it, do we go forward to truly fulfill the promise of life.

Ego development is much like balancing a set of scales. We seek to move forward with our will, but not be consumed by the need to accomplish our material goals over all others. The following exercise will help you develop balanced goals to encourage the healthy ego:

EXERCISE 3: GOAL LIST

Make a goal list, a list of things you wish to do, to accomplish. Take a few minutes to brainstorm, and write down all the things you want to do or want to have. Then divide them in terms of the four elements as follows.

---

1. Neil Gaiman, *The Sandman: Brief Lives*, trade paperback (New York: Vertigo Comics/DC Comics, 1984), 5.

What are your earth goals? Earth goals are the financial and monetary goals. They can include obtaining possessions, or anything involving home or food. Earth goals are the ones that make you feel stable and secure in the world. They are the practical, "down to Earth" goals that most people think of as their general goals. However, these are simply one fourth of our life goals.

What are your water goals? They are all your emotional and relationship goals. When people make goal lists, they often forget water goals, thinking that water goals are intangible. But if you are not specific in your intent regarding the types of relationships you want with yourself and with others, you won't create them. Water goals include resting, being still, and taking time for family, time for relationships, time for meditation, time for ritual and prayer, and time for simply enjoying life. Anything that brings a strong emotional reaction, or any circumstance you consider healing or rejuvenating, would fall under water goals.

What are your air goals? Air goals involve education and learning, but not necessarily degrees and formal schooling. We should always be learning about new things. Education is a very important part of life, and those who further their education on all levels are generally more successful in their careers, home life, and overall health and well-being. Air goals also include areas in which we learn to communicate better, such as our verbal and writing skills.

What are your fire goals? Fire goals include anything you have a vital passion to do. They can be career goals, beyond just the finances of earth in your drive to succeed. Fire goals also include romance and sexuality, creativity, art, music, creative writing, poetry, sports and games, as well as spiritual exploration. They are ultimately the activities through which you learn more about yourself and how you relate to others and the world.

Divide your list into these four groups, and then rank them in order of importance. Do you have goals that are not really important? Why are they on the list? Do other people think these goals are important, but you don't? Are they status symbols, but not indicative of what you really want? Are some goals more important to you personally, but you feel they are too selfish to ask for, so you ranked them lower? If so, change them. You must be honest with yourself if you are going to succeed. Rework the list until you are happy with it. Then give yourself *reasonable* achievement dates to accomplish them. If there are big goals, break them down into several smaller benchmarks, and tackle each piece one at a time rather than getting overwhelmed.

Keep your goal list someplace important, where you will see it every day. I put mine on my altar mirror and try to read it every day. Other people tape it to their bathroom mirror or bedroom mirror, knowing they will go there every day and be reminded to read their goals. Mirrors seem important in this process, as you are agreeing with yourself that these are your goals, looking yourself in the eye as you are reminded of them.

I usually take my goal list and rate my goals with year dates. Sometimes goals get lost as I realize they are not important to me any longer, so I change the list every year, keeping some goals and changing others. There have been quite a few I thought I would not accomplish, but somehow, through the power of my ego's will in the solar plexus, they were fulfilled before the year was over. As a witch, I list my year from Samhain to Samhain, but you should use whatever calendar you like, whether it is secular or magickal. Don't wait until Samhain to do it. If you need to set your goals now, set them now. You can always reevaluate later.

Heart

The heart chakra is located in the center of the chest, at the sternum, and energetically it is the link between the lower body, with its lower three chakras, and the higher body, with the upper three chakras. While most people associate the heart with the emotion of love (in terms of both personal relationships and divine unconditional love), thinking it has nothing to do with prosperity, our understanding of success, wealth, health, and the enjoyment of life is encoded in the heart. When you are centered in the heart chakra, you will find it easier to move from one chakra to the next in harmony, and access all of their powers.

The heart chakra is traditionally colored green in modern lore, sometimes with a pink center. Green is a traditional color for money magick, and many folk magicians will use green for attracting cash because paper money is green. Yet if you look across the world, and even with the recent redesign of United States currency, green-colored money is the exception, not the rule. Yet green is still a powerful color for money and prosperity rituals. To understand the green association with money and its link to the heart, we must also look at the Qabalistic color association with the heart.

In the Hermetic traditions of Qabalistic magick, the heart is associated with the central area of the Tree of Life, known as Tiphereth. Tiphereth is associated with the color gold, or yellow gold, and the Sun. The heart is considered the "Sun" of the body, because it is the center of the body, like the Sun is the center of the solar system. Prosperity on our planet is actually based on the solar model, empowering agriculture. Golden solar light is converted into the green of the grain, grasses, trees, fruits, and vegetables. Older societies either traded foodstuffs or the animals that ate the vegetation. Both became symbols of wealth, of what we value. Astrologically, green is also associated with Venus, the planet of attraction. Most magicians harness Venus's energy for love magick, but it can be used to attract anything you value, including money.

Gold and green are the colors of the spring—the golden yellow sunlight shining brightly after a dark winter and the green that grows on the land in the spring. Grains eventually turn gold too, at the end of the cycle. Green-colored things are used to attract value, as are gold-colored items, including the metal gold itself. Gold and green signify the power of new growth and vitality after a period of darkness and stagnation, and both colors are aligned with the heart, the place of expansion and vitality within the body.

The heart chakra regulates the flow of the divine energy that sustains us through the body. The physical heart pumps blood throughout the body, and through the blood, all the organs of the body are nourished. The heart takes the physical vitality of the lower three chakras and circulates it through the body, just as the Sun radiates life force out to the other planets in the solar system. Many metaphysical philosophies discuss the power of love, and how divine love is the cornerstone of everything. Witches call this divine love Perfect Love, a part of our concept of sacred space being a temple of Perfect Love and Perfect Trust. This isn't the personal love of daily relationships, but an embodiment of the divine life force that connects all things. While the physical heart pumps the blood, the heart chakra pumps this vital life force, spiritually nourishing the whole being.

When we truly feel spiritually loved, we know we are worthy of receiving anything we want and need. We know our natural state of being is to be whole, healthy, and enjoying life, and when we align with this love, we feel more whole, more healthy, and we enjoy more. This sense of life force nourishing us is what helps us align the lower and upper chakras into a state of expansion, so that we feel open to receive the bounty of the universe, and safe enough to let go of the things that no longer serve us, even when we do not know what is coming next. We do know we are loved and things will work out. Love is the key to not only prosperity and health, but to great spiritual evolution.

When people feel contracted in their consciousness, money is not the only thing that stops flowing. People with money or career problems often also have relationship problems, family issues, and even physical health issues. When you don't feel loved, safe, and open, you block yourself off to this flow of life force, and many areas get stagnant. To truly be open and loved, you have to choose love. Choosing love can be very difficult when you are not feeling loved, and particularly if you come from a family background or series of life experiences in which you were not exposed to love and good health. But once you understand that love is a choice, you know enough to choose it, and you must take the steps to embody this love. For some it is simply a new life attitude. For others it may involve deeper healing and counseling, and finding a support system of friends and family who can provide models of healthy, loving relationships. All of the people I know now who had a difficult family background and lived a life of poverty consciousness, unhappy relationships, and ill health are better today only because they chose to be better and stopped blaming their past. Once you know that there is a choice, you have the freedom to choose, but you must choose. You can no longer claim ignorance.

The heart represents the center of the chakra system, and in various versions of the system, it has been associated with all four of the metaphysical elements. Traditionally, a center of emotion is related to the element of emotions, the water element. Because of the green color and its associations with vegetation, elemental earth is also linked with the heart. The green color is associated with Venus, the planet that rules both of the signs Taurus and Libra, earth and air signs respectively. The golden Sun obviously has fire associations, and older Vedic lore on the chakras maintains that the color red, not green, corresponds to the heart. Ideally, because the heart is the center chakra, we must be balanced in all four elemental powers—emotions, body, mind, and soul—to truly be open to the blessings of the universe.

I was friends with a metaphysical store owner who was having a lot of prosperity issues and problems in her store. She hired me to cleanse her store and ward it from harmful energies. She told me a bit about the problem and said that previous cleansings were unsuccessful, so she wanted to bring in somebody who really knew what he was doing.

We did the traditional cleansing with the four elements. We used incense for air, and a blend of frankincense and myrrh and a red candle for fire. We mixed salt and water for earth and water, to asperge the area and cleanse it. Then we used a mix of rose water for peace and healing, a spicy prosperity incense (see chapter 6) for inviting in financial blessings, and a series of visualizations to create semi-permanent wards of protection.

No sooner were we done than the store owner started to rehash all the problems she had had in the store, and started to discuss all the people who were causing her problems, filling the room with those contracted and destructive vibrations. Regardless of people wishing her harm or misfortune, she was really her own worst enemy. We had cleansed the space of all unwanted energy, and we had invited blessings, and then she immediately focused on all the things that had gone wrong and could go wrong again. She invited back her misfortune by contracting her consciousness, and no amount of incense, holy water, and visualization would be able to change her store until she chose to change. She was not open and balanced enough in the heart center to change her reality, so her reality remained unchanged, and a few weeks later I heard from others that my wards were not good and her problems were back. Despite being surrounded with metaphysical philosophy and all the tools she would need to change and transform the store, it would not change. The true cause of the situation was her relationship with prosperity, and she needs to heal herself instead of focusing on the outside sources of problems. Once she becomes centered in herself, her problems will most likely disappear.

The next exercise is a simple folk ritual to help you physically align with the four elements to open the way to blessing.

EXERCISE 4: ELEMENTAL BLESSING

Make a copy of your thankfulness journal and your goal list. Read them and then burn the list in a cauldron or other flame-roof container. Take the ashes and mix them in a bowl with honey and milk. Honey and milk are associated with the Sun and Venus, and they are used to bring blessings and prosperity. In this ritual, they are an offering to the universe. By holding something of prosperity and sweetness, you can embody prosperity and sweetness and receive their blessing in your life. As you mix the ashes, honey, and milk, think about all the blessings in your life that you have received and all the goals you hope to accomplish with the divine's help.

Take the mixture to a place of fresh, flowing water, like a river. Pour the offering into the river, and offer your blessing to the water spirits and the goddess of fresh water. Let the offering flow. As the water flows and goes outward, perhaps to the ocean, it will eventually evaporate and take your blessing into the sky with the clouds. The next time it rains down upon the land where you live, step out into the rain, even for a few minutes, and imagine receiving the blessing of the divine. While many of us shun rain today, not wanting to get wet or cold, in most magickal societies rain was a great blessing, for it was a symbol of fertility and health. If the land only had sunshine and no rain, there would be no crops. Notice how your attitudes about prosperity, health, and happiness change from when you start this ritual to when you next walk in the rain. Does life seem sweeter to you? Do you flow better with the powers of the universe? Do you feel more balanced with the four elements?

This ritual traditionally requires a source of fresh running water, such as a stream, brook, or river. If you live in a particularly arid area, you might have to adjust this ritual to suit your own environment. Some urban practitioners will use flowing sink water, but toilets should never be used, for they do not invite in blessings. Although the ritual calls for a source of fresh running water, if all you have available is a lake or the ocean, it can also be used, but swamps or other very stagnant bodies of water should be avoided. Like toilets, they do not invite blessings, but are used in purging magick.

Throat

The throat chakra is the first of the upper three powers, which practitioners traditionally consider to be more "spiritual." No chakra is more or less spiritual than another, even though many of us seeking enlightenment are more impressed with the abilities conferred by the upper chakras. However, without the lower chakras, we cannot ever develop the higher ones.

The throat chakra is associated with the power of the magician and the magick word. Those who can communicate what they want to the universe, or to other people, have an infinite advantage over those who cannot communicate what they want. Magick, in essence, is the ability to communicate to the universe what you want in an effective way, so that the universe can then respond and create what you desire.

We envision a special key language or set of magick words that accomplish miracles—the classic image of the magician saying, "Abracadabra!" and something wonderful happening. There are indeed systems of sacred languages used to heal, transform, and accomplish magick. Modern magicians use Sanskrit mantras, Hebrew names of God, and

Norse runes to create change. Yet much of our modern magick is merely communicating with the universe through simple petition spells, speaking what we want in plain English or through visualizing what we want while lighting a candle, burning incense, or saying a prayer.

Speaking up to harness the power of the throat chakra is not always esoteric and magickal. Sometimes magick occurs between people, and miracles are accomplished by effectively speaking up and communicating your needs. I had a great teacher who said, "If you can't ask for it, you won't get it." I'd like to say it was a profoundly spiritual esoteric teacher, but he was a music business teacher in college, teaching his students how to negotiate a contract. If you want something, such as greater prosperity, or the money or resources you feel you deserve, and you can't speak up and say you want it, you won't get it. Many people will complain about what they didn't get to friends and family, people who aren't necessarily in a position to give it to them, while they are silent when speaking to employers, teachers, or others in a position of authority. Speaking up is a key to true prosperity. We believe we are deserving of what we want, but we do not necessarily believe that we are deserving of instant gratification without any work or effort. Just because we "deserve" something doesn't mean we will receive it because we've been "good," without expressing to someone what we want. We are not rewarded with prosperity when we are good and punished with poverty when we are bad. We have to learn to flow with the energy of prosperity, and one of the ways of directing energy is with our minds, our words, and our intentions in harmony.

The throat chakra is linked to the element of air and our concept of the mind, the mental body. All of our thoughts, beliefs, and perspectives are aligned with the throat chakra. While many focus on the concept of speaking up with the throat chakra, it truly governs all forms of communication, and communication requires both speaking and listening. The ears are also associated with the fifth chakra. You must be able to not only speak to the universe and other people, but also listen to and truly understand the messages of the universe and other people. If you can't, you are not truly communicating. In the case of the hearing impaired, information is received and sent via different methods without the use of sound, but both processes are still important for true and effective communication. Many magickal trainings, including the ones I teach, focus on meditation before doing ritual magick. While many aspiring witches seek out the latest spell book, it is just as important, if not more important, to learn how to tune in and listen to yourself, others, and the gods before running off half-cocked to do a spell you think is right. Listening first can save you a lot of trouble.

You must also learn to listen to what is already within you, and discern what is true wisdom and what are the collected programs you've gathered in your lifetime. Just because you think something, it doesn't mean it's true. Just because you believe something, it doesn't mean it's true. Magical training and self-help books suggest that you always listen to your first instinct, and in most cases, that's true. Your first instinct is usually right, but a good psychic or intuitive reader learns with proper training to discern what is a true message coming through the psyche, and what is a message from the accumulated programs of hopes, dreams, fears, and trivia in the psyche. We carry a lot of programming from our family, friends, religion, and society. Some of that programming is useful and helpful; it aids our functioning and provides us with support in accomplishing our goals. At other times the programming hinders us. The programs were created to control us socially, politically, or religiously.

When I first began my teaching career, I struggled with the issues of money and spirituality. Much of my own practice was based on donation, and when I was first invited out into the "professional" world of metaphysical stores, I liked to work with a sliding scale. A sliding scale means that a person pays what he or she can afford within a suggested range, and nobody was turned away because they couldn't pay for a class, reading, or event. Although I never took any vows against accepting money, and I myself paid for many classes to advance my witchcraft and herbal training, I still had a societal and personal block regarding money and spirituality.

One student in particular helped me get over this block. She told me she couldn't afford to pay the minimum of the sliding scale for a seven-week class when the class began, but she still wanted to come. We agreed that she would pay me a little bit every week, whatever she could afford, until she paid it off. She went several weeks without paying me anything. First she gave me excuses of why she couldn't pay me, and then she stopped with the excuses and simply didn't mention it. In this extended class, we'd begin by going around the circle with a check-in, and each week she would tell us about her adventures out having a good time. The last week of the class, she "checked in" to tell us how she had gone out clubbing and drinking one night, and the next day she bought over two hundred dollars' worth of new books, including some witchcraft books for the class that she wanted. Two hundred dollars was well above the maximum of the sliding scale I was charging, let alone the minimum. I was angry. At the time I was "poor" because of my block to prosperity, and I couldn't afford a weekend of partying and book buying. At the time I hated confrontation, and felt that if I was being "good" and flexible to others, then they should be good to me, and week after week, I couldn't understand how she could be so rude and disrespectful to me and not even know it. But the point was, she didn't really know it. She was just being herself, and I needed to speak up, since I was the one who felt like I was being taken advantage of.

We had words at the class break, and the student apologized and promised to pay me as soon as possible. The class ended. Weeks turned into months, and I still didn't receive anything from her. For the first and only time with a personal student, I sent an invoice and continued to send one once a month until the minimum was paid off. Since that time, I've been much more clear in my financial arrangements with students. I still often make special exceptions and sliding scales, but we have a clear written agreement, and I've never had to speak up with an individual student again.

Later I had a similar situation with a store where I taught some very successful classes. The store was having financial problems overall, however, and they always paid me late. I assumed that they would pay me when they could, but I later found out that all the other teachers were getting paid before me, because they all complained to the owners whenever their checks were late. Since I didn't ever speak up, I didn't get my check on time. Once I spoke up and they realized they could jeopardize our relationship, I got my check on time, or at least more promptly than before. Speaking up and making a clear agreement that everyone understood was the key.

Life reveals to us the unconscious, unhealthy programs we carry with us, and once they become conscious, it's important to then work on reprogramming the psyche so it operates in harmony with our stated goals and intentions. One of the most effective ways of reprogramming the psyche, to add new and better programs, is to use affirmations. When I first learned affirmations from a witchcraft teacher, I thought they were too disingenuous. How could I repeat phrases that didn't match my reality? How can I say, "I am prosperous" when I can't pay my bills? Yet witches are ultimately practical people, and we use what works, even when drawing through popular psychology. If you look back to the old spoken charms or runes (not Norse rune symbols, but spell poetry), you will find that they are constructed much like poetic affirmations. My teacher encouraged me to try them, and I did so diligently, if only to prove to her that they didn't work. I found that they did work for a variety of areas in my life, and I continue to use them to this day as a part of my own daily magickal practice.

EXERCISE 5: REPROGRAMMING CONSCIOUSNESS

1. Start by closing your eyes and relaxing your body. Give your entire body permission to relax, starting at the top of your head and relaxing down through your body, down to the tips of your fingers and the tips of your toes. Imagine waves of relaxation sweeping through your body and releasing any tension or stress out to the universe.

2. Relax your mind. Imagine that your mind is like clear, blue, bright sky. Any unwanted thoughts are like white, whispy clouds, and your will blows through the sky, clearing it until it's completely peaceful and empty.

3. Feel your heart beating with love. Feel the love flowing through your body, circulating around and inside you. Feel the love you have and the love the universe, the divine, has for you.

4. Within your heart, feel the light of your soul, your inner fire. This inner fire will guide you and protect you in all things, leading the way.

5. Imagine a screen in your mind's eye, and on that screen draw the number twelve. Hold it for a moment and then erase it. Draw the number eleven. Hold it and erase it. Continue downward in your count until you reach the number one. You are now in a meditative state in which everything you do is for the highest good of all involved.

6. Release the screen of your mind and hold no image. Simply and silently count backwards from thirteen to one, going deeper into meditation, where anything is possible.

7. While in this meditative state, repeat the following "I am" affirmation statements at least three times in a confident manner, either out loud or silently but strongly in your own mind:

   I am prosperous in all ways.

   I am open to the abundance of the universe.

   I have all the money and resources I could ever need or want.

   I have everything I need and want.

   I am in the right place, at the right time, doing the right thing.

   I am successful in all that I do.

   I enjoy my daily work.

   I am compensated more than fairly for my work.

   I am fulfilling my soul's purpose.

   Feel the affirmations become "planted" in your mind, like seeds, and when you repeat this exercise, you are watering and nourishing these spiritual seeds. They will soon take root and grow strong.

8. When you are finished, count yourself up, from one to thirteen and then up from one to twelve, with no visualizations. When you reach the last "twelve," feel your fingers

and toes, arms and legs. When you are ready, open your eyes.

9. Bring both hands above your head, with palms facing the crown. Sweep down the front of the body, over the face, neck, heart, belly, and groin, pushing out and then down toward the ground. Say:

> *I release all that does not serve my highest good.*

Repeat the sweeping motion two more times, following each with one of these two additional statements:

> *I am in balance with myself.*
> *I am in balance with the universe.*

10. Ground yourself as needed. Feel your feet extend down into the ground like roots, anchoring your physical body in the physical world.

Brow

The sixth chakra is located between and slightly above the eyes, on the brow of the head. This power center is also known as the third eye, as it is related to a gland within the body, the pineal gland, which is sometimes thought of as a vestigial third eye, capable of sensing both the light of day and perceiving the "astral light" of psychics and magicians. Those with a developed third eye are capable of having psychic visions of the past, present, and future, though one doesn't have to be a professional psychic, witch, or magician to work with the power of the third eye. Everybody has a third eye chakra, and everybody deals with inner vision.

When someone says, "Picture this" or "How do you see yourself?" you are using the brow chakra, whether you realize it or not. The brow is our psychic connection to the universe, and like the throat center, it helps us communicate with others and the divine powers. When we receive an image and interpret its information to help us, we are receiving a psychic impression. While many of us work through a visual medium, psychic impressions can come in words, feelings, inner voices, gut impressions, or just a sense of intangible knowing. They are all psychic skills. When you remember or envision something, even fleetingly, you are using your third eye. When you envision the future, daydream, or imagine how things could be different, you are using the third eye.

The brow chakra holds the archetypal interface we have with the world. While we use words to communicate with the universe, an even "better" medium in which to communicate with the intangible forces is through image and symbol. Many rituals combine both symbolic action and words to make a truly effective spell. Our dreams, meditations, visions, and stories speak to us through archetypes. The archetypes we hold about ourselves in regard to prosperity are important to understand, and perhaps change, if we want to change our fortune.

While metaphysics teachers will say that the astral body is the ego self-image, the personal self-image, the third eye is where we hold the greater archetypes that go into our self-image. We can tap into the power of archetypes, and like mental programs, if they are helpful archetypes, they are helpful to our goals. If they are archetypes that are contrary to our intended goals, they work against us. Unlike mental programs that reside solely in our own personal consciousness, the brow links us to the greater collective consciousness, and the reservoir of power behind universal archetypes. When an image is known to many people, in many places and times, it gathers a momentum. When you tap into that symbolism, or way of doing something that has been done in the past, you tap into that momentum. Witchcraft author Raven Grimassi refers to this phenomenon in magick as the "momentum of the past." It is important to know that the momentum you are tapping is going in the direction you want to go, rather than taking you further and more quickly away from your goals.

Review the financial archetypes earlier in this chapter. Think about which ones you identify with, and if the archetype that best describes you is truly the one you wish to manifest in your life. The following exercise helps you to change your financial archetype if needed and empower the archetype you have chosen:

EXERCISE 6: EMPOWERING YOUR ARCHETYPE

1. Perform steps 1–6 from Exercise 5: Reprogramming Consciousness.

2. Envision a mirror before you. Even if you don't see it clearly, feel it. Know it is there. In the mirror, see your reflection as your archetype. What archetype do you think is most like you? How do you look? How are you dressed? How are you different from your everyday self? Sometimes the archetype that appears in the mirror is different from the one you think you conform to. Go with the image that appears in the mirror instead of the one your mind has chosen consciously.

3. If the archetype is something you wish to embrace and work with, keep it. If you need to, change it slightly with your will and imagination to create the divine persona that suits you. Create something you aspire to grow into, particularly if you are seeking to increase your prosperity, rather than something you already are. If the archetype is one you want to release, draw a Basic Banishing Pentagram (fig. 2, also known as a Banishing Pentagram of Earth) over the mirror and let the image disappear. Choose your new archetype. Think of it. Feel its qualities. Draw a Basic Invoking Pentagram (fig. 3, also known as an Invoking Pentagram of Fire) over the mirror and let a new image appear. How does it look? Repeat steps 2 and 3 until you create an image that is satisfactory.

4. Imagine walking through the mirror and embracing your mirror image. Merge with your mirror image and become it. When you look into the mirror, you see your transformed self. Stay with your transformed self, asking yourself how you feel differently. How will you approach life now? How will you approach your job, your finances, your goals, and your home?

5. When you are done with this image, don't banish it with a pentagram, but simply release it. Imagine your archetype stepping back into the mirror. Say goodbye to this counterpart, and let the image and the mirror vanish from your mind's eye. Whenever you need to see things from

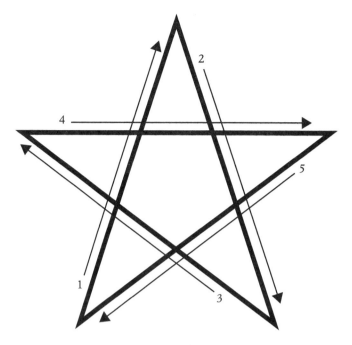

Figure 2: Basic Banishing Pentagram

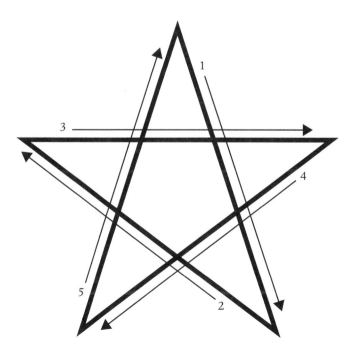

Figure 3: Basic Invoking Pentagram

the perspective of your magickal persona, imagine you are merging with it again to deal with your situation.

6. Perform steps 8–10 from Exercise 5: Reprogramming Consciousness to end the vision work.

Sometimes changing your life is as simple as changing the way you see yourself and how you interact with the world. Magick is all about perspective, about how you see things. Change the way you see the world, and you'll change the way the world sees you.

Crown

The final chakra in the traditional seven-chakra system is the crown. Found at the crown of the head, this chakra rules our spiritual connection to the source of creation. While the root deals with our physical and material survival, the crown is said to rule our spiritual survival.

In terms of transforming our relationship with prosperity, it is in this chakra that we must change our consciousness to truly understand that prosperity is a spiritual energy, and like any spiritual energy, it is available to an energy worker to bend, shape, and partner with. We must learn that prosperity and fulfilling our material needs is just as sacred as any other magick.

The color of the crown chakra is usually described as violet or white. Many people who come to explore witchcraft are very concerned about doing only white magick and avoiding what they see as black magick. To the practicing witch and magician, such divisions are really artificial. Some schools of ceremonial magick define white magick as theurgy and all other magick as thermaturgy. Theurgy is god magick, and in such modern schools, any magick that helps you connect to the divine, to the gods or your own higher self, is white magick. Any magick that harms or destroys is black magick. Everything in between is gray magick, and there is a lot in between. Thermaturgy, or low magick, also considered to be practical magick, encompasses both black and gray magick.

With these definitions explained, I ask new students concerned about doing only white magick what kind of magick is healing magick.

Nine out of ten will reply, "White magick," because of course, white magick is "good" magick and healing is good. These students are relying on their pop-culture, movie definitions of magick, or medieval images of white and black witches, and ignoring what we just discussed. I have to inform them that healing someone physically, or even spiritually, is gray magick. It is not for you to commune with the divine, but to effect change. It's gray because we don't always know the effect of it. What if that illness is "teaching" its recipient a valuable spiritual lesson? By ending it prematurely, are you doing harm? Most magicians and witches only use the labels of white, black, and gray magick as an initial teaching tool, and then discard them, explaining to their students that all operative magick is gray magick, or better yet, the range of magick includes the rainbow, not just the two shades of light and dark. We must be responsible and careful in all we do, even when we think it is good. Yet everything is potentially good if we approach it with that intention. No desire is inherently evil.

It is the absolute black-and-white definitions in pop culture, in movies and television, that have given us the erroneous belief that witches and magicians cannot use their abilities to help themselves financially or accept compensation for professional services. We have this collective archetypal mental program in our culture that equates poverty with spirituality. If we are spiritual magicians and witches, we think we have to be poor. While abstaining from worldly goods and pleasures is one path of spirituality, it is not the only path, nor is it the best path for everybody. It requires a very specific desire and temperament. In any other indigenous culture with a magickal worldview, these ideas are ridiculous. A magician who cannot provide for himself or his family is obviously not a very good magician.

I have a student and client who is very accomplished in the world. She has an amazing education and works in the medical field, doing great healing work in her practice, trying to unite traditional Western medicine with holistic concepts. Yet despite her vast accomplishment of completing medical school and getting established in the medical world, she found herself facing financial difficulties as well as her own personal and health-related issues. She turned to the study of witchcraft to help her with her problems, but she still had the idea that magick could not help her financially. When she finally broke down to do a money spell to get out of debt, her spiritual guides and patrons thought it was no big deal, and were just waiting for her to ask, to be actively engaged in her own prosperity. She was dumbfounded, thinking her guides were okay with spells for healing and enlightenment, but not money. Yet she couldn't stop worrying about her debt and could not work on her healing and enlightenment until she did get out of debt, or at least on the right path. With her spell and the aid she received from her spirits, her finances began to improve, and she formulated a plan to get out of debt and reshape her life and job in a way that would be more healthy and self-sustaining.

The repeated messages I hear, both personally and from many other students, friends, and fellow practitioners, is that the spirit world has no problem with your prosperity as long as you want it. There is nothing evil or wrong with having the things you want if you truly want them and can live in harmony. Money magick is no more good or evil than healing, love, fertility, protection, or enlightenment magick. All of these areas are connected, and part of the human journey. The human journey, like the journey of any being, is sacred. All of it is sacred and an opportunity to learn, grow, and experience.

The following exercise for the crown chakra helps us understand how everything is connected:

EXERCISE 7: CHAKRA WEB MEDITATION

1. Perform steps 1–6 from Exercise 5: Reprogramming Consciousness.

2. Focus on the space between your feet. Or if you are sitting cross-legged, focus on the base of your spine, the root chakra. As you inhale, imagine drawing up the energy of the deep earth through your legs, and bring this energy to the root chakra. Feel it turn red and energize the area at the base of your spine. Think of your physical space and how sacred your body and your home are.

3. Inhale and draw the energy of the root up to the belly area, turning it orange. Feel the energy in your belly chakra, and think of all the things you are thankful for in your life. Think of all the blessings you receive daily and how you can trust the universe to take care of you when you are in relationship with it.

4. Inhale and draw the energy up to your solar plexus, turning it yellow. Feel the energy of the solar plexus chakra, and think of your will, your healthy ego, and all the goals you wish to accomplish. Feel the energy of the universe supporting your goals.

5. Inhale and draw the energy up to your heart, turning it green. Feel yourself in harmony and balance with the four elements: earth, your body; water, your emotions; air, your mind; and fire, your soul. Feel yourself open to the blessings and guidance of the universe.

6. Inhale and draw the energy up to your throat, turning it blue. Feel your channels of communication open, and think of how clear your mind is, programmed toward your own success and well-being. Think of your favorite prosperity affirmations.

7. Inhale and draw the energy up to your brow, turning it indigo or purple. Feel yourself open to the vision of the universe. How do you see yourself? What is the archetypal power you are tapping into? Feel that power flow through you and move you toward your own success and well-being.

8. Inhale and draw the energy up to your crown, igniting the crown area with white light or white flame. Feel yourself connected to the divine source. Feel the light and fire flow out of your head, and connect you to the universal web of the gods, the web of fate. You are like a spider hanging from the web of life, hanging by a strand from your crown chakra. When you are one with the

web and weavers of fate, you play a role in changing your own fate. Imagine yourself ascending into the center of the web of light. You can see, feel, and hear everything in your life. You sit in the center, and all things revolve around you. You are divinely connected, and all things are possible. Ask yourself, what is your purpose in this time and place?

9. Feel the power of the web flow through you, down from the web into the crown, down through the remaining chakras—the brow, throat, heart, solar plexus, belly, and root—down through your legs, and grounding you to the Earth.

10. Perform steps 8–10 from Exercise 5: Reprogramming Consciousness to end the vision work.

You can practice this chakra/web meditation anytime you need to be centered and understand your place and power in the universe. It is most effective if you have already done the previous six exercises.

CHAPTER 3

THE POWER OF EXCHANGE

One of the key concepts of true prosperity that many of the self-help books on creating abundance overlook is very pagan in nature. You get nothing for nothing. Some pagan wisdom teachings tell us that life feeds life, which is another way of emphasizing the importance of exchange. One must be able to give and offer to the universe in order to then receive from the universe.

Exchange is not necessarily payment or reward, as some would have you think. Good people are not rich while bad people are poor. You do not necessarily get what you deserve. Many books and teachers have simplified the Eastern teaching of karma, or the Western Law of Return, into a reward/punishment system. You get what you earned. If you are having a "good" life, then you must have been "good" in the past, or in past lives, and if you are having a "bad" life, then you must have been "bad" in the past, or in past lives. You are now reaping what you have sown.

Esoteric laws of exchange do not label experiences as good or bad. Who's to say that having a million dollars is good if you are unhappy and lonely? Who's to say being a peasant is bad, if you don't even know you are a peasant and you have a loving family? Esoteric laws simply say that the results of your actions will manifest in your life, and you learn from your actions because their results show up in your life. If you invest wisely, your investments pay off as a tangible result. If you invest poorly, then the result is a loss of assets. The result is based on your action, but it is not necessarily moral. The concept of investing in life has given us terminology of karmic "credits," "debts," and "balance," as if we are balancing the personal or cosmic karmic books like an accountant. It's a metaphor, and it's as good as any other, as long as you don't equate credit with "good" and debt with "bad."

From the highest spiritual view, a true spiritual master is seeking to be in balance at zero, having neither credits nor debts, but to be in harmony, doing as his or her soul dictates. When you are indebted to someone, or if someone is indebted to you, you are attached to the world of form. You are stuck on the wheel of rebirth. You must come back time and again to live your lives, to find balance. When you are at zero, you have the spiritual freedom to go wherever you want, to do whatever you want, all being guided by the will of your soul.

Exchange is the mechanism of flow, and in our case, the flow of prosperity energy. To emphasize that attraction and abundance are not moral laws, some empowerment teachings will say that you don't necessarily have to do anything, or at least that is the way the teachings are understood. Due to the popularity of such modern works as *The Secret* by Rhonda Byrne, people are attracting what they want by using the principle "Ask. Believe. Receive." Yes, those are three important steps, but there is a bigger picture. There is follow-up. What are you doing to set these forces in motion, and what are you doing to make the room to receive?

Success is preceded by planning and hard work. Sometimes you experience some failures before you fully succeed. You can get what you want. It is easier than most people think. But today we have a world of people focused on what they want, rather than on a larger picture or any higher ideals, and we have a world that is in a difficult situation environmentally, socially, economically, and politically. I'm not sure I'd want to arm a world of selfish, self-absorbed people with the laws of spiritual success and not at least talk about the bigger picture of life.

From the pagan point of view, life is a continuing series of exchange with the universe, and the universe's representatives—the physical people, animals, plants, and even the very land itself, and also the invisible spirits of the Otherworld—the ancestors, faeries, angels, and gods. We look to our partners in exchange—physical and immaterial—as our teachers.

On a physical level, prosperity is the fertility of the land. Our coins and bills are symbolic of the value of the solar energy in the land and animals, and the mineral energy of valued metals from the land. We work in partnership with the land through a cycle of resting, ploughing the land, planting seeds, tending crops, gathering the harvest, and saving seeds for next year. We plan for the future, but we do not hoard seeds. Many of the seeds will be used in food. We find balance. Without the plants, we would not eat. And with our help, they are tended and cared for, and their seeds are spread.

When we look at the plants themselves as teachers, they are certainly creatures of exchange. They absorb nutrients from the land, taking from the soil. Yet when they die, they enrich the soil with their decaying bodies. They take solar light and turn it green, to be consumed by animals, humans, and the land itself. They absorb the carbon dioxide of the animal world, a toxin to us, and exchange it for oxygen, a life-giving nutrient for us. A plant with all its needs met doesn't continuously take and take from the environment like an ever-consuming black hole. It gives back as well, and what it takes, it takes in balance, in measure for what it needs—no more, no less.

Animals are great teachers of exchange as well. When we speak of a zero karmic balance, I think animals are the best teachers of that. Some traditions call them "furry sages" or "furry Buddhas," because they intuitively have such a grasp of things we struggle with, for we have logical thought along with animal instinct. Animals in the wild usually do not struggle with debt or credit to other animals. They do as their soul dictates. When an herbivore eats a plant, that animal is not karmically indebted to the plant. When a carnivore eats another animal, that carnivore is not karmically indebted either. They are simply following the cycles of nature. In this level of awareness, they deeply know that life feeds life, and that is simply the cycle of exchange. It is not personal. It is not malicious. It is simply the cycle of life. It is what is necessary at any given moment. In following their instincts, they have everything they need, unless they are disturbed by humanity's expansion into their land. When we don't live in balance, we upset the balance of everything else. Generally animals do not hoard resources or compete in the way that humans do, unless that is a part of their nature. Squirrels hoard nuts not because they are greedy, but because it is a part of their instinctive or soul nature.

As witches, we are highly interested in the exchange with the spiritual world. When we first get involved with magick and spirit guides, we are continually asking for things, from new jobs and improved love lives to healing and happiness. Do you ever wonder what's in it for the spirits, fey, angels, and gods? Why are they so eager to help us?

Those of a pseudo-scientific background will look to magick and the spirit world and say that these guides are simply thoughtforms, fulfilling the programs we have put into them. They are constructs following orders, be they newly created thoughtforms or those existing in the astral for thousands of years. While that's a valid view, it's not mine.

Those who are spirit walkers would disagree, seeing these otherworldly beings as separate and distinct entities, with their own motives, learning, and paths to follow. They are very eager to help us because they, too, are looking for spiritual partners and allies on this side of the veil, the physical world. While they can set forces in motion to make major changes, they need someone to open the door. Because these entities lack hands, feet, mouths, and eyes, there are jobs we can do more easily and efficiently than they can do. We are allies. They spend a great amount of time getting us "better" in our own lives so that we will be in a good place to help them, to serve the divine. If you don't have your basic health and needs met, you are not a very good partner in spirit work. Sadly, most witches are so focused on their own lives that they never get to the point where they become good partners, but that is what we need, a balanced exchange with the spirit world.

Witches celebrate the Wheel of the Year, eight seasonal holidays amalgamated from several ancient calendars, including the solar equinoxes and solstices and the Celtic fire festivals. While most think of these celebrations as fun rituals or parties, ways to attune yourself with the changing seasons, or opportunities to do personal work and healing, they are really moments of exchange with the spirit world. There is a belief that we must do our part in "turning" the Wheel of the Year, and if the energy is not raised at these rituals, the wheel will not turn. Indigenous people who have been celebrating the solar and agricultural cycles have been bearing the burden of this global responsibility, keeping the wheel going. But because those of us in modern societies have larger populations, we need more turning, more exchange with the spirit world, to keep things going. The people with the largest populations unfortunately do the least, spiritually and environmentally, to keep the wheel turning.

During the Wheel of the Year celebrations, also known as Sabbats, the energy generated by the revelers is directed by the priests and priestesses to the spirits and gods of the Otherworld. The image of the spirit world is traditionally viewed as backwards to ours, behind a veil or mirror. When it is day here, it is night there. When it is spring here, it is fall in the spirit world. The spirits' own wheel of life runs counterclockwise, the direction opposite to ours (fig. 4). When we offer energy to them by turning our own wheel, we help move their wheel. Our energy seems intangible and insignificant, but it is very important to the spirit world. They return energy, which is what helps sustain the fertility of the land and the health of the people. Without this exchange, this partnership, both worlds would suffer. Many of our tales and traditions of ancient paganism were meant to keep a good relationship between humanity and the spirits of the Otherworld, as the Otherworld was often seen as beneath the land, as much as in the heavens.

By looking at our land, plant, animal, and spirit teachers, we have a wider community to think about, and while prosperity for the individual is important, we also have to think about the prosperity of all levels of creation.

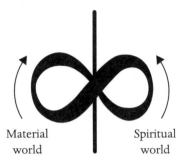

Material world   Spiritual world

Figure 4: Wheels of the Material World and Spirit World

ETHICS AND VIRTUES

The concept of "good and bad" is what holds back much of our success, even though success is not dependent upon morality. Yet morality, or our own ill-defined sense of morality, is what prevents our success. If more people thought about their own concepts of good and bad, and acted upon it, I think we'd be living in a better world. Unfortunately, we don't have a great understanding of our own concepts of good and bad, or good and evil, and we become bound by some strange notions that do not serve us and do not really make the world a better place.

Novice students come to me wanting to learn magick, and with a sincere effort to be ethical and spiritual people, and they are aghast to find out that I've done money magick. "Why would you use your powers for selfish gain?" one asked, making me sound like a character out of a comic book or movie. While you can think of magick as a power, such powers are natural. While some people have the talent in abundance, anybody can learn the skills of magick and have success with them. And if you look at the long-standing traditions of folk magick from all across the globe, even exotic places we'd like to think of as "spiritually pure," such as India, Tibet, or Peru, you will find traditions of money magick being performed by respected practitioners, not necessarily illicit and unholy sorcerers. Having enough is one of the basic needs of life, and magick helps us fulfill our needs. If you can't put a roof over your head and food in your belly, you don't really care about enlightenment. You don't have that luxury to care, because you need to focus on survival. Still, we have a stigma around the ethics of money magick.

The primary concern among those who are doing money magick is expressed in the following question: *If I'm doing magick to make money, am I "taking money away" from someone who needs it, or deserves it, more than I do?* That's a good question. You should consider all the consequences of your magick, but it's much like asking, if you're breathing now, are you taking oxygen away from somebody who needs it or deserves it more than you? Technically, yes. Once you breathe that oxygen, nobody else will be able to breathe it. You still need it. Why shouldn't you have it? You are not maliciously taking it away from someone else right now. It's not like you are stealing the breath from another person. It's your nature to breathe, so breathe. It is equally your nature to fulfill your desire and have the resources you need, so fulfill your desire and needs.

We fear that our very nature will unfairly take something away from another person, and not wanting to take something away from someone because we wouldn't want something taken away from ourselves, we become paralyzed, afraid to do anything because we might do something wrong. I hate to break it to you, but I can almost guarantee that you will do something wrong. You'll make mistakes. You'll screw up. That's life. That's one of the ways we learn. Far better that you learn from your desires, and your mistakes, than you do nothing at all. If you do nothing, then why are you here? You are here to learn, to explore, to make mistakes, and to do things "right," whatever that might be for you.

Once we decide we are "good" people, we fear "darker" or more basic emotions and try to deny that we have them. In that denial, these emotions grow and become a part of our shadow selves. If we were able to fess up to these emotions and believe that simply having them doesn't make us a "bad" person, they wouldn't cause so much trouble. It's the repression of these feelings that gives them strength and power over us.

We fear greed, but we also get caught up in it. We desire something so strongly, and we want more and more of it. When we deny ourselves something we want, the greed builds and our intensity of the seeming need grows stronger. We feel that greed is something "dirty" or "wrong," and such labels also make it stronger. We struggle to deny ourselves of something we perceive as bad for us, and we put this struggle at epic proportions. So when we fail, our failure is equally monumental.

Greed never leaves us satisfied. Once the intensity builds up, greed simply leads to more greed. We are seeking to fill something in us, and we somehow come to the conclusion that whatever we are lusting for will fill that empty space in us, yet it never does. The guilt of our greed generates an even stronger sense of emptiness that needs to be filled, perpetuating the cycle.

The cure for greed is satisfaction, true satisfaction. When we want something, we have to look at that want in an honest way. When we think of our wants as less than spiritual and deny them, the cycle begins. If, instead, we could look at desires as sacred and holy, we'd see them as the teachers they are. From the pagan perspective, everything is made from the body of the Great Mother and Great Father, and all things, material and immaterial, are divine. That would include your desires. You have them for a reason. Rather than deny your desires, explore the reasons you have them. Become conscious about your desires.

1. *Acknowledge the desire*. What is it you want? Is it possible to fulfill this desire, or is it a fantasy beyond fulfillment? Is it something prohibited by society's standards or laws? If so, do you hold to society's standards? Will it harm you or another?

2. *Analyze the desire*. Why do you feel uneasy about fulfilling it? Will the desire hurt you or someone else in some way? Were you told you can't have it, and now you want it? When you think of yourself, your past, and your family history, where do you think this desire is coming from? Would fulfilling this desire be healthy for you or not?

3. *Fulfill the desire*. If possible, without hurting another or yourself, or breaking any laws, fulfill the desire in moderation and really reflect and meditate upon it afterward, or through journal writing.

All three steps, when possible, are critical to this healing and necessary for resolving the problem of greed. I find step 2 particularly helpful. Can you get to the root of the desire? If fulfilling the desire gets to the root of the problem and solves it, you are doing well, but you must acknowledge when fulfillment of the desire has simply confused one need with another. If you feel a true sense of satisfaction, then you have found a successful and healthy desire to fulfill. If it still leaves you feeling empty, realize that the solution is something else, not more of the same thing. Many people get stuck in a desire and believe that if they didn't feel true satisfaction and fulfillment from it, they simply need more of it, not something better.

For example, if you really want a new computer, analyze the desire. Do you need a new computer? Would your work or leisure time benefit from it? Can you afford it? Is there a pattern here? Have you bought a new computer every three months, getting further and further into debt, or are you a computer programmer who needs to have the latest equipment and can easily afford it? Do you want it simply because it's new and buying things brings you momentary happiness, distracting you from other problems? Do you want it because someone else has it and you don't want to be the only one without it? If you are shopping from a sense of distraction or insecurity, or addiction, a new computer is not going to help you, and you should know that before buying it. Buying something is not inherently wrong, but if it takes you further out of alignment with yourself, then it is not "good."

None of your desires are inherently bad. They are not all meant to be fulfilled, but usually if you become conscious of your desires, you can explore the reasons behind them. You will find them to be sacred teachers. Desire for wealth, sex, security, or anything at all is not bad. Everything is divine. Everything is a gift from the gods, from nature. Learning to experience but not get attached to, or get stuck to, a desire is the key to exchange and learning to flow with nature.

It is important, however, to distinguish need from want, as it's easy to believe that we need something when we only want it. Our needs are relatively simple. Neither needs nor wants are wrong, as long as we are honest with ourselves and our motivations.

Paganism doesn't have one set standard of ethics. In fact, as a whole, we do not believe in absolute good and absolute evil. We look to nature as our teacher, and in the natural world, our experience of something,

and our judgment of it, lead us to label it as good or bad, but it is not inherently good or evil. All aspects of nature simply fulfill their function.
A sunny day is good if you enjoy it and your flowers grow, but it's bad
if it's a continuation of a severe drought. A hurricane is bad if it blows
away your house, yet good if it ends the drought. It's perspective that
helps us define good and bad.

While we don't believe in an absolute divine source of evil, such as the
Christian concept of the Devil, we do believe in evil. The creatures capable
of the most evil are humans. That's why we fear evil so much. Evil is really
not being in alignment with the divine. When you are not in alignment,
when you are not in connection, then you are in the place where evil occurs. Nature is in alignment with the divine. It is not evil, even when it
does unpleasant things. It does so in accordance with divine will. When
nature gets out of alignment, particularly through environmental deterio-
ration, it is usually because of humanity's actions. Unlike the angels and
spirits who are automatically in divine alignment, we must choose to be in
alignment, and that takes work. That's part of our journey here.

Pagan myths, stories, and poems have our ethics subtly ingrained
upon them, particularly when in regard to the physical world. Nine
Noble Virtues are drawn from the Norse traditions with the Poetic
Edda, Icelandic sagas, and Germanic folklore. These nine points were
codified by John Yeowell and John Gibbs-Bailey in the 1970s. They sum
up quite a bit about pagan ethics. Although they are not a teaching of
every pagan tradition, I have found them most helpful.

Courage

Truth

Honor

Fidelity

Discipline

Hospitality

Self-reliance

Industriousness

Perseverance

Our pagan ancestors have traditionally been traders in their econo- mies, trading goods and services for other goods and services, either within a tribe or village community, or dealing with other tribes and cultures. The concepts of truth and integrity play a strong role in all of our dealings. Although it is easier to bend the truth in today's culture, or cloud the truth in legal mumbo jumbo, the intention of truth is your word and your bond, and you say what you mean. Holding to my sense of truth and integrity in my business dealings has been tough, particu- larly in industries that have strong legal backgrounds and are known for their strange negotiation tactics. But I've found success in being honest and forthright, saying exactly what I mean, and backing it up with my actions. When you live your truth and have integrity in your actions, then you can perform your business, or business magick, and know that you are doing the right thing.

Some practitioners worry about making financial gain unethically through magickal techniques. Conversely, others use magick to pur- posely bend their ethics, believing that if they themselves break no vow or law, they were not being unethical. Integrity involves the spirit, as well as the letter, of the law. If your actions, magickal or otherwise, create an unethical situation, it is your duty, as a person with integrity, to rectify it. The classic textbook example is a money spell for fast cash. You need to pay your bills. You do your spell, and you find a wad of cash, rolled up on the ground, and the person, who obviously dropped it, walking away from you. Some would think, *My spell has brought this to me. This is for me. The universe wants me to have it.* Yet when you know someone else lost it, and you have the opportunity to return it, honor demands that you do. While it is not required, it is good ethics.

Prosperity magick, or any magick at all, is not necessarily based on moral earning, but many witches believe in a principle called the Law of Return or Law of Three. Like the law of karma, it believes what you do returns to you, but in this case, magnified threefold. It simply means that your action comes back to you stronger than when you released it. The vibrations of your consciousness, through your thoughts, words, and actions, return to their source of origin. It's not the punishment and reward most people think of, but simply a return of energy of the same quality. If you label that quality of energy good or bad, you think of it as a reward or punishment. In the preceding example, perhaps the magick gave you the opportunity to return the money, so three times as much, literally or simply figuratively, could be "returned" to you, fulfilling the spell. The catalyst for the fulfillment of the spell was returning the money. The spell brought the opportunity, but you have to fulfill it. Not returning the money creates a certain energy that would also return to you, but not likely in a pleasant way.

The pagan virtues of self-reliance, industriousness, and perseverance play an important role for anybody looking to be successful in life. You are your number one asset. If you cannot count on yourself, your hard work, and your ability to commit to something for the long haul, then you will never be a success. Learning to build these virtues over time, with smaller tasks, builds the fortitude to have these traits when they really count. Look for experiences that are truly challenges to your self-reliance, but not challenges that are unearthly and impossible to overcome. Accomplish these goals and move on to other, more challenging goals. Successful people are constantly setting goals for themselves, to move forward and take on new tasks. You might occasionally fail, but you learn something even when you do, and you are better prepared to tackle the next challenge, as learning to fail is an important skill as well. You must know how to learn from your mistakes if you truly wish to succeed.

Hospitality is also a key virtue that is often forgotten in modern pagan culture. Older societies offered food and shelter to any peaceful traveler. In the Greek myths, the gods disguised themselves as beggars, and those who offered charity and hospitality to the lowest beggar were offering it to the gods. That is also a metaphor in our time. If we see everybody as an aspect of the divine, an expression of the Great Spirit, the gods and goddesses, then those who are in need deserve our compassion and hospitality. Sharing our good fortune with others is important. In this modern age, opening your home to strangers might not always be the wisest course of action, but we also have modern agencies to help shelter and feed others. Both donation and volunteering at such organizations is a fine way to share your bounty with your community. In return, this bounty given returns to you threefold, increasing your blessings with the power of exchange and reciprocity. Taking care of each other helps us take care of ourselves, creating a community win-win paradigm, instead of a scarcity/me-against-them paradigm.

From the pagan tradition of Wicca, we have an ethical guideline I was taught and I subscribe to, known as the Wiccan Rede. A rede is a suggestion, not a law, and while the Wiccan Rede is a considerably long poem filled with lots of folk wisdom and good advice, it is most popularly boiled down to "An' it harm none, do what ye Will" or "An' ye harm none, do as ye Will." Most of us simply say, "And it harm none, do as you Will." On a basic level, it means you should use harming none, including yourself, as your guide, your yardstick for any action. If your action is causing harm, or more harm than good, then don't do it.

The Wiccan Rede is seen as a variation of the Golden Rule in Christianity—treating others as you wish to be treated. If you believe things return to you and return threefold, then perform actions that you would want returned to you. On a deeper, more magickal level, the word "Will" is purposely capitalized, to emphasize that you are not doing your personal ego will, but the True Will or Mystic Will, the will of your soul, not your personality. If you are doing what your soul calls you to do, you will be harming none. You will be doing exactly what you need to be doing.

WICCAN REDE (FULL VERSION)

Bide the Wiccan laws we must
In Perfect Love and Perfect Trust
Live and let live,
Fairly take and fairly give.
Cast the circle thrice about
To keep all evil spirits out.
To bind the spell every time,
Let the spell be spake in rhyme.
Soft of eye and light of touch,
Speak little, listen much.
Deosil go by the waxing Moon,
Singing out the witches' rune.

Widdershins go by the waning Moon,
Chanting out the baneful rune.
When the Lady's Moon is new,
Kiss thy hand to her, times two.
When the Moon rides at her peak,
Then your heart's desire seek.
Heed the north wind's mighty gale,
Lock the door and trim the sail.
When the wind comes from the south,
Love will kiss thee on the mouth.
When the wind blows from the east,
Expect the new and set the feast.
When the wind bows from the west,
Departed souls will have no rest.
When the west wind blows o'er thee
Departed spirits restless be.
Nine woods into the cauldron go,
Burn them fast and burn them slow.
Elder be your Lady's tree,
Burn it not or cursed ye'll be.
When the Wheel begins to turn,
Let the Beltane fires burn.
When the Wheel has turned to Yule,
Light the log, the Horned One rules.
Heed ye flower, bush, and tree,
By the Lady, blessed be.
Where the rippling waters flow,
Cast a stone and truth ye'll know.
When ye have and hold a need,
Hearken not to other's greed.
With a fool no season spend,
Nor be counted as his friend.
Merry meet, merry part,
Bright the cheeks and warm the heart.
Mind the Threefold Law ye should,

Three times bad and three times good.

When misfortune is enow,

Wear the blue star on the brow.

True in love ever be,

Unless thy lover's false to thee.

Eight words to the Wiccan Rede fulfill

An' it harm none, do what ye will.

The Wiccan Rede also says, "Fairly take and fairly give," reminding us of the fundamental principle of exchange. In the magickal tradition of the Qabalah, the Tree of Life is a map of the universe divided into three pillars. While the Middle Pillar is one of balance and integration, the outer pillars are named Severity and Mercy, and they are seen as dual powers of taking and giving. They are seen as divinity at its extremes as darkness and light, or Goddess and God. More specifically, these two pillars are divided into three sections, or sephira, each. The middle section of the Pillar of Severity is known as Geburah, and it is the power of strength and destruction. The middle section of the Pillar of Mercy is known as Chesed, and it is the power of mercy and compassion. Together they are truly seen as the powers of taking and giving, destruction and generation, catabolic and anabolic.

Encoded in this map of the universe is the idea of creation, destruction, and exchange. Just as science says, nothing is truly destroyed, but its form changes. Prosperity is knowing how to change the form of our resources.

LUCK AND FATE

A topic strongly related to our magickal concepts of prosperity is the force of luck. People will come to the local witch, be it the traditional village witch of years past or the modern practitioner, and ask for a good-luck charm. Sometimes this request will be specifically for gambling luck, while other times it will be to change their general lives, to grant them overall "good" luck and stop their previous "bad" luck.

Luck is a tricky concept. I have to admit that I don't really believe in luck as most people describe it, as metaphysical force. Luck is generally thought of as a series of circumstances or events that operate by chance and change the outcome of a situation or the fortune of an individual, for good or for ill. Individuals generally seem to be disassociated from these circumstances. They are not responsible for their luck; it seems to "happen" to them, and it is not caused by their actions. I don't believe in that kind of luck.

Luck is associated with another tricky concept, but one I do believe in: fate. But I don't believe in fate the way most people believe in it. Most people use the terms *fate* and *destiny* to describe what is "meant" to happen, regardless of their actions. I don't believe that luck, fate, destiny, or any other force makes things happen, or is disconnected from our actions.

I believe in the fate of magicians and witches. Witches are often said to worship a goddess or triple goddess of fate, who is described as a weaver. One aspect of the goddess weaves the thread of your life. Another measures it out. The third cuts it and ends life. They are known as the Fates, the Norns, or the Wyrd Sisters, for *wyrd* is the Norse/Saxon concept of fate. Together, they determine the course of your life, but the pattern they weave is based upon the sum of all your past actions. What you have done determines what you will most likely do, and how your fate will mostly likely turn out. Yet if you choose and follow through on new actions, you take a hand in weaving your own fate, and you change the pattern. You partner with the goddess of fate, and write your own fate, or at least co-write it. To do so is the secret of magick.

I don't believe in luck because I don't believe things happen randomly. I think things appear to happen randomly, but I also know the secret of magick is aligning things that appear to be random or unrelated in order to manifest your will. Magick is not fireballs from your fingertips, but aligning forces to be in the right place and the right time, doing the right thing, to fulfill your will. The universe is filled with patterns upon patterns that appear to be chaos, yet with everything connected through this web of life, also known as the web of fate or the web of wyrd, there is a pattern, even if we are too close to it to see it clearly.

When someone isn't aware of magick, and doesn't have a relationship with the goddess of fate, then there appears to be luck. Much like we do with karma, we label luck as "good" or as "bad," depending on how it affects us. Are the results pleasant or unpleasant? When we want good luck, we want to bend these forces to our will, to get what we want, or at least create boons and blessings that will manifest in unexpected ways. Sometimes "good luck" brings us things we didn't even know we desired. Luck is directly related to the level of life force and connection an individual has. Someone who is healthy, strong, creative, and optimistic appears more lucky than someone who has low self-esteem and is ungrounded, pessimistic, and overly sensitive to his or her environment. The one with good luck appears to be blessed with virtues, perhaps from the gods, perhaps based on the work of previous lives. This power seems to be inherent in the individual's makeup. In modern takes on Norse metaphysics, the term *hamingja* refers to the individual's "luck" and ability to get things done in the world. As an aspect of the soul, it is something one is born with, yet it can also develop with brave and virtuous deeds in life.

If we think of this luck, this fate, as the sum of our previous actions, and if that energy is influencing the future (even if most people are unaware of it), we can treat it like any other energy, and use ritual to transform it. Because we seem to exchange this energy with the unseen forces of the universe, we can change it like any other energy. This process is described as "turning your luck." Although you can turn your own luck, or help turn someone else's, it is important to realize that there is a bigger spiritual picture to fate, and that the true goal of a witch is to be a partner, a co-creator with fate, rather than be subject to seemingly outside forces.

Transforming "bad" luck is much like removing a curse, be it a self-inflicted curse or an energy that has been directed to you. Energies are directed to us all the time, mostly from nonmagickal practitioners, yet they can still have an effect if there is a strong emotion behind them and we are not centered in our own power. If the energy is malicious, angry, or fearful, it can affect us in a harmful way and require us to remove it. Magickal practitioners will often cleanse themselves and their homes of unwanted energies. If you've never done any cleansing magick, here are some ideas based upon the elements:

Air

Traditionally, one smudges a space or a person in order to change the energies and lift heavy, unwanted ones. To smudge means to burn an incense or herb and circulate the smoke in an area or around a person. Some witches use a feather as a fan to spread the smoke. The concept is that some herbs and resins, when burned, release a high vibration that removes lower, unwanted vibrations. Good smudging herbs include sage, sage/cedar/sweet grass combinations, frankincense, frankincense/myrrh combinations, lavender, pine, cinnamon, clove, basil, copal, dragon's blood, and mugwort.

Fire

Charging and burning candles, particularly white, blue, and purple ones, to cleanse an area or person of unwanted energies can transform energy. Some traditions use black candles to absorb the harmful energy. To "charge" a candle, hold it and clearly think of your intention. You can visualize your intention, imagining the candle flame burning up the unwanted energy, or state your intention in clear terms, out loud or silently in your mind. Many practitioners would suggest clearing the candle of unwanted energies first, by smudging it or using water and/or salt.

Earth

Earth cleansing is done by leaving a bowl of sea salt in the area you wish to clear. When you are clearing a person, that individual can sit in front of a bowl of salt, meditate, and breathe deeply. Then you can remove the salt from the area and dispose of it by pouring it down a drain. Alternately, you can lie outside on the ground and intend that the land absorb your unwanted energy. It won't hurt the land, as the land transforms refuse, in the same way that it turns dead leaves into soil.

Water

Clean, pure water can be used to clear and bless a person or area. The water is charged for cleansing and then sprinkled upon the individual, or sprinkled around the area to be cleansed. Water is most often mixed with sea salt or kosher salt in order to combine the powers of earth and water. This makes the water particularly purifying. Floral waters, also known as hydrosols, can be used as well; they can be added to the cleansing water, or you can use commercial spray bottles to spritz a room or person. Rose water, lavender water, and orange water all have cleansing and blessing properties. Other strong agents to break unwanted energy are vinegar and ammonia. Sometimes a few drops of one (not both) can be added to the water. If you do use one of these additives, be sure not to get it in your eyes.

When you fear that energy directed to you was intentional and malicious, you might need something a little stronger than a simple home-and-self cleansing. You might need an uncrossing ritual. To be "crossed" means that someone has crossed your path with ill intent and left you cursed. It doesn't have to be a formal curse placed upon you by an experienced practitioner. This can be what many cultures call the "evil eye." Its effect is much like bad luck. Things don't go your way. Problems are attracted to you. You might get sick or have a headache/nausea for no apparent reason, or you might suffer from nightmares. Even if someone hasn't purposely crossed you, and you only think they have, an uncrossing ritual can be used with no ill effect. It acts as a super spiritual cleansing and blessing.

UNCROSSING OIL

This is one of my favorite uncrossing oil recipes. Start with a base of olive oil or any other base oil you desire. When the Moon is waning, grind the herbs and soak them in the oil for at least four weeks. Then strain out the herbs, and add the salt and ammonia to the oil before bottling it.

> 2 ounces of olive oil or another base oil, such as grapeseed, apricot
> kernel, or jojoba oil
> 1 teaspoon of hyssop leaf
> 1 teaspoon of sandalwood powder
> 1 teaspoon of patchouli leaf
> 1 teaspoon of myrrh resin
> 1 teaspoon of vervain herb
> 1 teaspoon of cinquefoil
> 1 pinch of sea salt
> 13 drops of household ammonia

The ammonia can be substituted with a traditional commanding agent: urine. Although it sounds gross, it's a very powerful method of uncrossing. Use thirteen drops or a teaspoon of your own first urine of the day. Upon rising, you must stay silent until the urine is collected and added to the potion. Then you can speak. If you plan on sharing the oil with anybody else, helping them become uncrossed, you probably want to stick with the household ammonia. If someone else uses your urine, you are putting that person under your command, not freeing him or her from unwanted forces.

You can use the potion whenever you feel you are crossed, shaking it vigorously and dabbing a few drops on your wrists, brow, or neck. You can add a few drops to bath water and take an uncrossing bath. You can also anoint your clearing candle with uncrossing oil, to empower it with this intention. If you need an uncrossing potion immediately, and you don't have time to make the preceding one, use the following mixture:

> 5 drops of hyssop essential oil
> 3 drops of myrrh essential oil
> 1 drop of lemon essential oil
> 1 pinch of cinquefoil herb
> ⅛ ounce of jojoba oil base

Uncrossing rituals are often followed by blessing rituals, to bring blessings in to fill the space of the energy you just removed, to prevent any further ill wishes or bad luck from attaching to you. Splashing on or bathing in floral waters, particularly rose water, are particular blessing rituals. Also adding some honey to the bath, to bring the sweet blessings of life to you, helps generate good luck and fortune. Bringing flowers into your living space, particularly the bedroom, is also a way of bringing blessings. Some witches choose to dip flowers in floral-honey water and use one of the flowers as an asperser to sprinkle scented honey water on a person.

If you feel that you are simply unlucky in life, and it's not something that has changed recently, there are rituals to transform your luck. I've found that the most effective ritual for my clients has been creating a "scapegoat" of sorts, which takes their bad luck. Usually we use a stone, slightly larger than the size of a fist. Go out into nature and locate the appropriate stone, ideally when the Moon is waning in light. When you think you've found it, sit down with the stone and meditate with it. Ask to communicate with the spirit of the stone. Explain your lifelong misfortune. Think about the events you would consider bad luck. Talk to the stone, out loud or internally, as if the stone were a good friend. Ask the stone if it will help you by taking this bad luck and giving you good luck. If you feel that the stone agrees (the spell only works when the stone agrees), hold the stone close to your heart. Imagine pouring out your bad "luck" into the stone. Then take a journey, walking someplace you never usually walk, and when you find the right spot, leave the stone there. Some people drop the stone from a high place, or into water, or they bury it. Any of those techniques would work. You might want to ask the stone where it wants to be left, or ask it to help you know the right place. When you release the stone, thank it again, turn your back, and don't look back on it, or you might take back your bad luck. Take notice of the changes in your life after that, and look for your "luck" to change for the better.

There do seem to be individuals who have a specialized relationship with this force we are calling luck. There are some people who, by their very virtue and presence, seem to bestow luck on others. They are also very healing and inspiring individuals, but for some reason, "good" things seem to happen when they are around, and some have the ability to have their own good luck rub off on others with whom they come into contact. Once you've made contact with them, you seem to have blessings and good fortune, at least for a short time. Many of these individuals appear to be spiritually "advanced," yet they are not necessarily esoteric practitioners. Perhaps they simply have strong hamingjas, and their energy jumpstarts the hamingjas of others.

Other individuals are, for lack of a better word, luck "vampires," or luck stealers. I generally hate using the term *vampire* in any derogatory way, as many people identify with the vampire as a positive magickal archetype, but the word gets across the apparent mechanism that is occurring. "Luck vampires" generally might be unlucky, but when they are around those who generally seem to have good fortune, the luck vampires appear to gain good fortune while the other people appear to lose it for a time. This doesn't always correspond with people who would be identified as psychic or emotional vampires—those individuals who do not process life energy well and need an alternative source of life-force energy to successfully function. In the Norse cosmology of the soul, what is often referred to today as life energy, ki, chi, prana, or mana is known as Önd or Athem. While psychic vampires have difficulty processing Önd, perhaps these luck vampires are born deficient in hamingja in some way. I've found that general psychic self-defense techniques seem to protect your hamingja as much as your life force. More about psychic self-defense can be found in the previous book in this series, *The Witch's Shield*.

While rituals of luck and clearing are helpful to improve our quality of life, good witches seek out the mystery itself, to learn to move with the wheel of fate, the loom of life itself, and spin their own destiny with the Wyrd Sisters guiding them.

EXERCISE 8: MEDITATION ON THE WHEEL OF FORTUNE

1. Perform steps 1–6 from Exercise 5: Reprogramming Consciousness.

2. Imagine yourself walking toward the west, facing the setting Sun. Imagine walking toward your future. Think about your goals. Think about your future. What are you walking toward?

3. As you walk, feel the ground beneath your feet become unstable. As you think of your future, what you are walking toward? Think about how none of your goals and none of your plans are guaranteed. Many unforeseen things can happen. Blessings you can't even imagine now can come your way, and many things can go wrong. Feel the ground shake and move.

4. Notice that the ground beneath your feet is transforming into the rim of a wheel, as if you are walking the edge of a wheel, precariously balanced on the edge. If you make a mistake, you'll fall off the wheel.

Figure 5: Wheel of Fortune

5. Feel yourself fall from the top of the wheel. Now you are walking on the lower, inner rim of the wheel. You can't see where you are going or what you are doing.

6. As you walk and focus on your life, you go up and down on the wheel, just as you go up and down in life.

7. Look at the center of the wheel, and see yourself, another part of yourself, what is called the higher self or Bornless Self. Feel yourself become one with the higher self. If you identify with only your personal self, you will continually go up and go down, with no sense of security. If you identify with the higher self, you sit in the center of the wheel, the center of the web of fate. You find security in your higher self, and you simply observe the part of you that goes up and goes down, yet you are the part of eternal center. When you identify with the eternal self, you have a greater partnership with the forces of fate, and you can do anything.

8. Feel yourself in the center of the wheel, observing your personal self going up and down with the cycles of life. Again think about your goals for the future, what you are working toward. Then be open to the messages of the eternal divinity. The messages you receive will tell you how to better partner with fate to achieve your goals, or when and how to change your goals to align with your higher self.

9. Feel the presence of the turning wheel gently fade from you. You are always in the center of the wheel, but you now bring your awareness from your visionary state to the physical body.

10. Perform steps 8–10 from Exercise 5: Reprogramming Consciousness to end the vision work.

THE QUEST OF SERVICE AND SECURITY

Each of the four elements represents an area of consciousness we are all experiencing. Each of the four contains a sacred quest, a journey we undergo several times in our lives in a desire to pierce the four mysteries, to understand them and integrate their wisdom in our lives. Nowhere are the four quests better depicted and explained than in a deck of tarot cards. The minor arcana, the "minor" or daily struggles of life as opposed to the "major" life lessons of the major arcana, depicts the four quests.

The minor arcana is divided into the four suits, one for each element. The wands are associated with the element of fire. The swords are linked with air. The cups represent the quest of the element of water, and the fourth suit, known by names such as Pentacles, Discs, Coins, Shields, or Stones, is the suit of the earth element. The quest of earth is usually depicted as the quest for security.

In the tarot, the earth suit (of Pentacles) is about money, and how you make money to feel safe, comfortable, and secure. The image of the pentacles are used as discs, because the pentacle, the five-pointed star in a circle, embodies all the elements. To manifest something in the material, earthly realm, you need all five elements—spirit, fire, air, water, and earth. The pentacle represents the highest, most subtle and divine forces, as well as the densest, earthiest, and most physical manifestations. That is why it is a symbol of both protection and money.

But when you really look at the quest, it is not only the quest for security, what you are getting from the universe through your hard work and planning, but it is the quest of service, what you are offering to the universe, through the medium of your community, your vocation, to receive that security. It is the power of exchange in this quest that is so important. Each of the four quests is about exchange and relationship, but in particular, this earth quest, this prosperity quest, is about your relationship with the universe and the true source of prosperity.

When you look at the suit of pentacles, starting from the Ace to the final card, the Ten of Pentacles, you have an understanding of the quest of service. The wonderful thing about the deck of tarot cards, as opposed to a book, is that the deck reminds us that the quest doesn't always happen in sequence. All of our lives take unique twists and turns, but the tarot does provide a pattern in understanding our lives and those turns, particularly in regard to money.

Ace of Pentacles

The Ace of Pentacles is the root of the powers of the element of earth. It represents a boon from the divine source of earthly power, talent, and resources. The classic Rider-Waite tarot image has the "hand of God" extending from a cloud and holding a golden pentacle. On the sacred quest, the Ace represents whatever blessings and talents we've been given in the world, and whatever resources we've been given without necessarily having to work to receive. The Ace can be your personal skills and talents that you later develop, or the circumstances of your family and its financial status. It's not to say that you then have to use your resources and put work and effort into them, but they are the resources you are divinely granted. Whenever you get a windfall of cash, good luck, or any other good fortune, the Ace is the card indicated.

Two of Pentacles

The Two of Pentacles is known as the change card. From the blessings of the Ace, you must do something with your resources, and action always sparks change. The traditional image of the card has a figure who appears to be juggling two pentacles. The juggling of resources is necessary in order to make changes. We must take risks for any advancement in finances and security. Those who pull the Two of Pentacles typically feel that they are in a financially risky place, yet without risk, there can be no gain. You must take a chance and actually use your resources.

Three of Pentacles

The traditional name of the Three of Pentacles is Work, though it is sometimes called Craftsmanship. The figure is working his craft, using his talents and learned skills to "carve" out three pentacles in a church, while two people, apparently in a position of authority, are supervising or inspecting his craftsmanship. Just as you might expect, one has to put hard work and effort into any vocation. When starting out on the path, you have to be open to observation, criticism, and guidance. We look to those who have expertise or knowledge in an area, and if we can accept their feedback and put effort into perfecting our craft, we can improve. This stage is a lot of work, and we can wonder if we are really going to get a payoff and when, but hard work is a necessary stage to our success.

Four of Pentacles

The Four of Pentacles is a consolidation card. After the Three, we want to gather up whatever we have "earned" and hold on to it, fearing that we will not make it again. The Four is called the Power card, because we are gathering our power, our resources, and preventing unnecessary expenditures. Staying too long in this stage creates a contraction, and we hold on to things we must use and spend in order to go further. The classic image is of a fairly well-to-do man sitting in a fancy chair, holding four coins—two beneath his feet, one in his arms, and one on his crown. He looks like he's not giving them up. The Four of Pentacles can be described as a miser, as we don't want to part with what we have. There is a temptation to rest too long at this stage and become stagnant. Again, we just remember that change brings us forward. The secret of true security lies far beyond this stage.

Five of Pentacles

Worry is the name of this card, for it indicates worries about finances, loss, and insecurity. Fives are generally unstable cards, yet they have an energy to move us forward, being halfway between the Ace and Ten. The traditional image is of two ragged, indigent people, one seemingly crippled, wandering out in the snow beneath a church window of stained glass, with five pentacles above, yet they never look up to see them. When we worry about losing our power, from the fourth stage, and don't look up to see higher guidance, the higher plan of our immortal selves guiding us from "above," we experience fear, and we think that there will never be enough food, money, or anything else we need for security.

It's interesting to note that this card signifies worry, not disaster. What you are worrying about is not necessarily a reality. The card indicates the worry of the situation.

Six of Pentacles

The Six of Pentacles is the Success card, showing up when we have moved through our worry and realized a certain measure of success in our chosen work. The best known image of the card gives us two potential perspectives, as one rather rich-looking figure is holding a scale and giving four coins to two poorer-looking figures, perhaps the two from the Five of Pentacles. The card gives us two meanings, as you can be the successful one with enough to share with others, for charity, knowing that charity and giving mean that you can receive more. Success means a cycle: you give to others in order to receive what you need. Or you could be those who are receiving, having success by getting help from those around you, as the divine works through those around you, offering you the resources you need to aid your path.

Seven of Pentacles

The Seven of Pentacles can be called the Failure or Fear of Failure card, and in many ways it has similar lessons to the Five, as both Fives and Sevens are inherently unstable, yet they eventually move us on to the next step. The traditional image is of a farmer looking at his "crop" of seven discs, appearing melancholy. After your work and initial successes, there is a tendency to think, *That's all?* or *Shouldn't I have more?* Things are not proceeding as fast or intensely as you'd like, and without overwhelming success, it can be easy to think of yourself as a failure and have your fears and insecurities downplay your accomplishments, so that you focus on what you haven't done. If used correctly, however, this new insight can jump-start your goals and enable you to succeed on even deeper levels.

Eight of Pentacles

As the Seven mirrors the Five, the Eight of Pentacles mirrors the lessons of the Three. While the Three of Pentacles represents work scrutinized by others, the Eight signifies work scrutinized by yourself. You have reached a level of competence, if not mastery, and you now are both your best and worst judge. This is a time to put work and effort into your goals, because slow and steady wins the race. The card is called Prudence, for now is a time for caution and frugality. Many think that this card indicates impending loss, but it tells us that if we are cautious and practical now, particularly in regard to long-term goals, there will be no loss.

Nine of Pentacles

The Nine of Pentacles is known as the Gain card, for we have gained a greater measure of financial success and security. The common image is of a well-dressed woman in a garden filled with dark grapes and nine pentacles "growing" around her, in a place that suggests an estate or villa, and she usually has a hooded falcon on her hand. The falcon is the animal self that has a high vantage point to see the big picture. When we learn to listen to this type of intuition, we can succeed and truly gain, yet there is one more step to go.

Ten of Pentacles

The Ten of Pentacles represents the culmination of the quest for security. It is called the Wealth card, though I often call it the Secret to True Wealth, or the Secret to True Security. An old man is surrounded in seemingly opulent environment, with a nice robe, crests on the archway, and architecture that suggests a grand, if not royal, home. He has younger figures around him, who are usually interpreted as his family, as well as two dogs. The ten pentacles make up the Tree of Life pattern. The "secret" is that wealth does not come solely from money, but also from family, comfort, quality of life, and your ability to relax, enjoy it, and share it with others. Success is living a long, happy, healthy life doing what you enjoy and sharing your enjoyment with your loved ones.

The four remaining court cards of the suit are also a part of the quest. Court cards have a wide range of interpretation, making them some of the most difficult cards to read. There is some confusion to their titles, as different decks name them differently, but usually there is an adult male, an adult female, a young male, and a young female or androgynous figure. They can represent people in your life, and those who knowingly or unknowingly are influencing you on the quest for security. They can also represent the roles that you take while you are on the quest.

Some readers look at the court cards as extensions of the suit, with the Page/Princess as Eleven, the Knight/Prince as Twelve, the Queen as Thirteen, and the King/Knight as Fourteen. Tarot traditions drawing upon the teachings of ceremonial magick align the court cards with secondary or sub-elements. The King/Knight is fire, the Queen is water, the Knight/Prince is air, and the Page/Princess is earth. Thus the Queen of Pentacles would be the water of earth, or the emotional aspect of the material world, health, and prosperity.

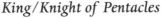

King/Knight of Pentacles

The adult male figure of the pentacles is traditionally thought of as the fire of earth, the will and drive to succeed and get things done. The Rider-Waite image has him on a throne, surrounded by dark grapes and growing things, with a scepter in one hand and a pentacle in the other. He is on solid ground, with a castle in the background and looking down to the source of his security, the land. When read as the fourteenth card, he is seen as not just the success, but now the burnout, as he's accomplished everything, and unless he starts a new quest, there is nothing left for him.

Queen of Pentacles

Like the King, the Queen of Pentacles is also sitting firmly on her throne, with only a pentacle in her lap, looking down lovingly at it, like a child. She is out in nature, surrounded by wild greens, not a cultivated garden. She is the water of earth, the emotional nature of the security quest, seeking emotional security along with the physical. As the thirteenth card, she represents the true fulfillment of the quest, and the satisfaction that comes from the fulfillment.

Knight/Prince of Pentacles

The young male figure is usually seated on a horse, or on a chariot, charging forward to his next journey. The Knight/Prince is the air element, so the Knight of Pentacles is the air of earth, the intellectual side of security. Generally he represents a realistic view on life, focused on understanding the task at hand. He uses the tools of analysis to determine what needs to be done before doing it. Once he has made a decision, he can be stubborn, and often overlooks the creative, artistic, or ethereal and concentrates on the down-to-Earth, practical, and concrete idea. When read as Twelve, he is the knight on the quest, charging forward into the world, seeking something new.

Page/Princess of Pentacles

More traditional decks depict this figure as the androgynous page or even a princess, while others plainly use a male figure as the Knave. The Pages offer advice and wisdom, traveling far to deliver a message, be it a literal message or a spiritual message. The Pages are the earth element, so this is the earth of earth, the seed of all earthly wisdom. The advice of the Page or Princess of Pentacles is usually practical and trustworthy. As the Eleven, she represents the message, or impetus of the "king" figure in the Ten of Pentacles, to go forward and go deeper into success, to seek out the higher spiritual meanings. But the first steps on such a quest are practical, concrete ones.

The quest for security is really a lesson in understanding the relationship between yourself and the universe. Security doesn't come from outside of yourself, from money, possessions, and job. While your business agreement might be with an employer, your sacred contract is with the divine, the gods, and the universe. It takes a quest of security to understand that. Those who can move through the steps of the question in meditation and ritual, or those who can see the quest as it is already playing out in life, have an infinite advantage over those who cannot, and they are able to act in harmony with the universe.

TRUE WILL

While we have alluded to it in other sections, the true power of exchange comes from knowing and performing our True Will. Our True Will is also known as our Mystic Will or Magickal Will. In the East, the Hindu term *dharma*, or "right action," is similar to our Western understanding of True Will. (Buddhism's concept of dharma is different, specifically seeing right action as following Buddhist teaching.) While your personal self, your ego self, wants certain things, these wants are informed by your personal life—your hopes, dreams, wounds, and failings. Often what our ego wants is to improve or salve the ego, to make the ego feel better and more important.

The True Will is the will of the soul, the impersonal self or higher self, known as the Bornless Self or Holy Guardian Angel in ceremonial magick traditions. It is what your soul wants for you, your purpose in this incarnation, and the theme of your soul's learning and work. It is not affected by your personal experiences, hopes, dreams, wounds, or failings. All those things can help lead you to the True Will, and they can help inform you, but they do not shape your True Will.

It is said that there are two types of consciousness we can be living in, as incarnated humans: karmic consciousness and dharmic consciousness. *Karmic consciousness* is the level of debt and credit, of cause and effect, as we stumble through life, searching. Everything we do has a repercussion we must deal with. These repercussions are neither good nor bad, but they are labeled as such, or as credit/debt, depending on whether we find the experience pleasant or unpleasant. It is the level of consciousness that is very attached to what we are doing, and attached to the ego.

Dharmic consciousness is the unattached view, doing our soul's work in any given moment. We are in the right place, at the right time, doing the right thing. We follow the urgings and yearning of our soul, even when it doesn't make conscious or practical sense. We are open and guided, and know how to flow with the tides of life. Dharmic consciousness is living the life your soul wants for you, and having clear communication with your higher self and other spiritual guides. That's not to say there are not consequences to your actions, for there always are, but dharmic consciousness results in more dharma for you to do. However, the actions are a joy, for they are what your soul wants.

One can be in karmic consciousness in one area of life, and dharmic in others. You can experience True Will in your career and struggle in your relationships, or vice versa. The more you understand the quality of life, and its flow in one area of your life, the easier it is to bring it to other areas. Dharma, following our souls' will, is always a decision, and our spiritual practices make the decision easier, as we can each hear the voice of our soul better. But we can slip in and out of dharmic consciousness as we go through our lives, or even as we go through our day. There is no "getting it" and no more work. It constantly requires a choice.

This choice is the best method of exchange we have with the universe. When we choose to carry out our dharma, which takes quite a quest itself, not only through the pentacle's quest of security, but through the quests of the other three suits—fire/wands/identity, air/swords/truth, and water/cups/compassion—we exchange our energy with the universe, and the universe provides us with everything we need to fulfill our dharma. We still have to do follow-up and real-world action, and we still do our magick, but things line up much more easily for us, as the universe supports us in all we do when we are in dharmic consciousness.

We can make money in karmic consciousness. Lots of people do. Yet it's not the full success of those truly visionary people, who, whether they realize it or not, are in dharmic consciousness. Dharmic consciousness doesn't always give us massive wealth, but it does give us massive satisfaction, balance, and happiness to fulfill our work and have everything provided for without worry. That is the true power of exchange.

CHAPTER 4

PLANNING, TIMING, AND LOCATION

Everybody who has done any real-estate investing, searching for a home or other property to buy, knows the overused phrase "location, location, location!" Where you find your investments is very important and can determine their future value. Yet those truly versed in real estate know that it's not just location—it's also timing. Real estate moves in cycles, and those who know when and where to buy can cash in on those cycles.

All investment is ruled by timing and location. Everything has cycles, and everything is affected by where it operates. Even when you are doing stock-market investment, and think location doesn't matter, the company you are investing in is affected by where it is based, the local and national laws governing it, and the employees who come to work. Even though location may not seem to play into your assessment, it does affect the situation.

Just as all investment is ruled by timing and location, so is all prosperity magick. Learning to plan your magick with the proper flow of spiritual energies, and learning to do such workings in places of power, in harmony with your intention, will help you have a much greater chance of success.

FINANCIAL ASTROLOGY

Most magicians and witches study a bit of astrology, for astrology is an art and science that allows us to understand the patterns and flow of energy at any given time and place. All magick is influenced by these tides of energy, not just prosperity and money magick. The basic idea behind the working of astrology comes from the second Hermetic Principle, a wisdom teaching that says, "As above, so below. As below, so above." The apparent patterns of planets and stars in the sky correspond with patterns of energy that are on the Earth, and in human society. Because we are so close to the earthly energies, we cannot see the larger pattern, or use it to make predictions very well. However, if we can see a larger pattern that is farther away from us, such as that of the sky, we can use it to help us make decisions regarding earthly matters.

Each of the planets, signs, and their locations in the sky correspond with an area and function in our world. While astrology is a science, it is also an art form, for we must creatively interpret these signs and omens, and that gives us a wide range of possibilities, even when we are dealing with specific patterns. Some critics of astrology erroneously think that astrologers believe that we are controlled or compelled by the stars. The stars do not compel. They correspond with what is already happening. The patterns occur simultaneously, even though with all rational explanation, they seem unconnected. There is no logical reason to connect a particular part of the sky with your financial health, yet there is a part of the sky that indicates your finances.

While the scope of this work is not to give you a crash course in astrology, I do hope to give you enough of an understanding of the financial pieces of the astrological puzzle to allow you to put them to use in your magick. You will know enough of the concepts to then seek out more detailed astrological information, and you will be able to apply it to your financial magick and goals.

Two basic forms of astrology concern us in financial magick. Astrologers can read your natal chart, and with it, they can determine your innate abilities, talents, and propensities in the area of finance. Your *natal chart* simply means your birth chart, and astrologers worldwide believe that the moment when you are born encapsulates many of the blessings and trials you will face, your life "lessons." They also believe that an understanding of the natal chart gives you a great awareness of yourself and how to function better in your life.

The second function of astrology is to look at the current patterns of the sky and use those patterns in a variety of ways to pick auspicious times to do things. The general patterns of the sky are read to determine times when financial magick will be more successful, or more difficult. This is the form of astrology most witches and magicians are concerned with, as they can tell when to do their rituals simply by reading an astrological calendar. In more complex forms, the current pattern of the sky can be compared to your natal chart, and the relationship between the two can tell an astrologer when the timing is particularly good or difficult for you personally, because your own individual natal chart is involved.

If you want to get deeper into financial astrology, you can consider any company you invest in to be an individual being, with its own blessings, traits, and lessons. You can create a natal chart for when the company was founded or "born," or for the stock market itself, or for any other financial "entity" you will be dealing with, and you can use the natal chart and the current patterns to help you predict the best times to buy, sell, or make other financial transactions.

While financial astrology could be a whole book in itself, let's simply start by looking at the most important factors of astrology that pertain to finance and money, for both astrological timing and natal chart interpretation. First we have to start with a very basic introduction to astrological terms.

We have four major divisions, or parts, in our understanding of astrology. They include the following:

Planets

Planets are the heavenly bodies in our own solar system. Each has their own orbit, except for the Sun, and while we know intellectually that the other planets orbit the Sun, from our perspective they appear to orbit the Earth. Astrology is all about how the patterns of the sky appear to us on Earth, so we act as if they do orbit around us. Each planet embodies a component of ourselves, of our psyche. Each has a different function and purpose in our lives. The ancients knew seven basic planets. They include the Sun, the Moon, Mercury, Venus, Mars, Jupiter, and Saturn. Technically the Sun and Moon are known as luminaries, but they count as planets by their function in astrology. With the additions of modern discoveries, astrologers also use Uranus, Neptune, and Pluto, as well as some other smaller heavenly bodies, such as Chiron and the larger asteroids of the asteroid belt. Although the technical definition of a planet is debatable, with new scientific rulings promoting and demoting planetary status, anything with its own orbit in our solar system can be seen as a planet in astrology.

Signs

The signs occupy a specific area of space around the planet and appear to rotate around us from our earthly perspective. The "belt" of the signs is divided into twelve segments, each thirty degrees. Each sign is associated with one of the twelve stellar constellations of the zodiac. There is a pattern to the signs. Taurus always follows Aries. Aries always follows Pisces. Pisces always follows Aquarius. The planets appear to occupy a sign, and that sign is said to influence the way that planet operates. The Sun in Libra operates very differently from the Sun in Scorpio. The band of zodiac signs also revolves around the Earth.

Houses

Houses are fixed areas in the sky that the signs and planet seem to occupy. Astrologers mathematically divide the sky into twelve sections—six above the horizon and six below. Unlike the signs, they do not rotate. Different systems of calculation, such as the Placidus or Koch systems, yield different types of houses, and astrologers each have their own favorite method, but generally the houses are fixed areas in the sky that appear to be larger or smaller, depending on where you are on the planet. The houses look different near one of the poles than they do at the equator. This is why most astrologers ask for a birth location as well as a time and day to create a natal chart. The Equal House system is different from the more traditional Placidus or Koch, because it simply uses houses of thirty degrees and does not vary their sizes.

Aspects

The aspects of a chart are specific angles made between planets. If you consider the planet Earth to be the center of the chart, the joint that connects two other planets creates the angle. Not all angles are considered aspects, only very specific ones are, and the angle between the planets determines whether the energy of each planet supports or conflicts with the other. When planets are not making these specific angles, they are considered fairly neutral toward each other. Magickal timing comes from maximizing the times when the planetary energies you need for your intentions are in harmony and supporting each other, and minimizing the times when the planets you want to call upon are conflicting.

Keeping track of seven to ten planets, twelve signs, twelve houses, and a variety of aspects, and all their potential combinations is a daunting task for the aspiring astrology student. One astrology teacher gave me a great analogy to understand the basic parts of an astrological chart.

The planets are like actors. They can play any part, but each has its specialty, its own persona as an actor, and some roles fit better than others. The signs are the roles. They determine how the actor acts. What quality will the actor have? As the planet moves through its orbit, it will have a chance to try all twelve roles. Some the planet will naturally like, and others it won't. The houses are the scenes, the stages where the actors are playing their roles. Each house is a realm of life, a scene where things happen. The aspects are the kind of dialogue the actors are having with each other. Are they antagonists, friends, lovers, allies, or sworn enemies? But as the roles change, the relationship and dialogue between the planets change, so no role or dialogue stays the same for long.

The birth chart is a snapshot of the actors playing their roles in the scenes of your life. Their energy will be with you in some way for the rest of your life. Each planet is acting out a part of your psyche, and understanding how each part is working, or not working, with every other part will help you make the best decisions in life.

For financial matters, as well as general timing matters, the important planets to look for in your natal chart include the following:

Sun

The Sun is your core identity in astrology. Arguably the most powerful planet, as it denotes your personality and the identity you are developing in this lifetime, the Sun magickally indicates your potential energy to do things, and it is called upon in matters of wealth and good fortune. The Sun's metal is gold, the most valuable metal, prized the world over. It's valued for its color and resistance to tarnish, rather than its usefulness, as it's a soft and pliable metal. Light and beauty are linked with financial value. That is why we value beautiful shining gems, metals, and artwork.

Venus

Venus is usually seen as the planet of love, but it is the planet of attractions first and foremost. Venus's energy will attract whatever you want. If you value money, it attracts money. Venus's color is green, and we traditionally associate money, and money magick, with green. It's the green of nature, of vegetation, and of the nature goddess Venus that is the true prosperity symbolism here. Money is associated with Venus because once we attract it, we don't want to let it go, unless it's to purchase comforts and luxuries, expressions of material wealth.

Jupiter

Jupiter is the most important planet for prosperity magick. Beyond the energy of success, or the ability to attract what we want, Jupiter is the planet of expansion. It is generally a planet of blessings, and it is said to confer blessings from all four of the elements when used properly. Jupiter is the planet of material wealth in the earthly realm, and its color is royal blue. It is the planet of power with the fire element. It is the planet of health and well-being in the watery realm and the planet of wisdom with the air element. Those who are aligned with Jupiter's blessings have health, wealth, power, and the wisdom to use it all. Jupiter is the planet of the inner teacher, the Eastern guru or master. When we tap into the power of Jupiter, we tap into the power of our inner teacher. In the natal chart, it gives clues to our higher self, our higher purpose, and our dharmic vocation.

Pluto

Pluto is a "newer" planet currently classified as a dwarf planet, yet to modern astrologers, it is still a major power. Named after the Roman god of the dead, with his Greek counterpart named Hades, the planet is associated with death and transformation. Its movement marks areas of great change, of letting go and rebirth. Such change comes with the feeling of destruction, to make something new. The god Pluto is also the lord of hidden riches, as the deep Earth, where the dead are said to reside, is also the source of metals, minerals, and gems—signs of wealth. In many cultures, particularly those of the East, the realm of the dead is associated with the wealth and well-being of the living. Magick involving Pluto also adds power and force to any spellcrafting.

When you seek to do astrological magick, pay particular attention to where these planets are. Each will occupy a zodiac sign. Does that sign match the intention of your magick? As you explore astrology, look at these four planets in your own natal chart. What sign does each one occupy, and does that sign give a better understanding of how your identity and energy are, how you attract things, and what your higher purpose is? These signs will give you clues as to how your own relationship with wealth is operating. For more information on all twelve signs, look to the appendix.

The houses that are most important in financial matters are the houses of material reality. They are "naturally ruled" or in harmony with the earth signs of the zodiac, since earth influences financial matters. In our tarot, the pentacle suit is the earth suit of finance and security. The earth signs are the second sign of Taurus, the sixth sign of Virgo, and the tenth sign of Capricorn. The houses are numbered, and these three signs rule or are in harmony with the Second, Sixth, and Tenth Houses, respectively.

Second House

The Second House is where you have your resources. The sign on the cusp of this house will tell you how you work with your resources and give you an idea of some of the resources you have. Often called the house of money or investment, it is so much more. Some astrologers read it as the house of the body, for the body is the first possession, the first resource you own in this life, and the last one you give up as you die. It is your physical resource and your health. It is also where you find your skills, talents, and abilities that help you earn money.

Sixth House

The Sixth House is the house of daily work, sometimes known as the house of daily service. In this house we find how you work every day. What is your job like? How are you a part of society, and how does your job help to serve society? The sign that is on the cusp of this house gives you a greater idea of how your day-to-day work life will be and how to work best in that framework.

Eighth House

The Eighth House is not naturally ruled by an earth sign, but by the water sign of Scorpio. It is included in financial astrology because it is the opposite to the Second House. The Second House is the house of what you have and what you plan for, while the Eighth House is what you have to let go of, or some unexpected financial matters. It is known in older teachings as the House of Sex, Death, and Taxes, because we can't truly and absolutely control any of those things, yet we desire to control them. We now call it the House of Transformation, but taxes, debts, and unexpected inheritances can show up in this area of the chart.

Tenth House

The Tenth House is the house of your career and vocation. The four houses on the cardinal directions of the chart are often given special names and greater importance. The Tenth House is the only finance house in this category. Its cusp is also called Midheaven, as it's the highest point in the heavens when the chart is cast. In a natal chart, it represents where you are going, or what you are here to do. I think of it as the house of career and career responsibility, where you have to do your work in the world.

Look at your natal chart, if available, and determine what sign is ruling the cusps of the Second, Sixth, and Tenth Houses. What do those signs tell you about the resources you have, the way you go about your daily work, and the way you go about your vocation? Each will give you clues, and each is linked to the next financial house. Look to see what planets, if any, are in these houses. The planets, and their aspects, can represent

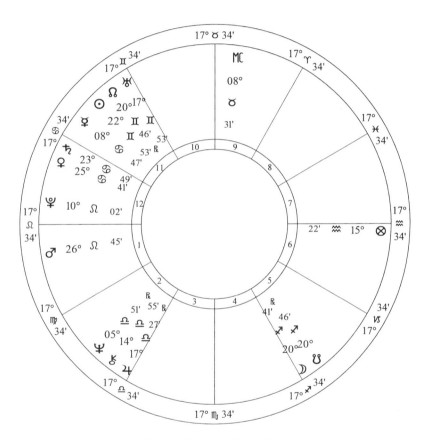

Figure 6: Example Natal Chart
Birth Date: 06/14/1946 (June 14, 1946) / Birth Time: 09:51 AM EDT
Birth Place: Queens, NY / Geocentric / Tropical / Equal House / True Node

blessings in these areas, or challenges to work through and overcome. For more information on all the houses, look at the appendix.

When we look at the example in figure 6, we can start by taking note of the houses associated with finance. The Second House, the house of resources and what you have, is ruled by Virgo. Virgo is a mutable earth sign, with a capacity to hold and manage a lot of details. Virgo is the power of process, or being meticulous in the process. Virgo is an asset for this person. Inside the Second House is Neptune, Chiron, and Jupiter, all in Libra. Libra is the sign of balance and justice, the power of equality. The inner vision of Neptune is one of balance, and it manifests in the arena of resources. Jupiter's ability to expand and bring luck indicates areas of luck in relationships, and the balance of relationships. While many people think of relationships as purely personal, in the Second House, they would also include business relationships and business partnerships. Both are assets for an individual. Jupiter is also making trine aspects, beneficial aspects with Uranus, the planet of inspiration and unconventional thinking, and a point known as the North Node of the Moon, the direction where one should be headed. Both are in Gemini in the Eleventh House of social service and societal interaction. Chiron, the planetoid that indicates where you need to heal and share that healing with others, is also in Libra and the Second House, indicating a lot of energy being placed on balance and finance, possibly from past-life issues where money was a problem.

We can also see that, in this example, the Sixth House of daily work is ruled by Capricorn. Capricorn's nature is one of responsibility and structure. While mythically Capricorn is the sea goat, many astrologers simply use the image of the goat—with its nature of climbing the mountain, to be at the top—as a more easily understandable image. Daily work will be the disciplined climb to the top, continuously looking for new challenges. In this example, no planets are specifically in the Sixth House. The Part of Fortune, signified by a circle with an X, is an Arabic Point, a popular point that is not a planet or an asteroid, but a calculated "sensitive" point in the chart, based upon the position of the Sun, Moon, and ascendant. It indicates worldly success, health, innate talents, natural abilities, and general "good fortune." Here in the Sixth House, a house of work, it indicates success in day-to-day work, and reveals that the work has an innovative, individualist Aquarian flair.

Here, the Tenth House of career is ruled by Taurus, the fixed earth sign. Taurus is about gaining and holding on to resources, holding on to luxury and wealth, and using it in the manner that most suits you and your temperament. Careers that are Taurean will be have qualities such as strength, stubbornness, and practicality. The bottom line of profit or loss will be emphasized.

Other planets associated with finance are the Sun, Venus, and Pluto. The Sun is in Gemini in the Eleventh House. This person will be a creative thinker, he will be able to see both sides of a situation, and he will be in the public or social eye. His Leo ascendant, the rising sign ruling the First House, will show that he will enjoy the public attention, and, on a side note, he will have interesting hair, as Leo rising can indicate an unusual "mane." Pluto is also in Leo, in the Twelfth House, giving a lot of power and transformative energy to the public persona. Venus is in Cancer in the Twelfth House, showing that what he values, from money to romance, will have a strong emotional and protective quality.

While this short interpretation focusing on financial matters only scratches the surface of this person, it does give you some insight as to how to interpret your own chart in regard to financial strengths and weaknesses. Who does this chart belong to? None other than Donald Trump, famous self-made millionaire in real estate and now pop-culture icon.

Astrology is an art as well as an esoteric science, and not all astrologers will agree upon how to calculate and interpret a chart. If you use another house system for this chart, such as the Placidus or Koch house divisions, Trump will only have Neptune in the Second House with Chiron and Jupiter moving to the Third House. I generally tend to prefer the Placidus system, but I've noticed that many astrologers advocate the use of the Equal House system for this particular chart.

Of course, to have the best understanding of your personal chart in its entirety, not just in regard to money—as money is only one facet of life, and it is interconnected with all others—I highly suggest seeking out a reputable astrologer who will do a personal consultation of your natal chart, and visiting this astrologer regularly to discuss the current movement of the planets and how they are affecting you and your life. I go roughly once a year to understand the upcoming patterns in my life and to be able to take full advantage of the easy moments and learn more from the difficult ones.

The practical magickal timing comes from looking at the planets in their signs and the current aspects that are occurring. Most magicians who look at an astrological calendar for simple spellcasting timing do not draw up a chart or consult the house placement for any given moment when the ritual will take place. We use simpler techniques and overall, intuition is the most important thing. Decide what planets fit your intention best, and look to see what they are currently doing. Or when you learn to scan a calendar, you can take advantage of good opportunities for spellcraft as they arise, and plan your spells around what fortunate alignment is about to occur.

If you can't find a technical reason to do a ritual, but you intuitively feel called to do it at a specific time, you might psychically know something that you can't find on a calendar intellectually. Likewise, if you have a strong feeling about when *not* to do a spell, though you don't know why and there is no overt reason on the calendar, you should still follow your intuition. The tides flow in and out, and there will always be another time to catch a wave of beneficial energy for your magick.

With this in mind, here are some general guidelines to help you plan your rituals better:

Moon Phase

Witches teach that when you want to increase or attract something, you should do your magick as the Moon is waxing or growing in light. If you want something powerful really quickly, you should do it as close to the full Moon as possible, and ideally start before the Moon has reached its peak. If you want to get rid of something, you should do it when the Moon is waning in light, and if you want to banish something immediately, you should do it as close to the dark Moon as possible, before the Moon starts waxing again. Modern astrological calendars divide the Moon cycle into four quarters. First and Second Quarters are waxing. The end of the Second Quarter is the peak of the full Moon. Third and Fourth Quarters are waning. The end of the Fourth Quarter is the peak of the dark Moon. Generally, money magick and prosperity magick are done during a waxing Moon, and the full Moon is regarded as a growing silver "coin" in sympathy with your intentions.

Planetary Days and Hours

Magicians have traditionally assigned one of the seven ancient planets to each of the days of the week, believing that each day is overtly influenced by the corresponding planet's power. The best days for prosperity magick are Sunday, the day of the Sun; Thursday, the day of Jupiter; and Friday, the day of Venus. Monday, the Moon's day, is a great day for any type of magick. Saturdays are generally avoided, as its planet, Saturn, is the planet of contraction and loss, unless the Moon is full or another alignment is occurring at the time. The days are also divided into planetary hours. (A variety of complex formulas for calculating planetary hours can be found in my previous book *The Outer Temple of Witchcraft*.) The easiest way to work with planetary hours is to know that the first hour, at sunrise, of any given day is ruled by the planet of that day. If you want extra Venus power, doing a spell at sunrise on Friday will give you the added benefit of doing the spell in the hour, as well as the day, of Venus. If you want more Jupiter energy, do your spell at sunrise on a Thursday, for both the hour and day of Jupiter.

Signs

All the planets occupy one of the zodiac signs at any given time. Some spend a long time in a sign. Others change quite rapidly. The Sun takes a year to go through all twelve signs, while the Moon takes slightly less than a month, so usually magicians are most concerned about Moon signs, as the Moon rules all magick. For prosperity magick, you will also want to find out what sign the Sun, Venus, and Jupiter are occupying. For strict money magick and wealth magick, to increase financial gain, your magick will be more successful if the Moon, Venus, or any of these other planets occupy earth signs—Taurus, Virgo, and Capricorn. Taurus is the ideal sign because it deals with financial comfort and luxury. Virgo helps us gain through day-to-day work, and Capricorn deals with financial gain through our vocation. If you are doing career magick, the fire signs are better, because they give us an impetus to take action. If the planets, particularly the

Moon, Sun, or Jupiter, are occupying fire signs, your career spells will be more successful.

Aspects

In terms of spellcasting, aspects can be divided into those that are helpful or beneficial and those that are more detrimental to our magick. When you are doing prosperity magick, you want the planets involved in your spellmaking to be in their fortunate aspects. Or, at the very least, they should make no detrimental aspects with any of the other planets you are using. They could be making detrimental aspects to other planets that are not involved in your magick, and that's all right.

Table 1: Beneficial Aspects for Spellcasting				
☌	0°	conjunction	direct support and communication, intensity	same sign
⚺	30°	semi-sextile	minor support, neutral, reactive	adjacent signs
⚹	60°	sextile	compliment, understanding, minor support	two signs apart, same gender, opposing elements
△	120°	trine	support, strong understanding	four signs apart, same element

Table 2: Detrimental Aspects for Spellcasting				
∠	45°	semi-square	friction, irritation	adjacent signs
□	90°	square	tension, obstacles, block	three signs apart, same quality
⚼	135°	sesqui-square	abrasive, difficult communication	five signs apart
⚻	150°	inconjunct	misdirection, misalignment	five signs apart
☍	180°	opposition	conflict, no support, cross purposes	six signs apart, opposite sign, same quality

The only exceptions are the Sun and the Moon, for the Sun and Moon are in opposition, technically a detrimental aspect, when the Moon is full, yet it's the most powerful time to do magick.

Retrogrades

A *retrograde* occurs when a planet appears to be going backwards in its orbit when viewed from Earth. We know it's an optical illusion, but the basic principles of magick often work on appearances from a certain perspective, rather than the actual phenomenon. Since the planet appears to be going backwards, its energy and influence are said to be moving backwards as well, and many astrologers interpret retrogrades by focusing on past events regarding the planet's sphere of influence in our lives. For example, a Venus retrograde can trigger unresolved issues and memories involving past romantic relationships because Venus is the planet associated with love and romance. This often creates some difficulty for people. All the planets except the Sun and Moon have times of retrograde, and the calendar will mark these periods with the symbol "℞." Then, many weeks or even months later, a "D" will indicate that they have gone direct again. When one of the financial planets is in retrograde, it's a good time to think about your past decisions, learn from them, and contemplate your relationship with money, luxury, and career. It's a time of introspection, not new actions.

Void of Course

You want to avoid times when the Moon is *void of course*, meaning that it is not making any major aspects before it enters the next sign. Its energy is said to be ungrounded, and magick done at this time is usually unsuccessful. A calendar notes this condition with a "v/c" and a time. Void of course lasts until the Moon enters the next astrological sign. Once it does, the Moon is no longer void, as the energy has shifted, and you are free to do magick.

Your astrological calendar or day planner will give you specific instruction in reading its individual layout, but here is an example using a fairly standard layout, to give you an idea how to read your calendar and look for financially advantageous times:

Table 3: Thursday, December 20, 2007		
Second Quarter	☽ in ♉	Moon in Taurus
Moon trine Saturn	☽ △ ♄	6:41 a.m.
Mercury enters Capricorn	☿ enters ♑	9:43 a.m.
Mercury conjunct Jupiter	☿ ☌ ♃	4:54 p.m.
Mercury sextant Uranus	☿ ✶ ♅	5:14 p.m.
Sun conjunct Pluto	☉ ☌ ♇	7:14 p.m.
Moon opposition Venus	☽ ☍ ♀	10:41 p.m.

The day given in table 3 would be a good day for prosperity and money magick. Let's look at its qualities in detail, so you can learn how to determine the best days for your magick. First, it's a Thursday, the day of Jupiter, for expansion and abundance. The Moon is in the Second Quarter, approaching full. The Moon goes full on the twenty-third of December, that Sunday. The Second Quarter means the Moon is waxing, so it's a good time for gaining things through magick. The Moon is in the sign of Taurus, an earth sign of luxury and financial gain.

As for the aspects of the day, the Moon is trine Saturn. While Saturn is the opposing force of Jupiter—contraction rather than expansion—Saturn is making a beneficial aspect to the Moon, meaning that it is not working against the Moon but is in harmony with the Moon. It is a time of manifestation.

Mercury is conjunct with Jupiter, meaning that our thoughts and words (Mercury) are fused with the power to expand (Jupiter). Whatever we think and speak will grow bigger. Mercury has also entered Capricorn, the sign of the sea goat, the archetypal image of the father, or the main "bread winner" of the family. Capricorn deals with responsibility, and often the responsibility of a job. Mercury is also making a minor beneficial aspect to Uranus. This aspect does not deal with money particularly, but Uranus is the planet of inspiration. Perhaps this spell will give us new insight into our financial situation.

Most powerfully, the Sun (which is in Sagittarius, the sign naturally ruled by Jupiter) is conjunct with Pluto, which is also in Sagittarius. For two planets to be conjunct, they must be in the same sign. Pluto brings absolute power to the magick, linking the success and energy of the Sun with the regenerative riches of the Underworld.

The only ill-advised aspect is with Venus, which is opposed to the Moon later that evening. While Venus rules fast money and quick cash, this day would be best for larger issues of career, finance, and long-term wealth.

WIND AND WATER

While timing plays an important role in Western magick, our knowledge and teachings about location and placement are a little less sophisticated. We have teachings of geomantic magick—understanding the nature and flow of the landscape, particularly through what are usually referred to today as ley lines—but much of these teachings are half forgotten, and those individuals with detailed knowledge usually feel that it's unwise to reveal too much to the general public.

Our Western ways make an unusual counterpoint with the Eastern teachings, which are so widely available today. The Eastern teachings have made their way into Western world, filling the gaps of our esoteric teachings. We know these teachings under the name *feng shui*, usually translated as "wind and water." Developed in esoteric traditions of China, feng shui is an art and science used to shape the flow of energy in the landscape, including in and around human dwellings. It is used to promote the healthy flow of chi, or life-force energy, and block the flow of poisonous chi that would harm or stagnate your health and good fortune. Life force is said to flow with wind and water, giving us the association with the term feng shui. Its original Chinese characters were associated with the connection of the heavenly forces with the Earth. While today we think of it as an adjunct to home decorating, feng shui really involves a variety of deeply esoteric subjects, from astrology and numerology to the properties of medicines, stones, plants, and spiritual philosophy.

How does the study of feng shui today help us in our quest for prosperity and good fortune? While many schools of feng shui have developed, the use of the geometric figure known as the *Pa Kua* has become

Figure 7: Pa Kua

Wealth	Home	Love
Family and Health		Creativity
Knowledge	Career	Mentors and Friends

Figure 8: Modern Pa Kua

very popular (fig. 7). The eight trigrams of feng shui are arranged around the octagon of the Pa Kua, and they organize the esoteric forces.

The Pa Kua is laid out over a home or office, and the areas in the building that correspond to the esoteric forces are decorated with appropriate images, symbols, and objects to promote the strong and healthy development of these forces. Obviously there are places on this Pa Kua for our career and good fortune. A modern Pa Kua with nine squares has been developed for the ease of practitioners doing this work (fig. 8).

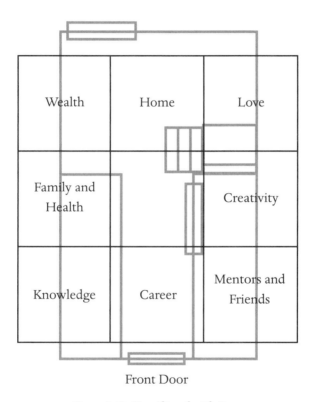

Front Door

Figure 9: Pa Kua Aligned with Door

Two different techniques exist for aligning the Pa Kua with your building. In the Black Hat Tibetan school, the side of the Pa Kua (usually called a *Bagua* in this school) indicating knowledge, career, and mentors is usually aligned with the front door designed by the architect. The idea is that the front door, being the door you use most often, is bringing in the most chi with its use, and it is the place of alignment. We typically bring the most chi to our careers. The career section is usually aligned with the front door, but sometimes it's closer to one of the sides, knowledge or mentors (fig. 9). Some feng shui practitioners believe that if there is a door or other opening to your home that you use more often than your front door (for instance a garage door), then that entrance should be aligned with the knowledge, career, and mentors side.

The second method, from the Compass school, aligns the Pa Kua with the cardinal directions of the map. Career is always in alignment with the north, usually the northern wall of the building, regardless of the door placement. Some will align it exactly with magnetic north, rather than relying on the rising and setting of the Sun.

Both techniques can be used not just for an entire home, but to break down a particular room. Each room can have its own sub–Pa Kua. If you rent a room or have an apartment, your own personal feng shui starts there. Usually the front-door method of the Black Hat school is more popular in Westernized feng shui systems. Either system can work, but practitioners trained in a particular tradition have their own preferences and teachings behind it.

While the entire Pa Kua represents a balanced life and should be looked at as a whole in order for it to bring harmony and prosperity, the sections of the Pa Kua that specifically deal with our topic at hand include the following:

Wealth and Prosperity

Direction: Southeast

Colors: Green, Purple, Red

In the prosperity section of the Pa Kua, place objects that symbolize or resonate with money and good fortune. A picture of someone who is highly financially successful could go in the area, as well as an expensive item, like a piece of art. Objects that are colored purple, green, red, or even gold, or that are otherwise rich or luxurious would also do well in the area. A red string tied to eight gold or brass coins—for instance, traditional Chinese coins that have a hole in the center—in this area of the home is used to bring wealth. Bamboo wind chimes, as well as water fountains, are used to promote success in the wealth area, because they both promote the movement of wind and water, of life force, in the area where life force is needed for successful growth.

Career
Direction: North
Colors: Black, Blue

In feng shui, if not Western magick, water symbolizes wealth. Having pictures of water, or actual water in the career or wealth sections of your home or office is very beneficial. Goldfish in water also increase finance and prosperity. Having nine fish—eight gold and one black to avert bad luck and petty crime, is a traditional feng shui technique. If you live in a dangerous neighborhood, you could keep eight black fish and one gold to prevent theft. Plants and flowers are symbols of health and prosperity and growth, and they can be used in the career section or any other section of the Pa Kua where you want growth. They must be healthy; if they are sick, they must be replaced. Living plants are used, particularly evergreens and bamboo, as well as cut flowers. Artificial flowers supposedly have the same effect as living ones.

Fame and Recognition
Direction: South
Colors: Red

Place red objects in the fame and recognition section to attract attention. Symbols that get attention, such as a solid, high-backed chair, will help you resonate with the energy of solid attention in the world, as if you were always sitting in that chair. In that section of the home, do anything you wish to be recognized for. If you are a musician, write your music there. If you are an accountant, do your accounting there, if possible. Whatever you do that you wish to receive recognition and praise for, do it in this section, and surround yourself with eye-catching and strong objects that will get attention. Fountains can also be used to increase fame, just as they can in the wealth section. In fact, a fountain can be used in any of these sections listed to promote the flow of healthy energy and increase prosperity.

Mentors and Networking

Direction: Northeast

Colors: White, Gray, Black, Gold, Metallic

In the mentors section, put anything that represents your faith and philosophy in life—the kind of mentors you are hoping to attract. You want mentors that are compatible with you and your worldview. Quartz crystal can be used to activate this section. Anyone who is looking to find mentors should spend time in this section of the home, but especially teens. Metal wind chimes are particularly useful both for mentors and for career, and they are more beneficial than the bamboo wind chimes of other sections. Metal helps activate these sections, where it would be detrimental in other sections, based on the Chinese five-element system that includes metal and wood.

Feng shui is a complicated art of interrelated correspondences, and this hasn't even scratched the surface. If you are interested in more, I suggest starting out with *Feng Shui for Beginners* by Richard Webster. By acquiring more complete knowledge, you can balance aspects of your entire life—not just prosperity.

Many witches dislike the use of feng shui in Western magick and witchcraft. The core ideas of feng shui were based on weather patterns over the Chinese landscape thousands of years ago, and do not speak as strongly to the Western psyche already versed in the land-based traditions of paganism. The Eastern elemental system is different, using metal and wood instead of air and spirit, and the arrangement and correspondences are different. I have a friend who is a very adept high-level magician, and she says that feng shui simply does not work here in the Western world.

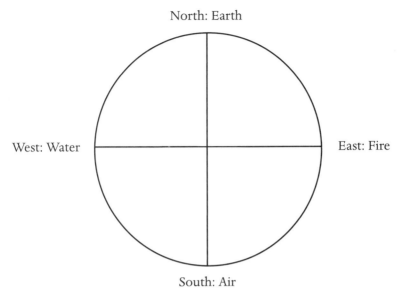

Figure 10: Witch's Circle

The basic idea behind feng shui is creating harmony and flow in the energies in your environment. It uses an Eastern mandala to order and organize the universe. A Western mandala could be used just as easily and successfully. I know it can, because I've arranged my own home and office around the Western mandala of the witch's circle (fig. 10).

Use the circular mandala laid out with the elements in place of the Pa Kua when designing your home. Rather than align it with the front door, I align it with the true directions of the compass. Then I place objects that have magickal significance to me—decorating with the appropriate colors, symbols, stones, and plants in those areas. Although my house is pretty "witchy," many of the objects just look like decoration.

There are several different elemental orientations for the witch's circle. While the most common has air in the east and fire in the south, I prefer fire in the east and air in the south, as I was trained. If you have a different orientation, use the one that works best for you and your family. Lay the circle over your home, or in microcosm, over any room. Use the directions to help you arrange and decorate your home.

Table 4: Elemental Associations			
Earth	North	Black, Green, Brown	Solid, Heavy, Dark, and Grounded. Hematite, Jet, Jasper, Smoky Quartz, Black Tourmaline, Onyx, Emerald, Dark Agates.
Fire	East, South	Red, Yellow, Orange	Energizing, Warming, Sharp, Eye Catching. Garnet, Ruby, Fire Opal, Amber.
Air	South, East	Blue, Yellow, White	Clear, Tranquil, Mentally Stimulating. Blue Lace Agate, Kyanite, Turquoise, Amethyst.
Water	West	Blue, Green	Cooling, Soothing, Opening the Heart. Moonstone, Selenite, Chalcedony, Rose Quartz, Peridot.

For the work of this book, pay particular attention to the areas of earth, for wealth and finance, and to fire, for career. Take note of when those areas of the home become cluttered or dirty. When you change them, do those aspects of your life change? Notice your house as a microcosm for your life.

As you explore other spellcraft in this book using herbal charms and crystals and making specific talismans for wealth and success, you can enhance the effectiveness of these items by placing them in the earth or fire area of your home. They can be used much like the traditional feng shui remedies to alter the flow and harmony of energy in your environment and your life.

For those wanting a greater depth to this technique, I suggest you learn whatever you can about feng shui, but then apply the ideas of it to a symbol system that works best for you. Observe. If it worked, then you are effectively altering the flow of energy in your space. If it didn't, perhaps the choices you are making are not effective and you need to do further research before you start making your own creative decisions in this technique.

THE MAGICK CIRCLE

The most important alignment of time and location for a witch occurs in the magick circle. The magick circle is a sacred space created through ritual, said to be a space beyond space and a time beyond time, a temple between the worlds. It grants both protection and focus, helping us gather power and direct it toward a specific goal. The circle contains both the power generated by our bodies and minds, and the powers we've summoned through evocation, such as the elements and divinities. While magick can be done at any time and in any place, our best magick is done between the worlds, because we have clearer communication with all the beings of the Otherworld, to partner with us, and we are in alignment with the timeless forces and better able to make change in the world of time and space.

While there is nothing specific to prosperity magick in the teachings of the magick circle, if you plan on doing powerful prosperity magick, it would be good to know how to cast the circle. Learning it now will help you focus on more specific prosperity magick in future chapters. The circle elevates simple folk magick to the realm of theurgy, a magickal partnership with the gods. Casting the magick circle often in your home or outside on your property elevates the vibration of the area, inviting in good spirits, divine protection, and blessings on many levels. Regular ritual can be a "remedy" for difficult energies as much as any feng shui placement in the home.

Circle magick is found in most forms of modern witchcraft today, and it can trace its roots back to both a ceremonial magick influence on the modern Craft and also folk rituals of circle dancing and tribal customs of gathering for ritual in the circle and honoring the four directions. The basics of modern witchcraft circle castings are fairly simple, and different traditions embellish them based on their own mythologies and symbolism. The instructions here are very basic, and not steeped too deeply in any one tradition. They constitute a stripped-down version of my own circle-casting methods, so some things are particular to the ways I've been taught and the way I practice. If you already know how to cast a magick circle, feel free to use the methods and traditions that already work best for you in conjunction with the prosperity magick of this book.

Most witches use a tool to cast the circle, such as a magick wand or an athame that has been ritually cleansed and blessed, but you can start out with just your finger. Most witches will also use a full altar as a workspace, with candles, a chalice, stones, bowls, oils, and incense readily available. If you are just starting out, don't worry too much about having an altar, but as you progress and learn spellcraft, gather all the tools you would need for the spell and place them on a simple work table.

First, face north and hold your casting tool northward. Imagine a beam of light coming out of it, creating a ring of light as you slowly move clockwise, reciting the words to consecrate your circle. The light is traditionally visualized as being blue, though it can be of any color, with white and violet being popular choices. The circle is traditionally nine feet in diameter, but you can make it fit your room space if you are indoors. Cast the circle three times around you, clockwise, reciting one of the following three lines for each cast circle:

> *I cast this circle to protect me from all harm.*
>
> *I cast this circle to attract only the most balanced energies and block all harm.*
>
> *I cast this circle to create a temple between the worlds.*

Second, face north again as you began, and invite in the elements from each direction as you move clockwise. Different traditions associate the elements with different directions, and specific beings, but the following lines are standard quarter calls that can work for anybody. (If you have relationships with specific elemental beings or deities aligned with the elements, you could call upon them. For prosperity magick, try calling upon gods listed in the next chapter. For a Greek-inspired circle, you could use Gaia or Hades for earth, Hermes or Zeus for air, Hephaestus for fire, and Aphrodite for water.)

> *To the north, I call upon the guardians of the element of earth. Guard and guide me. Hail and welcome.*
>
> *To the east, I call upon the guardians of the element of fire. Guard and guide me. Hail and welcome.*

To the south, I call upon the guardians of the element of air. Guard and guide me. Hail and welcome.

To the west, I call upon the guardians of the element of water. Guard and guide me. Hail and welcome.

Third, invite in the divine as Goddess, God, and Great Spirit, in any forms you recognize, as well as your own spiritual guides and protective guardians, angels, and animals. Witches usually see the divine as both male and female, and they recognize a whole host of spirits from the otherworlds, as well as the spirit of nature all around you. As you learn about specific gods and goddesses associated with prosperity, you might decide to call upon them specifically at this point in the ritual. If you have any other candles, incenses, or tools that need to be lit, sprinkled, or scattered, such as salt, water, or oil, do so now. A black candle is often lit for the Goddess and placed on the left of the altar, while a white candle is lit for the God and put on the right side of the altar.

Fourth, give a traditional blessing of protection before doing any magick. Usually a protection potion is used, anointed on the wrists and sometimes the brow or other chakra points. If you have *The Witch's Shield* or *The Outer Temple of Witchcraft*, you will have the formula for protection potion, but many witches simply use a pinch of sea salt in clear spring water as their protection-blessing potion. For tradition-specific magick circles, other religious elements would be added at this point, such as the Great Rite, offerings, or the blessing of cakes and ale. Since this is a simple outline, I've omitted those parts, but you can add and extend the ritual based on your own guidance, tradition, and previous experiences.

The fifth step is called the work, and at this point you would perform any spellwork, meditation, or any other work to be done in the circle. This is the point when you would do the prosperity and money magick spells found in the upcoming chapters.

Sixth, if you are doing simple spellwork, raise the cone of power to send out your intention. If you are empowering a physical charm or potion, raising the cone of power is not always necessary and is up to your discretion. Empowering an object (also called charging, blessing, hallowing, or consecrating) simply means holding it in your hands, thereby directing energy into it via your hands or third eye, with a specific magickal intention. I visualize the energy that would have gone into the cone of power going into the object I wish to empower. If you do raise the cone of power, raise your arms up and sweep the energy out the top of the circle, in what is called the Goddess position. When you bring your arms down, cross them over your heart—the God position, mimicking the pose of an Egyptian mummy—to reflect on your work. Then ground yourself as necessary.

Seventh, start to release the circle as you built it. Some traditions thank and release the spirits first, then the quarters, while others thank and release the quarters first, then the spirits. As long as you release both, it works. For this version, first thank and release the powers and spirits who have gathered with you, including the Goddess, God, and Great Spirit. Any entities you have called by name, thank and release by name.

Eighth, release the quarters, starting in the north and going around counterclockwise to dismantle the circle. (If you called on specific guardians, make them a part of your release of the quarters.)

To the north, I thank and release the guardians of the element of earth. Hail and farewell.

To the west, I thank and release the guardians of the element of water. Hail and farewell.

To the south, I thank and release the guardians of the element of air. Hail and farewell.

To the east, I thank and release the guardians of the element of fire. Hail and farewell.

Ninth, release the circle. Start with your casting tool facing out to the north and move counterclockwise one time.

I release this circle out into the universe as a sign of my magick. The circle is undone, but not broken.

While these abbreviated instructions are complete by themselves, if you desire a more detailed lesson on casting a magick circle and an understanding of each step, review the lessons in my book *The Outer Temple of Witchcraft*. You can use the basic ritual outlines here for all the spells listed in the next chapter.

THE GODS OF PROSPERITY, WEALTH, AND SUCCESS

All across the world, and in all of the many religions, people have always prayed for success, good fortune, and money, no matter how they have seen the divine. When looking to one or more divinities envisioned as the ruler or rulers of all the world, controlling the tides of good fortune and abundance, as well as misfortune and scarcity, devout practitioners often believe that the right prayers will ensure their success. While this idea is not wholly without merit, the better concept is that when we are in right relationship with the divine, we will have the resources we need and want, so as to fulfill our own divine mission, our own magickal fate.

Pagan people worship many forms of divinity and see the rulership of fortune and success under the auspices of several gods. First off, if you have a deity with whom you have a primary relationship, a patron you are partnered with, whose will you help fulfill in the world, that god or goddess is one of your best allies for success. It doesn't matter if that deity is traditionally aligned with wealth or not. A deity is a deity, and a deity who wants you to succeed will aid you in whatever way is needed to fulfill your work. Your relationship with the divine is paramount. Many of the old European pagan myths have the gods asking each other for favors or boons. Your own personal gods will move the gods who rule over fortune and success to get you the resources you need.

Beyond your personal relationship, in the world of the ceremonial magician's magickal correspondences, the gods most traditionally associated with wealth, success, and good fortune are those aligned with the planetary archetypes of the Sun, Jupiter, the planet Earth, and the Underworld. Each godform governs the powers of fortune in a different way. Solar and fire figures are rulers of health, wealth, and success as gods of primal energy. Everything on our planet ultimately derives its life force from the Sun. It grows and prospers, or withers, depending on the right balance of solar energy. Jupiter is the power of expansion. It takes what you have and brings blessings to amplify it. Those gods of the planet Earth are the fertility of the land itself, as manifested through the plants and even animals. To the ancient pagan, abundance of wealth and a good harvest went hand-in-hand. The gods of the Underworld govern the deep Earth, from which the hidden wealth of the land is revealed, in the form of precious metals and gems.

In various ways, through modern and ancient associations, the following gods are patrons of wealth and success. You can build a relationship with these gods to aid in your magickal endeavors and spells for prosperity.

GODS

Aphrodite

While we tend to think of Aphrodite solely as a goddess of love, romance, and sex, she is also the goddess of fulfilling desires. Her planet Venus rules the power to attract what you want, whatever that might be. When your heart's desire is for success, fame, and fortune, she can be a powerful ally to help you get what you want.

Bel

Bel is the Celtic god who is honored in the fire festival of Beltaine, the fires of Bel. Also known as Belanus, he is considered a god of fire, light, and the welfare of cattle and sheep. The herds are run through the fires at Beltaine to purify and heal them. Bel is also associated with the light of the Sun, and in that regard, he can be considered a god of wealth, health, and good fortune.

Cernunnos

Cernunnos is the horned god of the early Celtic world, believed to be depicted on the famous Gundestrup Cauldron discovered in Denmark. As a god of the hunt and animals, he is also the god of death and Underworld, encompassing fertility and material wealth.

Cronus

The Greek Titan Cronus, equated with Saturn in Roman mythology, is the figure who ruled over the Titans before the rise of Zeus. In Roman mythology, Saturn is the god of the grain, and he ruled over the Golden Age of myth. As a ruler over grain, a symbol of material resources as well as the wealth and prosperity of the Golden Age, Cronus can be asked to aid in creating your own golden age. Cronus has been equated with Chronos, the embodiment of time.

Dagda

Dagda is the Irish all-father god, son of the Goddess Danu. He is a master druid, and father of life, death, and magick. He owns a magick cauldron known as the Undry, which contains an inexhaustible supply of food, like a cornucopia. Although he is not a storm god in modern magick, he's seen as a Jupiterian figure because of the ever-expansive nature of his cauldron and his abundant good nature and power.

Fortuna

Fortuna is the Roman goddess personifying fortune, particularly good fortune. She is prayed to for blessings and fertility, and her worship is particularly associated with women, specifically mothers.

Freya

Freya is the Lady of the Vanir, the land-based gods in Norse mythology, who was adopted by the sky-based Aesir gods after their war together. A goddess of fertility, sexuality, love, and magick, she is a powerful and all-encompassing goddess. The tears she sheds for her lost husband are said to turn to gold when they hit the ground, and amber when they hit the sea. Gold and amber are both tokens of wealth.

Freyr

Freyr is the Lord of the Vanir, a race of earthy gods in Norse mythology, linked with the Aesir, the sky-god race. Freyr is the god of agriculture and the bountiful harvest. He is also said to be the most beautiful of the Vanir men, matching his sister, the Lady Freya. In cultures where the bounty of the land is reflective of wealth, Freyr can be a great ally in making sure all of your material needs are satisfied.

Gaia

Gaia, or Gaea, is the Greek Earth Mother, one of the first beings born in creation. Gaia is the planet itself, or in some neopagan theologies, the material universe itself. She is the source of all bounty and the ultimate mother of all—gods, mortals, animals, and plants.

Ganesha

The Hindu elephant-headed god is the remover of obstacles. He is entwined in the lives of millions of people in India and across the globe, and he is respected and loved by all who know him. Modern pagans have found a devotion to him, and we have incorporated him into our practices. Although he is not specifically a wealth god, he removes any obstacles to wealth, or anything else, when asked. He shares traits with Hermes, and in ceremonial magick he is considered a Mercurial god-form. Business owners pray to Ganesha to remove obstacles to their good fortunes and success.

Hades

Hades is primarily known as the lord of the dead in Greek mythology. He rules with his queen, Persephone, and many minor gods ruling over aspects of the Underworld. Because he rules the depths, he is also considered the ruler of material wealth, of the riches from beneath the land, such as metals and gems. Although he is a ruler of wealth, he is also a god of death, and many people have an aversion to him. Some avoid speaking his name and avert their eyes when making sacrifices to him. If you don't have a personal connection to the Underworld, perhaps Hades would not be the best patron of wealth.

Hecate

Hecate is the Greek triple goddess of the crossroads and witchcraft. Many modern witches equate her with the triple goddess image of maiden, mother, and crone, but older images have her three faces as a dog, snake, and horse. She appears as maiden as often as crone, specifically as the handmaiden of Persephone, who helped Demeter find Persephone after Hades abducted her. Although not specifically a goddess of wealth, she is a goddess of the Underworld, and the granter of wishes and magickal powers. Many modern and ancient witches have worked quite successfully with Hecate to receive whatever they desired.

Hermes

Today Hermes is primarily known as a messenger god, and a god of magick, but he was the Greek god of travel, communication, shepherds, and athletics. More importantly for our purposes here, the fleet-footed god is the patron of merchants, gamblers, and thieves. He is the god of cunning and shrewdness, and he favors those with such attributes. The exchange of goods, legally or illegally, is a way to honor Hermes, because he is a god of change. I've made purchases a form of "offering" to Hermes, since a priestess of Hermes once told me that commerce and travel were the two best ways to honor him.

Isis

Although not specifically a goddess of wealth, Isis is an all-encompassing and powerful goddess much loved by modern witches and pagans. She is a goddess of magick, power, and fertility, equated with many goddesses over time, and she enjoyed a great deal of popularity throughout the Roman era, having temples across the empire. Her name is associated with the throne, suggesting that she is the ultimate power granting sovereignty to the ruling pharaohs.

Jupiter

The Roman god Jupiter is equated with the Greek Zeus, as both are all-father figures to their respective pantheons. He is not only the god of sky and storm, but god over society, law, and the empire. He is petitioned for success and victory in any societal endeavor.

Lakshmi

Lakshmi is the Hindu goddess ruling over good fortune and beauty. In ceremonial magick she is equated with Venusian figures, both for love and for receiving what one desires. In Hindu myth, she was born from the churning waves of the milky ocean, much like Aphrodite rising from the foam of the ocean. She is the consort to the god Vishnu.

Mercury

The Roman god Mercury was later equated with the Greek Hermes, and he shares many of the same traits and descriptions. He is the god of trade, particularly trade in corn, and a god of profits and merchants. One of his symbols is the money purse, further illustrating his connection to monetary exchange.

Nerthus

Nerthus is a Teutonic goddess most often associated with the Earth Mother by scholars and neopagans alike. She is the patron of fertility, peace, and wealth. The Roman historian Tacitus gives a now-famous account of how her statue was paraded around the land to be worshiped in a time of peace.

Osiris

Osiris is the king of the dead in Egyptian mythology. He was given this title after his death and resurrection. Osiris is still depicted as a god of vegetation and fertility, and in this aspect, he brings wealth and good fortune through the blessings of the land rising up from the Underworld.

Pluto

Pluto is equated with the Greek Hades, sharing many of the same attributes. Both are gods of the dead, and both are gods of the material riches of the Earth. And like Hades, Pluto is also shunned by gods and mortals alike. Additionally, Pluto is associated with the Underworld/wealth figure-diety Dis Pater, whose name is a contraction of *dives pater*, or "wealthy father."

Ra

Ra is the primary Egyptian god, cited as the creator of the universe and embodied by the Sun—or the Sun was a part of him, such as his eye. He is the god of light, civilization, power, and the pharaohs. As a Sun god, he can be called upon for power and success in any endeavor. Usually he is depicted as a man with a falcon's head and the Sun disc on his crown.

Saturn

Saturn is the Roman figure equated with the Greek Cronus. Saturn was the god of the harvest and the ruler of the Golden Age before he was deposed by the younger gods. He is the god of grain and seeds, and later he was associated with restriction and responsibility. Saturday and the planet Saturn are named after him, and while he has a very popular festival near the winter solstice, the Saturnalia, he was not a very popular god. During the Saturnalia, roles such as master and slave were reversed. His temple in Rome was the Royal Treasury, the depository of wealth.

Tyche

The Greek goddess embodying fortune and luck is Tyche. She is also a goddess of prosperity in general, and she is depicted with a cornucopia, a rudder of destiny, and a wheel of fortune.

Venus

The Roman goddess strongly associated with Aphrodite is also a goddess of love and sexuality. Beyond her more well-known associations, she is also a goddess of herbal magick and cultivated gardens, and a patron of witches, who were known as *venefica* in the Roman era. Herbal magick for prosperity is particularly potent when working with Lady Venus.

Zeus

Zeus is the Greek father of the Olympians, ruler and king of the gods, considered the spiritual leader of both gods and mortals. He is the god of the sky, and specifically thunder, lightning, and storms. He oversees civil life, bringing peace where there is conflict and upholding justice, law, and morals. Linked with the Roman Jupiter, today he is called upon for success, blessings, and justice in all endeavors.

Realize that these are small, short descriptions of vast beings with a long history, and they are devoid of the original cultural and religious context. These descriptions encompass our relationship to the deities in regard to money magick, not devotional, religious practice. If any of these deities intrigue you, or their names and images speak to your soul, seek out more information on their nature, worship, and mythology.

JOURNEY TO THE TREASURE HOARD

The gods of riches and prosperity are sometimes considered to be chthonic, meaning that they are primal and chaotic, and find their home in the Underworld or Otherworld. They are described as dark and powerful, or holding the light in the primal darkness. One reason they are described that way is because humans value the light, and the metals and gems found in the land are the physical representation of the light within the Underworld. The true journey of prosperity is one of introspection. We must seek out the forces of the dark, the unknown, to find our true purpose. Through the journey of purpose, we are "rewarded" with the resources to fulfill that purpose.

We might think of ourselves as being rewarded for our good behavior, but prosperity is really a function of our consciousness, of being in the right place, at the right time, doing the right thing that is in harmony with our soul. It is not a reward/punishment system for those who behave in a "good" manner. People with excessive wealth are not better or more spiritual people than those with less money. But those with excessive wealth need that wealth on some level to fulfill their soul's purpose, even if it's simply to know how to work with such vast material forces. Many mystics believe that working with such vast sums of material power is an early lesson on the soul's path, and those who are comfortable in their relationship with money seek a satisfying amount to fulfill their purpose, but they do not need an excess amount any more than they need to be poor. They seek the mean, and the middle path of balance is one of the core teachings of witchcraft.

The seeking of wealth brings us to the Underworld. Sometimes the need for wealth, or the greed for wealth, forces us to face the darkness within, and the guardians of the Earth's prosperity. The image of the dragon's hoard, the subterranean wealth guarded by a serpentine watcher, is famous in folklore and modern fantasy. Mortals must prove worthy, in alignment with their soul, their purpose, to claim the treasure, and then they must learn the lessons of how that treasure is used responsibly in the world.

The following visionary journey takes you to the Underworld hoard, through what I call the gateway of purpose. It takes you to what some of my students have experienced as a Temple of Prosperity. It contains no dragon hoard, but it is a lavish temple dedicated to one or more of the gods of prosperity listed in this chapter. In the Temple of Prosperity, the students are not so much challenged by guardians, but they commune with the gods of purpose and prosperity to find their next direction or "job" in life, be it their daily vocation or a spiritual quest that will lead them to understanding their true purpose. Whatever you might encounter in the gateway, face it with honesty, courage, and commitment to your true purpose.

EXERCISE 9: GATEWAY OF PURPOSE TO THE TREASURE TEMPLE

1. Perform steps 1–6 from Exercise 5: Reprogramming Consciousness.

2. Imagine a great tree before you, what is known as the World Tree. Its branches reach up to the heavens, to the Sun, Moon, and stars. The trunk is in the world of humans,

animals, space, and time. The roots dig deep into the Earth, and go deeper into the Underworld. Even if you don't "see" the tree in your mind's eye, feel it. Sense it. Know the great tree is before you. Imagine slipping through the screen of your mind as if it is a veil, and stand before the World Tree.

3. Ask the powers of the universe, your own higher self and guides, to go to the gateway of purpose. Ask to go to the Underworld treasure hoard, the Temple of Prosperity. Ask the tree to open the way to you, so you can learn more about your true purpose and how to find the resources you need to fulfill it.

4. Look around the massive roots of the tree, and within the roots, there will be an opening, like a small cave, leading to a tunnel into the Underworld. Enter this gateway of purpose in the tree's roots, and find yourself going into the dark of the Underworld, spiraling deeper and deeper.

5. Continue onward until you see a glowing light at the end of the tunnel, light like the Sun reflected off snow, metal, or gems, bright and shining. Go toward that light and into the Temple of Prosperity.

6. Look around. What do you see? Is it an ancient temple dedicated to the gods of riches and good fortune? Is it the massive hoard of treasure—gold, silver, precious gems? The rich colors of good fortune surround you, filling your sight. You smell the burning of rich incenses, spices, and woods, slightly intoxicating you.

7. Is there anybody there in the temple? Is there a guardian, a guide, a god or goddess? Who attends the Temple of Prosperity? Perhaps there is a familiar spirit who has aided you in other journeys. Perhaps there is someone new and unknown to you. Seek out your temple ally, and introduce yourself. Ask any questions you have about your own prosperity and your purpose. What must you do to

receive the treasure? What qualities and virtues must you develop? How must you use the resources you already have? Receive the wisdom and messages of your ally, giving you advice on how to proceed. They might come to you as words, images, or simple knowing. Follow your instincts, and do not try to analyze the information until after your journey is over.

8. You might find the ally of the temple giving you some of the temple's treasure, indicating a change and increase in your fortune in the material world. The energy of the temple will come with you, attracting what you need. You might find the ally of the temple giving you a challenge or requiring a promise of you before anything changes in your life.

9. When the ally is done communing with you, you are ushered to move back through the tunnel. Do you feel different? Perhaps as you exit the gateway in the roots of the tree, you will have a clearer sense of purpose. Once you exit the tunnel, you find the roots closing up and sealing the gateway until you return.

10. Thank the tree for this journey to the Underworld. Step back through the veil of your mind's eye and see the tree again on the screen before you. Let the presence of the tree fade from your mind.

11. Perform steps 8–10 from Exercise 5: Reprogramming Consciousness to end the vision work.

When you return from your journey, write down any impressions and messages you received to reflect upon or to put into action in order to change your prosperity and embrace your purpose.

CHAPTER 6

THE WEALTH OF NATURE

As the pagan model of prosperity and abundance comes from our understanding of nature and its seasons, some of our most valuable allies in prosperity magick come from nature. They are the plants and minerals used in wealth magick. Today we find magickal value in all manner of plants, including wild weeds, herbs, beautiful flowers, trees, and bushes. We use metals, minerals, and gems from around the world. They are not simply "tools"; although we use them as such, they are truly allies.

Many would consider these natural objects to be inert or lifeless, particularly stones or plants that have been picked and dried. Some magicians take the view of the modern chemist and look these items as tools, as ingredients for a magickal recipe, and they are, but they are so much more than that. Each one has a spirit within it, governing in magickal virtue and growth. Magick helps us align with those spirits, consciously or not, to find allies who will teach us how to be in harmony with the principle of natural abundance, to attract the things we desire and create the life we want.

Many of the substances used in magickal formulas and charms are highly valued in and of themselves, creating a resonance with the principles of wealth. In magick, we say that "like attracts like," so things of value can be used magickally to attract other things of value. Many of these substances have been used for exchange in human culture. We use metals to make coins, and metals and gems to make valuable jewelry. Although it seems strange to our modern standards, plants—particularly in the form of spices, tea, and wood—have been valuable commodities for centuries, and they have shaped our exploration of the world and our politics with other cultures. While they have been commodities in and of themselves, their magickal virtue helps us align with whatever resources are valued in our own society.

Lore about the magickal uses of plants, stones, and other items has grown over several centuries. Modern witches draw from a variety of sources, including traditional Wiccan and ceremonial magick teachings on correspondences; ancient-world associations of Egypt, Sumer, Greece, and Rome; medieval magick; European folklore; and in America, the influence of the African diasporic traditions, New Orleans Voodou, and the American folk magick system of Hoodoo. Much of our lore on money magick, gambling magick, and overcoming obstacles comes from poor and oppressed people who had no other recourse but magickal charms. These systems of magick developed and changed in the urban environments of New York, Chicago, and Los Angeles, mixing with Wicca and European folklore of the occult shops. In this book, herbs and stones have associations that draw from all these sources, as they all have been influences in my magick.

WORKING WITH NATURE

Everything has its own energy—you, me, and every plant, tree, rock, and drop of water. Everybody's energy is different, but things that are of the same species or same minerals have similar energies. In modern magickal terminology, we say that everything has its own vibration. In older magickal thinking, we say that everything has its own virtue, its own special ability. Just as every person has his or her own aptitudes and talents, every part of nature has its own aptitudes and talents. Some of these abilities are indicated by their herbal or chemical actions. These are virtues that can be measured scientifically. Many plants and minerals also have a more subtle nature that cannot be measured by science as we know it today, at least not measured well. Yet magicians, healers, and witches know of this hidden nature, and it has become a part of our lore. Unlocking the hidden virtues of nature is one of the talents of the witch.

While much folk magick relies on the virtue of the plant or stone itself, it really relies on the spirit of nature animating the item. You simply carry it with you, eat it, drink it, or use it in any way that fits the substance. In modern practice, we often talk about charging the focus of our magick. Charging is known by many names, including *consecrating*, *hallowing*, *imbuing*, and *enchanting*. Some people think of it as simply using a substance to focus their will and mind, and the substance itself doesn't matter. I strongly disagree. Others think they are "charging" it like a battery, filling it with energy. Although it may seem to work that way, that's only part of the story. You are really giving it a charge, a mandate, a set of instructions. You are catalyzing its virtue to be in harmony with your will specifically. Any herb or stone can do many things, and charging it sets its energy, its spirit, to a specific task or range of tasks that you want to accomplish with the help of nature. To charge something magickally is to get into a relationship with it for your mutual benefit. Nature wants to use its virtue to better know humanity. By doing natural magick, we help the spiritual evolution of both nature and ourselves.

Charging a magickal object to align with your will has three basic steps:

1. To charge something, simply hold it in your hands. Many people will cleanse it first, either by passing it through purifying smoke or sprinkling it with salt water. For most herbs, these techniques aren't so great, so you can simply imagine the natural object filling with

light, and then imagine the light dissipating, taking the unwanted energies with it, or you can blow on it, blowing away the neutralized unwanted energies.

2. Once you feel that you are ready to charge the object, think about its virtue, its vibration. Think about its spirit, the energy associated with it. Commune with it. Imagine the vibration of your hands and body aligning with it, vibrating in harmony with it. Think about what you want the tool to do as a magickal charm. Imagine your instructions in visualizations or feelings. Think or speak the instructions in words. Simply know in your heart what you want the object to do, as clearly and completely as possible. Imagine this intention traveling through you, through your hands, and into the natural object. Some people imagine energy projecting from their eyes or third eye into the tool. Either way works; it simply depends on what feels more powerful to you. You might even speak to the object as if you were speaking to a friend, and ask for help. Traditional magick would have you flatter the object, speaking about how good it is with a particular area of work, and how you need its help, reinforcing the idea of whatever you want the charm to do. If you were doing a love spell, you'd tell the object how good it is at getting lovers and then ask its help to find you the right lover.

3. When you are finished, you will feel your energy and the object's energy separate. Then you can carry the charged object as a charm when you want its effect, or you can use it in a larger ritual, adding it to a greater formula or mixed charm.

You can use this technique for natural objects, or any ritual tool. From a magickal animist perspective, everything is alive. Everything has a spirit, but the spirits associated with nature usually have a stronger energy and virtue than items that are manufactured. A well-constructed magickal tool can have a very powerful spirit imbued in it as it was being created and forged, but still, I've found that some of the most profound magickal experiences come from communing with and charging simple herbs and stones.

PROSPERITY STONES AND METALS

The following minerals have a history, old and new, in prosperity and money magick.

Agate, Blue Lace

Blue lace agate is used in communication magick, and it can be used to communicate with your higher self in regard to what you should be doing in life. It aids communication in business and the home, and it is also associated with the angelic realm. It can be used to summon the angels to aid in your magick, or to commune with them for advice with finance.

Amethyst

The traditional use of amethyst is to keep a clear, peaceful head, as it is said to prevent drunkenness. Amethyst is astrologically associated with Pisces, and the traditional planetary ruler of Pisces, Jupiter, and the modern ruler, Neptune. Amethyst inspires higher visions of purpose and helps translate such inspiration into creative endeavors including art, music, and dance. Amethyst's hue is also associated with royalty, and the stone commands a certain personal power when worn as jewelry. It allows the inner light and power to shine and our innate divine "royalty" to be recognized by others.

Ametrine

Ametrine is a natural mixture of citrine and amethyst, combining the properties of both. It gives both energy and vitality to any magick, along with good fortune and expansion.

Aventurine

Used as a stone of good luck and fortune, aventurine can be successfully used in money magick, particularly when chance, gambling, or any form of speculative investment is involved.

Calcite, Blue

The entire calcite "family" of stones look waxy and somewhat reflective. Magickally, they are used to show us things we need to know but often don't want to know. Meditation with blue calcite can help you understand the blocks you have that are preventing both communication and prosperity.

Calcite, Green

Primarily used in removing blocks to love, green calcite can also be used in understanding and removing blocks to money and self-worth. It forms in colors ranging from a yellow-green to a deeper emerald green.

Chrysoprase

The apple-green chrysoprase helps us remove fears about prosperity, particularly those lodged in the solar plexus/heart area. It helps attract prosperity and new opportunities, usually by opening new social channels and attracting new friends and colleagues.

Citrine

This form of yellow-to-brown-tinged quartz is used to align with the energies of the Sun and all the bright blessings the Sun's power can bring. It can be used in any magick to increase energy and power to result in good fortune, wealth, health, and inspiration. Some say citrine is so bright and powerful that it is one of the few stones that never needs to be cleansed when used for magick and healing. Although I love its power, I think it should be cleansed before use as crystals are traditionally cleansed.

Copper

As the metal of Venus, copper can be used to attract whatever you value. It's generally better in quick money spells than in magick for the broader spiritual issues concerning career and purpose in life.

Emerald

Emerald is a prosperity stone in that it helps open your heart to feelings of worthiness and helps open your eyes to seeing the opportunities around you. It is a particularly good stone for changing careers or finding more holistic and empathic career choices, allowing you to see and feel the opportunities all around you.

Garnet

Garnet is an energizing, fiery stone that also has a strong association with the element of earth. It helps you be successful in your chosen profession by helping you put the necessary energy and focus into your business, and helping you manifest your intentions and goals for your work.

Gold

Gold, as the metal of the Sun, is the first and best metal to be used in money magick of all kinds, as it is the most valuable. But if you have enough gold to be using it a lot in magick, you probably don't need to do much in the way of money magick. Gold rings, charms, and necklaces can be enchanted as talismans for good luck and good fortune. Bottles filled with gold foil flecks can also be found in some mineral shops and used in talismans. Pyrite is also a good substitute for spells that call for gold.

Howlite, Blue

Blue howlite is sold as a peace, protection, and prosperity stone. It's important to know that blue howlite is actually white howlite dyed blue and sold as turquoise to unsuspecting folks. Although it is dyed, it still has magickal properties, but despite the color, those who know its true identity do not often use it in money magick. It is used for dream magick and some protection.

Jade

Jade refers to two similar-looking green minerals, one called nephrite and the other jadeitite. While other colors are available, jade is primarily green. It has been used as a talisman for many magickal effects, including good luck and prosperity, as well as peace, protection, love, wisdom, and longevity, and for increasing all spiritual endeavors.

Lapis Lazuli

Lapis is one of the favored stones of the Sumerian goddess Inanna. Lapis and malachite were used as eye makeup in Egypt and the Middle East, to add to one's attraction and allure. Lapis, sometimes flecked with pyrite, connects you to the power of Jupiter with its blue color, but also to the great Goddess in her forms of Queen of Heaven and Earth.

Lepidolite

Lepidolite is traditionally considered to be a luck stone rather than a money stone. Sharing rulership with Jupiter and Neptune, lepidolite can be used to improve your mood, lift depression and pessimism, attract good fortune and blessings, and manifest an optimistic view in the world. Its structure is a form of mica containing a quantity of lithium, which is well known for its medical use in easing the symptoms of depression. Carrying lepidolite is not a substitute for medical attention, but many individuals who suffer from depression believe that carrying lepidolite or gem silica lithium complements their treatment.

Malachite

Malachite is one of the more earthy stones for prosperity. It is also used in healing, grounding, and protection, and it can be called upon for drawing up the wealth of the land.

Pyrite

Known as fool's gold, pyrite is a substitute for gold in a lot of folk magick. When actual gold is not available, pyrite's similar color allows magicians to use the energy of gold.

Sapphire

Sapphire has many magickal properties, but for our work here, it is used to gain crystal clarity and clear vision to your purpose in life.

Silver

Although it is traditionally associated with psychic power and feminine energy, silver, particularly in the form of silver dimes, has been used in money magick. It is a metal second only to gold in terms of value.

Sodalite, Blue

Blue sodalite is another stone of Jupiter, and can be used in wealth magick to expand your fortune. It's also an excellent stone to improve communication, and it can be used when miscommunication is negatively affecting your finances.

Tiger's-Eye, Blue

Also known as hawk's-eye, the blue tiger's-eye can be used in much the same way as traditional tiger's-eye. The reflective nature of both varieties, but in particular the blue version, helps you reflect upon life and purpose, truly see things as they are, and determine where you need to go. Blue tiger's-eye can help you find your true purpose and will in the world and guide your manifestation of it.

Tiger's-Eye, Gold

Traditional tiger's-eye is ruled by the Sun, and therefore it can be used for wealth and success. Dark bands of golden stone are also a signature for helping you get everything ordered and into place. It is a solid grounding and protecting stone that does not diminish your energies, as some of the darker-colored protection stones do.

Tin

Strangely, the cheap metal tin is associated with the kingly Jupiter, and it can be used to invoke all the powers of Jupiter. Talismans of Jupiter are most effective when they are created from tin.

Tourmaline, Black, Blue, and Green

The entire tourmaline group of crystals facilitates the movement of energy and the removal of blocks from the human energy system. You can use blue or green tourmaline in alignment of the throat and heart chakras to be able to speak what you want, and to receive it. Black tourmaline helps remove blocks to manifesting your prosperity goals, and it also helps ground your intention in physical reality.

Turquoise

Turquoise is a great all-purpose stone used for a variety of reasons, but in prosperity magick it is aligned with both Jupiter, due to its blue color, and Venus, due to the content of copper in its chemical structure. Both planetary energies can be called upon with this stone in order to give you a powerful bonus in any magick—both expanding and attracting what you want.

PROSPERITY HERBS

Many different plants have associations with money, abundance, and good fortune. Here are some plants a prosperous magician will be familiar with when constructing prosperity charms. The fresh herbs, dried herbs, water infusions, tinctures, essential oils, and infused oils can all be used in magick, though certain herbs lend themselves better to certain extraction techniques, both magickally and medicinally.

African Violet

The common household plant African violet is usually associated with spiritual development, because its temperamental nature means that it needs constant care and balance in order to thrive. The color of its flowers, violet-purple, also associate it with Jupiter, as well as the forces of expansion and abundance. African violet is one of many plants over which Jupiter and Venus are said to share rulership.

Agrimony

Agrimony is an herb of the deep, and it is associated with sleep, dreams, the Underworld, and protection from fears and monsters. In money magick, it is used to help us understand the deep-seated fears and blocks we have to prosperity and fulfilling our True Will.

Alfalfa

Alfalfa is an herb of prosperity and abundance. The Earth itself abundantly bears this "grain," which is easy to grow and harvest. Keeping alfalfa in the cupboard traditionally keeps poverty and hunger at bay. It is best when grown yourself and harvested on the waxing full Moon.

Allspice

The flavor of allspice is said to be a combination of cinnamon, cloves, and nutmeg, hence being "all spices." It is another rich flavor that can be used in the enticement of riches. It combines well with any of the previous spices in teas, food, incense, and amulets. Its added benefit is as an herb of fire, granting vitality, energy, and creativity to the user.

Arrowroot

Arrowroot is used to change your destiny and avert tragedy. It helps you change the course of your life by picking a new direction with the "arrow" of your will. Ruled by Mars, the root should be powdered and sprinkled upon your body while you courageously announce the new direction of your life. It is also used to heal the heart and protect infants.

Basil

Basil is a powerful purifying herb—in some traditions, it is burned to banish unwanted spirits who flee because of its fiery nature—yet basil is pleasant to most humans. The fire signature of basil is also used to stir passion, and it's used in love and lust magick. Such energy and power can be directed toward the successful fulfillment of a job, and toward procuring money. Some magickal practitioners say that basil leaves used in potions and washes resemble green cash, which adds to the herb's money signature.

Bay

While bay is primarily thought of as a trance-inducing and oracular herb, it was also used in laurel "crowns." As such, bay can be used in rituals where one takes on an aura of success or royalty to inspire and command others. It is an essential ingredient in a Hoodoo formula known as Crown of Success, an oil used to bring success in any endeavor.

Blueberry

Blueberry is mostly used as an ingredient in psychic shielding and protection potions, but it can also be used in prosperity magick, as blue is the color of Jupiter in ceremonial magick, and the bunches of sweet berries indicate abundance. The berries or leaves can be used in magick.

Borage

Borage's main signature, as a tea, incense, or charm, is to stoke the fires of courage to face a difficult situation and triumph. It's particularly good in difficult business dealings, to bring about the courage to face and change the situation.

Burdock

A Jupiterian root herb, burdock's strongest magickal and medicinal signature comes from the seed "burs" that attach themselves to people's clothing and animals' fur, carrying the seeds far and wide. Burdock "hooks" and draws, either drawing things out of the system, or hooking you to, and attracting, things you want. Although the seeds and leaves also have magickal and medicinal purposes, the roots are where the power of the herb is mostly stored, and is the part of the herb that is most often available in magickal and medicinal shops. It can be used in teas, tinctures, and charms, though it doesn't smell particularly good in incense.

Cedar

Cedar is another aromatic wood indicative of wealth. It can be used to attract wealth, and it is also used with sage and sweet grass in tribal rites for cleansing and purification. Cedar is mentioned in the Old Testament, both as an element in purification rituals for lepers and also as a wood used in the lavish Temple of Solomon.

Chestnut

Both chestnut and horse chestnut are ruled by Jupiter and used in attracting good luck and money. Whole horse chestnuts and a variety of chestnuts known as buckeyes are used as protection charms, warding off the evil eye. A buckeye can also be used as talismans for luck in gambling when a dollar bill is wrapped around it with red thread. These nuts resemble the testicles, and they are also used in love and lust magick for male virility. They can be used as a substitute for the nutmeg in the creation of Gambler's Nutmeg (see the entry on nutmeg later in this chapter).

Cinnamon

Cinnamon is one of the most classic ingredients in money magick. The smell of cinnamon brings good fortune to whoever smells it. Add a little cinnamon to your morning coffee or tea. Cinnamon chips on burning charcoal make a powerful prosperity incense all by themselves. When something is cooked with cinnamon in a home that is for sale, or when cinnamon sticks are stewed on the stove, the home is more likely to sell, and at a higher price. This little bit of magick is used by real-estate agents everywhere. You can make an infusion of cinnamon, sprinkle it in your home, and anoint your doorways with it to attract success and good fortune.

Drinking a cup of spicy cinnamon tea is a classic money potion to focus your inner "fire" on your prosperity. If you are in a vocation that relies on the generosity of others—for instance, if you are a server in a restaurant and you rely on tips—add a cup of cinnamon tea to the laundry (not whites) when you wash your work clothing. If you have extremely sensitive skin, you can try soaking a handkerchief in cinnamon tea and let it dry without washing the cinnamon out, and carry it with you in your pocket. Either approach will help attract money and generosity to you.

Cinnamon can also be sprinkled in your shoe to bring you to new opportunities. (Caution: pure essential oils, particularly cinnamon, can be caustic on the skin and should be diluted with a base oil. Consult a reputable medical essential-oil text for more information on the effects of essential oils.)

Cinquefoil

Cinquefoil is known as five-finger grass and is another prosperity herb that also has a strong history in protection magick. It's a counter-magick herb, as it is most effective in removing curses and harm. Lore tells us that anything five human fingers can do, five fingers (grass) can undo. Cinquefoil is also used as a grasping herb, with the finger imagery helping us grasp what we want and value, particularly in gambling magick.

Clove

The spicy clove is naturally related to Jupiter because of its richness. It can be used alone or in combination with other spicy herbs, whole or powdered.

A powerful charm that is done around the winter holidays for success, friendship, and health is making a pomander. Simply stick the pointed ends of whole cloves into the skin of an orange until you cover the entire fruit, putting the cloves no more than an eighth of an inch apart. Roll the clove-covered orange in a mix of powdered cinnamon, nutmeg, ground cloves, and orris root powder (1 tablespoon each), and let it cure in a paper bag for about a month. When fully dry, it makes a spiced decoration that attracts health, wealth, and prosperity.

Clover, Red

Red clover is a versatile herb with many medicinal and magickal uses. In medicine, it is primarily used as a "blood purifier," and famous witch Sybil Leek suggested that witches should drink it whenever possible. In money magick, the flower globes or leaves can be used in charms for luck and to multiply the resources you already have.

Currant

Both black and red currants are ruled by Jupiter and used in a variety of success recipes. They can be used in the creation of wine and baked into pastries.

Dandelion

Dandelion is another Jupiterian herb, primarily used in medicine as a tonic to the liver, the organ ruled by Jupiter. Magickally, the root is used most. One folk name is *earthnail*, and it helps ground practitioners, as well as manifest desires in the material world. In magick, it not only serves as a flower essence, but it also helps remove blocks in the solar plexus, blocks to your own personal power and ability to create the life you want. The yellow flower indicates the ability to get in touch with the solar power to create and be successful. Dandelion seeds, with their whispy white tails, can be used in wish magick. Make the wish and then blow the white puff to the wind, letting it carry your intention.

Dill

Dill is an herb of abundance because of the abundant seeds it produces. It is used in magick to increase and multiply. A simple money spell using dill involves wrapping a teaspoon of dill seeds in a dollar bill and carrying it as a charm in your pocket, wallet, or purse, to attract money and increase the money you already have.

Fennel

Fennel is a powerful all-purpose herb used in many different ways. One of its most interesting uses in money and business magick arises from the fact that fennel seeds are said to confer the ability to charm others, persuading them to your point of view. It doesn't force their will or make them believe things that are patently untrue; it simply gives you a convincing "sweet" tongue. Politicians, lawyers, and teachers should all carry a small bit of fennel seeds to hold the attention of others and make their views clear. It is also used in protection, success, health, and counter-magick.

Fenugreek

The aromatic seeds of fenugreek, much like the seeds of other prosperity herbs, attracts money. Fenugreek seeds are particularly good in money jar spells, where you can add a few more seeds to the jar every day to magickally increase your wealth.

Fumitory

While fumitory is primarily viewed as a funerary herb, used in the rites of the dead or to commune with the spirits of the dead, it also has some history in money magick. Fumitory shows the link between hidden riches and the lords of the dead as the lords of the depths.

Galangal

Galangal root, also known as Little John root in Hoodoo, is used in court-case magick. The root, related to ginger, is chewed and the juice swallowed in the court room, with the remains spit discreetly onto the courtroom floor. With this ritual, the judge is said to rule in your favor. Some erroneously refer to it as Low John Root, which is technically a different species, according to most Hoodoo practitioners. Galangal is also used in the very powerful, spiritually uplifting ceremonial magician's oil known as Abramelin Oil, along with cinnamon.

Ginger

Ginger root is a powerful warming herb. Like many spices ruled by the Sun and Jupiter, ginger is a sign of wealth, but it has some particular properties. It is one of the most powerful herbs for stoking the fire of your will, to help you acquire the energy to go out and get what you want, creating the success you desire. It is also protective in that its inner fire wards off whatever unwanted forces are trying to impede your success.

Gravel Root

Gravel root is used in charm bags and incense to remove obstacles to your desires and purpose. Also known as gravelweed, Queen of the Meadow, and Joe-Pye weed, it can thrive in clay and gravel-filled terrain, and it is said to draw surrounding stones and gravel to it as it grows. It is used medicinally to treat kidney stones and urinary infections. Just as it can physically remove kidney blocks in the body, it can magickally remove other kinds of blocks, particularly the kinds of blocks in life that leave us angry, or, relating to the urinary tract, feeling "pissed." If you feel that something or someone is actively blocking you, gravel root is an excellent ally that can remove and break apart such active blocks or provide a route around them.

High John the Conqueror Root

High John root, a morning glory root also known as *Ipomoea jalapa*, is used in all forms of magick for success, victory, gambling, trickstering, protection, gaining mastery over the self and others, binding, drawing borders, sex, love, and generally strengthening "male" attributes. The root is carried like a charm, used in amulets, anointed with oils, and wrapped in dollar bills or other substances to draw out its properties. Beware of many commercial blends of oil made from this root, for many are fake and do not actually contain High John in them. Those in the Hoodoo tradition who prepare authentic oil will usually have a piece of the root in the oil.

Hollyhock

Hollyhock seeds and flowers are used for prosperity and material success. They attract the blessings of faeries.

Jasmine

A feminine Moon plant, jasmine has the power to raise the energy of anything to which it is added. Jasmine will raise the vibration of any money mixture, helping to make it possible for you to do what you really want to in order to earn the money. It brings in the forces of the Moon and is best used in prosperity magick when the Moon is waxing.

Juniper

Juniper is a sacred wood, burned in smudges to clear the space and invite blessings. The berries are used in medicine, and both the berries and the needles can be used in money magick to invite good fortune into your life. Juniper is also used to ward off thieves, letting you keep more of your riches.

Lavender

Lavender is an herb used medicinally to produce tranquility and peace. It helps clear the mind. In prosperity magick, lavender is linked to Jupiter with its purple flowers, and its strong but tranquil scent also gives Mercury domain over it. It can help provide the peace of mind to make appropriate decisions regarding business and money.

Lilac

Lilacs have a powerful smell that entices us and catches our attention. The color of lilac, a shade of purple, naturally gives Jupiter rulership over it, and its expansive smells help us expand our resources and sweetly get the attention of those whose aid we need. As a flower essence, lilac helps us stand up straight in our own personal truth, helping lead us to our dharma, our purpose in all areas of life.

Lovage

While most people think of lovage as an herb of romance due to its name in English, one of its greatest powers is to bring success in all matters of law and provide victory in court cases. In particular, it mixes well with frankincense and pine to create an incense to smudge, and thus enhance, talismans created to bring victory in court.

Marigold

Marigold is an herb of prosperity and riches. When it is planted in a pot outside your front door, your own prosperity is said to bloom as the plant blooms. The flowers of marigold and its European relation, calendula, can be used in charms to achieve victory in court.

Money Plant

Also known as moneywort, silver dollar plant, or lunaria, as the bright fuscia-purple flowers eventually create seed pods that can be stripped to look like silver-white coins growing on the plant. The seed pods are used to attract wealth, to decorate a prosperous home, and to heal, if they are used as a flower-essence remedy.

Mustard Seed

Mustard seeds are an ingredient in money magick, for they are tiny but abundant. The power of the mustard seed is commented upon in a parable by Jesus, comparing faith to the size of a mustard seed, and with that level of faith, you can still move mountains. Small things can have great power. Traditionally, mustard seeds can be carried almost invisibly in a wallet, purse, or shoes to attract money. Usually the money comes as lots of little sums rather than one large sum.

Nutmeg

Nutmeg is another easily available classic prosperity herb. Like cinnamon and mustard, it is also sprinkled in your wallet or in your shoes for good fortune. A particularly powerful old-world gambling charm is made from whole nutmeg. Known as Gambler's Nutmeg, this charm can be created by drilling into a whole nutmeg without cracking it. Into the hole goes a small amount of quicksilver—true mercury. Mercury is a toxic substance, and most magicians, witches, and root workers no longer use it. Bits of silver metal or silver filings can be used as a substitute, as they mimic the color of the quicksilver, and that silver color is what is most important here. Silver filings from a Mercury dime (see page 184) are best. Then the hole is sealed with red wax. Carry the Gambler's Nutmeg with you when you are gambling, and watch your luck improve.

Oak

The oak is a tree sacred to the Jupiterian gods, and it connects the blessings of the heavens with the Earth. While there are many different types of oak, the red oak is the best for making material changes and increasing power. Oak bark is traditionally used, though you can also use leaves, acorns, and powdered twigs.

Oakmoss

Like most mosses, oakmoss is associated with the element of earth and the Underworld. It can be used in all forms of Underworld magick, including working with the lords and ladies of the dead in order to obtain Underworld riches. It works well with patchouli as an incense base.

Orange

The citrus fruit orange is used for its connection with the Sun. It requires strong Sun, and it magickally absorbs the power of the Sun and expresses it in the fruit. While one might use the entire fruit or the juice in magick, more often the dried peel is used in potions, incenses, and charms, or the essential oil can be used in perfumes and washes.

Patchouli

The earthy scent of patchouli can be used in money magick, love magick, and protection magick. Ruled by Saturn, patchouli helps us manifest our desires and dreams in reality. It also helps connect us to earth gods and goddesses, as well as Underworld deities.

Pine

Pine is another tree ruled by Jupiter. The spirit of pine has a great disposition toward humanity. The needles, bark, seed cones, and resins can all be used in magick. They bring prosperity and clarity. The spirit medicine of pine aids in issues of leadership.

Rice

Rice, like most grains, is a symbol of abundance and prosperity. Many forms of Asian magick and American folk magick use rice as a staple of prosperity. White rice can be easily dyed with food coloring to add to the magick, as green rice is popular for prosperity. Rice can be gathered in a bowl for money magick, kept in a pouch, or scattered to offer blessings.

Sage

Sage popularly refers to both the garden-variety sage used in cooking and the various forms of sagebrush and white sage used in Native American smudging ceremonies, popularized by modern metaphysical groups and shops. Both can be used in money magick. Garden sage is a great restorer of body and mind, and it can be used after bouts of burnout or illness to prepare you to come back to focus on your work and purpose in life.

Add one tablespoon of dried garden sage to one cup of boiling water, and let it steep overnight. Drink this every morning for a period of one to three months. It is particularly powerful in the fall and spring as a way to prepare the body for the shifts in season. Those who are recovering from very serious bouts can take one to three cups a day, and for this use, sage mixes well with rose petals, jasmine flowers, and lavender. Mix three parts sage with one part each of rose, jasmine, and lavender, and again use the proportion of one teaspoon of dried herb to one cup of water. Coffee should be avoided. Both garden sage and sagebrush can be used in potions and incense to clear away unwanted energies and invite in blessings and good fortune. Sagebrush and California white sage work particularly well when they are burned with cedar and sweet grass. This invites in beneficial influences and the "sweetness" of life.

Sandalwood

Sandalwood primarily lightens and clears the mind. Because it is an excellent aid to meditation, in money magick it helps us clearly see the situation at hand and gain a sense of detachment to make an informed decision about our current issue. Sandalwood makes an excellent base for prosperity incenses, and it mixes well with other resins, woods, and spices.

Sarsaparilla

Sarsaparilla is ruled by Jupiter. The powdered root can be used in all incenses, teas, charms, and potions for Jupiterian magick. It is also used as an herb of increase, magnifying love magick.

Sumac

Sumac is generally thought of as a Saturnine herb, with the harsh power of Saturn deities behind it. It can be used in court battles, particularly to get the verdict you wish for, but it could also get a lesser verdict if the court case goes against you. It is used in potions of peace to end conflict with another person and bring a true and final judgment to the situation.

Sunflower

Sunflowers are naturally ruled by the Sun, and they are used in prosperity, success, inspiration, and health magick. The seeds are most commonly used, but the flower petals or leaves also carry magickal potency. Sunflowers you grow yourself are best for magick. The very act of planting a sunflower seed can be a spell. Your fortune grows as the flower grows. Just as we must find a stable place to grow our own natural prosperity in relationship with the land, sunflowers need a good spot to grow, and they do not like to be uprooted and transplanted. If you want sunflowers to bear seed, choose your spot well and water them often.

Tonka Bean

While Hoodoo traditions use the tonka bean in love magick, I was taught in the Cabot tradition of witchcraft to use tonka for prosperity. It has a sweet, rich flavor reminiscent of vanilla. It's ruled by both Jupiter and Venus, and it's used for prosperity and attracting the things you desire. A magickal ink for prosperity petitions can be made on a Thursday using blue vegetable dye or blue artist's ink. Add four tonka beans, whole or crushed, to the ink, along with a pinch of cinnamon and a chip of lapis lazuli. Use this ink to write out your money spells (see chapter 7).

Vanilla

Vanilla is another herb of both love and prosperity. There is an inherent power to the scent of vanilla, strangely causing some modern magicians to assign this seemingly benign ingredient's rulership to the planet Pluto, the planet of power, death, and transformation. The scent of vanilla is powerful and sweet, and it is used to attract blessings, good fortune, and sweet and pleasant things.

Vetiver

Vetiver oil and root has a strong earthy scent, used for the attraction of material wealth. It is also associated with Hermes/Mercury, as the patron of commerce and business, as well as thieves, so it can be used to repel thieves. It is also used in tranquility magick to calm the mind and ground the self. It can also be used in love magick.

Violet

Violet's natural magick is of encouragement, helping those who are overly sensitive. Due to the color of the blooms, violets, such as African violet, are also linked with Jupiter and the money magick of Jupiter.

Yellow Dock

Yellow dock is another Jupiterian root herb that is used for a variety of healing and magickal purposes. The seeds in particular are used in prosperity magick, as some say they resemble little coins. The magick is in the abundance of one plant to make so many seeds, and they are used to proliferate and multiply funds you already have. The seeds and the root can be collected in the fall.

CHAPTER 7

PROSPERITY SPELLS AND FORMULAS

Now that you have an understanding of the principles of prosperity, as well as place, timing, divine powers, and natural helpers, you are ready to do true prosperity magick. Being prosperous takes hard work. Even when you are not focused on money itself but your True Will, your dharma, it takes work to fulfill that dharma. Many people think that if they are doing the "right" things in their lives, money will just fall into their laps with no effort or work. There is a sense of entitlement. If magick teaches you nothing else, it should teach you about the cycles of exchange. You get nothing for nothing, even when you are divinely blessed and guided. Everything has its seasons in this world. Everything moves up and down with the wheels of life. If you are going to be in the world of form, you have to learn how to play by the rules of creation, sustainment, and destruction, transforming one thing into another. This is the way of magick.

Prosperity magick is a way of taking advantage of those cycles and seasons to get what you need and want. You can put a lot of work into something in your life and still not be prosperous, if you are not healthy and clear in your relationship with money. You can do a lot of work toward what you think is your True Will, but perhaps you are fooling yourself. Perhaps there is something truer for you to be doing that will also support you financially.

Most people are less concerned with the purpose of their soul and simply want to get by and be happy, and they get distracted in life. They say they want to be prosperous, but they lose interest in any one way to get there. They cannot put the necessary energy into their stated goals. Their wants change from day to day, or even moment to moment, and without that sufficient will and life force to back up their intentions, nothing happens.

While maintaining will over long periods of time is difficult for anybody, including magicians and witches, getting focused for a short period of time for a ritual is more reasonable. Sometimes you can muster enough energy (particularly when you've chosen the appropriate time, place, deities, and natural objects to help you), and with that energy you can change your life in a moment, when you are otherwise distracted and listless. Spells and rituals are technologies to make things happen quickly. As long as you can stay focused in the ritual, you can often forget about it afterward and the results will still be strong. In fact, most schools of magick encourage you to let go of your intention and forget about it, letting the universe (or your own subconscious, depending on the school of magick's own theology) manifest your desire.

Any of these spells can be done like simple folk magick, without a lot of ceremonial regalia or fancy setup. Some people prefer it that way. In general, I prefer a bit more formality in my magick, particularly when it is urgently needed to achieve a significant result. The extra time to set up adds to the energy for me. While you can do these spells on their own, as is, I do suggest attempting them inside a magick circle (see chapter 4), calling upon appropriate divinities, and choosing auspicious astrological times to do the spells. I also like using ritual clothing, either dressing in all black for magick, such as a simple black robe, or wearing prosperity colors, such as green, blue, and purple. If you have a favorite power color—a color that you use to feel strong or magickal—you could wear something of that color as well. The circle simply focuses your intentions better and blocks out unwanted interruptions. If the circle is too much for you to do, simply do the folk magick in an informal style. Take a few moments to acknowledge the sacredness of the space around you—the four directions, the Earth, the sky, and the center. Focus your attention on the work at hand, and begin your magick.

PROSPERITY PETITION SPELLS

The most simple form of spell is merely speaking or writing out what you want. I suggest writing it out, because the process of drafting your spell gets you to really think about what you want, and the best way to say it. Modern Craft petition spells usually consist of a statement of who you are, a call to the gods from whom you are asking for favor, a request for what you want specifically, a thank-you, and any stipulations. All of this is followed by a "So mote it be." It's like the pagan "Amen," stating "This is so," transforming the request into a positive affirmation that the request is the truth, it is reality. Here is the format I use:

> I, [state your name], *ask in the name of the Goddess, God, and Great Spirit* [or any specific deities and patrons] *to be granted* [list what you want]. *I thank you for all that I have and ask that this be for the highest good, harming none. So mote it be!*

An example of this type of spell personalized from my own past could be written as follows:

> I, *Christopher John, ask in the name of the Goddess, God, and Great Spirit, as well as the gods of Underworld riches, Pluto and Proserpina, to grant me a new job in the music industry that is completely acceptable to me on all levels, including location, pay, and job description, furthering my career. I thank you for all that I have been granted, and I ask this be correct and for the highest good, harming none. So mote it be.*

To do your own prosperity petition, simply tailor your own needs to fit the basic template. Ask for what you want, not necessarily the exact circumstances of how you get it. In the preceding spell, I asked for a job that is acceptable to me, fulfilling my personal criteria and advancing my career. I didn't ask for a specific position in a specific company. I could have, but that would close the doors to many opportunities that my magick could have manifested.

Ideally, you ask to manifest things on the waxing Moon and banish obstacles on the waning Moon. Once you have your petition created, write a final draft with neat handwriting on paper. The paper is traditionally a "parchment" available at paper stores, and can be colored to match your intention, using green, blue, or purple paper. You could also use green, blue, or purple inks to write your intention on colored or white paper. Generally we do not use recycled paper, because it has previous intentions in it. However, you could smudge recycled paper with purifying smoke, such as smoke from sage or frankincense and myrrh blends, to cleanse it.

Petition spells are done best in a magick circle, read aloud one to three times in the sacred space, and then lit on fire from an altar candle and burned in a flameproof cauldron or other burning vessel. Once the ashes are cool, they are kept in a sacred ash pot on the altar, scattered in the wind, buried, or released into running water.

A petition spell, like any other spell, can manifest quickly, within a few days, or it may take up to a few months to manifest. Some people like to put "time locks" into the spell, stating directly that the spell should manifest within a certain time period. If it doesn't, the spell has expired. What you want now is not what you want three years from now, and some spells are still working, but simply working at an incredibly slow pace. It's good to write down your spells in a journal or your Book of Shadows, a magickal book of rituals and formulas, so that when they do come true, you can compare what you asked for to what you got, and perhaps learn better ways to word and cast your spells.

LIGHTING THE WAY TO SUCCESS

Along with petition spells, candle spells are an easy form of magick, particularly with money and finance. As a professional tarot reader, I've found that many of the main questions people ask a reader are about money. They ask about jobs, raises, and selling their houses. Not only do I like to give readings on the events and potential futures people have, but I really like to help give solutions to their issues and problems. I've found that candle magick is quite effective for money issues, even for those who have no background in magick. I generally don't do magick for people, other than healing work, but I will either do magick with them, or give them a simple spell or ritual to do at home on their own. Most of my clients are not witches or magicians, but ordinary people looking for a little help, and most of the time a simple candle spell gives them the results they need.

Candles are so effective because they have all the natural elements in them already. The wax is for the earth element. The melting is for the water element. The fire is obviously for fire, and the oxygen consumed is for the air element. All four are needed for magick, and a candle has all four of these powers in its very nature.

Generally the color of the candle is aligned with the intention of the magick. For money spells to get quick cash, green is the most appropriate color. It is the color of Venus. Anything dealing with specific monetary values works best with green. If you are doing magick for success at your job, for a general promotion, or for "good luck," you might want to use blue or purple, the colors of Jupiter. Those using an elemental correspondence would use earth colors—green, brown, black, or any other earth tones—for general money and fire colors such as red, yellow, and orange for success and career.

Practitioners disagree on what type of candle is most effective. Most witches prefer candles made of all-natural ingredients, such as beeswax or soy, but they are more expensive. I generally prefer taper candles, as they are large enough to hold a magickal "charge" of intentional energy I think is sufficient for success, but they burn fairly quickly. The spell is not complete until the candle burns down and out. Because of this, some prefer smaller, birthday-size candles, to minimize time. Other practitioners believe votive candles in a glass, or larger seven-day glass jar candles are more effective, as they hold a larger amount of psychic energy and burn longer, maximizing the success of the spell. I tend to use seven-day candles for devotional offerings to the spirits and gods, and for long-term serious issues, such as critical healing.

While candle magick is even more effective in a magick circle, it's one of the few techniques I use regularly outside of the magick circle, and I encourage my clients who know nothing of formal ritual magick to use it at home. Here are the basic steps to candle magick, once you've chosen your candle, based on your intention and preference:

1. *Cleanse the candle.* Most practitioners usually skip this step, but just in case there are any unwanted energies on the candle from the store, or other people handling it once you got home, pass the candle over some purifying smoke (such as that of sage or frankincense and myrrh) to clear it. I had a student who rolled all her candles in fine salt before she used them. You could also hold it in your hands and simply blow on the candle, intending to blow away and neutralize all unwanted energy.

2. *Dress the candle.* Dressing the candle is an optional step to decorate it. Dressing adds more energy to the spell, but it is not absolutely necessary. As you learn more "advanced" techniques of magick, you can add this knowledge to your candle spells. Some people carve symbols into the candle that match their intention, such as the runes (see chapter 8). You can carve your initials and zodiac Sun sign symbol to show the powers of the universe that this magick is intended to benefit you. You can also anoint the candle with the infusions or oils of any of the prosperity herbs listed in the previous chapter, or any of the mixed formulas listed later in this chapter. Some magicians will even take an oiled candle and roll it in powdered prosperity herbs, covering the candle with a fine herbal powder. If you do so, make sure you have a flameproof surface underneath the candle. If the herbs fall, they might spark and smolder and create a fire hazard.

3. *Charge the candle.* Hold the candle in both hands and think of your intention. What do you want? Think it. Speak it. Visualize it. Use all three techniques in any combination. Imagine yourself with the intention fulfilled. What does that feel like? Imagine projecting that feeling into your hands and into the candle. Imagine you are "filling" the candle with energy.

4. *Light the candle.* When the candle is "full" with your magickal intention, light the wick. Keep it someplace safe, sheltered from strong breezes where there is little chance of catching things on fire. If you have an altar, keep the candle on your altar. Don't leave it unattended, but once it's lit, the ritual is done and you don't have to continue to focus on your intention. The candle is doing the work. Your job is done.

Let the candle burn continuously if you can, until it goes out on its own. If you have to leave the candle unattended, you can snuff it out to keep its energetic balance the same. Blowing out the candle or wetting it disrupts the balance of energy, while snuffing keeps things in harmony. Relight it when you can, and continue the process of snuffing and relighting as many times as necessary until the candle is out. Then the spell is complete and released to the universe.

Many of my clients write out a petition spell, replacing Goddess, God, and Great Spirit with however they see the divine, and place it beneath the candle holder. A few of my Catholic clients have had great success addressing it to "Jesus and Mary," "Father, Son, and Holy Spirit," or a specific saint. If you don't want to write a whole petition, my clients have also had success writing the dollar amount they needed on a piece of paper and putting that paper beneath the candle holder. One woman needed to sell her house that had been on the market for nine months. She put her ideal realistic price on a piece of paper, and the word "immediately." The candle burned all day and night. The very next day she got an offer, and they closed within the month. Even though she was not a witch, she became a believer in magick.

EMERGENCY MONEY CANDLE SPELL

This simple candle spell works very well when you need money in an emergency and don't have time to think of anything fancy. It would be done on the waxing to full Moon. Use a green candle and, with a pin, carve dollar signs into it. If you know the dollar amount of what you need, carve that into the candle as well. Also carve your initials or the initials of the person you wish to receive this money. Anoint the candle with a money potion or oil. Anoint from the tip of the candle down to the base, to ritually symbolize things coming to you. Take the dollar bill and rub it up and down the candle, wrapping it around the candle, and then place the dollar flat on your altar workspace with the candle holder and candle on top of it. Say this or something similar:

> *I ask the universe to immediately grant me* [state the amount] *for* [state the need], *in a manner good for all involved, harming none. So mote it be.*

Light the candle and let it burn, bringing to you the money you request. You will have the money you need. It may come in the form of a gift, prize, or, be forewarned, a loan from someone close to you. But you will overcome the emergency crisis.

BREWING FOR ABUNDANCE

Mixing substances together to create a synergistic blend is a time-honored tradition in all magickal cultures. While "simples," or potions made from one plant, were covered in the previous chapter, the strength of most potions comes from combining several different ingredients together. They work together to create something different. Just as when you cook, you mix together things that can be wonderful on their own, but together they make something new, complex, and filling. Certain herbs can trigger properties in other herbs, drawing out new or stronger powers from the plant spirits through teamwork, just as certain foods and spices mixed together in cooking draw out different flavors and textures they would not have alone.

Potions come in many forms, from blends of volatile oils primarily empowered through the use of scent to infusions of herbs in water, either used as anointing fluids or taken internally like a tea. You can also consider dry mixtures to be a form of potion, creating philters, powders, and incense. Potions work by aligning your own energy body with the vibrations of the plants and minerals used. It helps you align with the spirit of the plant, and the overall intention infused into the mixture. Traditionally, potions are said to last for four days, changing your vibration for that time, when anointed on the pulse points or chakra centers. Potions can also be a way to store energy for future use. If there is an astrological time that is great for money magick, and you have no need to do any, making a potion stores the energy of that moment and couples it with the energy of the herbs and other ingredients. You can use this potion whenever you need a little boost of its particular energy, as a daily oil or perfume, or you can use it to anoint ritual objects for bigger spells in your future.

You should be careful in using these powerful substances, just as you would with any other herbs. Many magickal herbs are toxic, and some people have allergies to common herbs and spices. Do not consume anything unless you are sure it is appropriate for you. When in doubt, check with a good medical herbal to see if there are any contraindications to your own personal health, or consult with a health care professional.

MONEY POTION

The following potion is not meant to be consumed, but made in a base of sea salt and water to preserve the infusion for several years and retain a magickal charge. You can use it as an anointing fluid for all your prosperity and money needs.

2 cups spring water
2 tablespoons sea salt
1 tablespoon cinnamon
1 tablespoon red clover
1 tablespoon cloves
1 tablespoon nutmeg
1 tablespoon patchouli
1 tonka bean
1 lodestone (natural magnet)

Prepare a heat-resistant container for this water-based potion. I usually use a large potpourri simmer dish so the mixture can be heated by candle flame, and I can keep it on the center of my altar with no other wires or devices to heat it. Other people like to use their kitchen stove. Traditional witches prefer the flame of a wood or gas stove to electric, feeling that the electric currents disrupt the magick of the ritual, but I've done some successful magick over an electric stove. Generally, non-metallic containers are used to brew potions. Although tin containers are not in use much anymore, tin, as the metal of Jupiter, would be appropriate for prosperity potions. I usually use an enamel, glass, or ceramic bowl to make my potions. Have all your other ingredients out and measured, and collect your basic tools for casting a magick circle before you begin.

First, cast the magick circle, as described in chapter 4. Then add your water and salt to the mixing container and heat it. I use about two cups of water with two tablespoons of sea salt, but go heavier on the salt if you fear that the potion will go rancid. Grind up each herb if you can. I like to use a mortar and pestle while visualizing or chanting my intention for the plant. Charge each herb for prosperity, money, and good fortune as you add it to the water. Stir in each herb. I stir in each of them with four swirls, because four is the number of Jupiter. Other witches like to use nine for the infinite power associated with nine and multiples of nine. Add the lodestone last. If you cannot get a natural lodestone, you can also use a household magnet. When you charge the lodestone, imagine it attracting the money and resources you need.

When all the ingredients are in, recite this charge over the potion four times:

> *The potion will bring money, prosperity, abundance, and good fortune to the user, in a manner good for all involved, harming none. So mote it be.*

Let the potion simmer for a while as the energies of all the ingredients mingle. Turn off the heat source and let the potion cool. You can release the magick circle at this time.

When the potion is cool, strain out the herbs and stone, and bottle the remaining liquid. Label it and date it. Dab the potion on your skin to increase your fortune, and watch the "lucky" coincidences occur for you. I've found that there is a balance to the universe, and using the potion every day tends to minimize its effect. So use it when you want or need something, but do not expect miracles of money every day if you use it every day.

MONEY OIL

A traditional money oil used at the famous occult shop Magickal Childe in New York City was revealed in *The Magickal Formulary Spellbook, Book I* by Herman Slater, the store's owner. Although many have discredited Slater and his formulary for a variety of reasons, including that he either got the traditional formulas slightly wrong, coded them with secret blinds (purposely misleading and ineffective information intended to divert the magickally uneducated), or greatly adapted many of the traditional formulas from Hoodoo and the African diasporic traditions to the point where they became something completely different, I have found that this traditional formula works quite well and have known many people to use it with success. It has become somewhat of a staple in American magick. I've altered the measurements to list the formula in drops, rather than parts, but the proportions are the same. I've used the old-time occult principle of half base oil to half essential oils, which most medicinally oriented practitioners frown upon as being too chemically strong for the skin (cinnamon essential oil is particularly caustic), so use the oil on your bare skin at your own risk, or dilute it with a larger amount of base oil. At times I've omitted the heliotrope due to not having it readily on hand, and the magick still worked quite well.

Money Oil No. 2

8 drops frankincense oil

2 drops heliotrope oil

1 drop bay oil

2 drops orange oil

    1 drop cinnamon oil

    4 drops sandalwood oil (optional)

    18 drops base oil, such as olive oil or mineral oil

    Green food coloring

A popular recipe for fast money oil shared by Scott Cunningham in *The Complete Book of Incense, Oils & Brews* is a version of the following:

Fast Money Oil

    7 drops patchouli oil

    5 drops cedarwood oil

    4 drops vetiver oil

    2 drops ginger oil

    ⅛ ounce base oil, such as olive, grapeseed, or jojoba

Cunningham's recipe is much easier on the skin, using a proportion of essential oils to base that is more in line with the principles of aromatherapy.

PROSPERITY TEA

The internal organ ruled by Jupiter, and thereby the principle of prosperity, is the liver. The old-world magickal notion behind this correspondence was the liver is the largest organ, and Jupiter is the biggest of the wandering stars, the planets. So it was natural to give Jupiter correspondence with the liver. The liver deals with filtering many toxins and impurities out of our system. When we eat rich, "kingly" food, we are taxing our liver. Herbal teas that are tonics for the liver can also double as prosperity teas. If you have any concerns about your physical health, or your liver, please consult an herbalist or medical professional before taking this tea.

    1 part dandelion root

    1 part burdock root

    1 part yellow dock root

    ½ part licorice root

½ part sarsaparilla

½ part cinnamon

¼ part ginger root

¼ part orange peel

Infuse one teaspoon of the herbs in one cup of boiling water for at least thirty minutes. Teas with a large amount of roots should be decocted for their herbal medicine, but here, for their magick, a regular tea infusion is fine. Take one cup every day for seven days, starting when the Moon is waxing and ending before the Moon begins to wane. Notice the changes in both your body and your consciousness to allow greater prosperity into your life.

MONEY-DRAWING POWDER

Seeds in general are used as a sympathetic draw for money and abundance, as the multitude of seeds coming from one plant is an indication of the multitude of money you wish to receive from one act of magick. One powerful technique involves making a powder of prosperity seeds and scattering it in the thresholds of doorways in your home, business, or around a room, or keeping it in a pouch as a charm. You can also scatter it in a ring around your home or office, encircling the whole area with good fortune.

Dill seeds

Fenugreek seeds

Mustard seeds

White rice (uncooked and dry)

Nutmeg (powdered)

Ginger (powdered)

Pyrite (crushed and powdered)

Grind together the dill, fenugreek, and mustard seeds in a mortar and pestle, along with the white rice. Some practitioners dye the rice green first with food coloring, for the color of money and Venus. Grind in a clockwise motion only.

Add the powdered nutmeg and ginger, which would be rather tough to grind by hand. You can purchase them pre-ground or use an electric grinder dedicated to your magickal work. You can also grind the white rice in the electric grinder.

Then add crushed pyrite (fool's gold) to the mix. Whole pyrite can be broken down with a hammer, or flakes can be scraped off. If you don't want to break any pyrite into powder, many people would substitute gold glitter for the pyrite, though I think there is better magick in natural pyrite than synthetic glitter.

Charge the powder while in a magick circle as the Moon is waxing, and use it as needed.

ABUNDANCE INCENSE

Many substances can be burned on charcoal to evoke the power of attraction, prosperity, and good fortune. Most incenses are a blend of woods and resins, which produce a pleasant smell and slower burn than incense made of only leaves and flowers. Wood-and-resin blends are often mixed with flowers, leaves, and stems of magickal plants with a high oil content, and fixed with essential oils. Traditionally, such blends should sit in a jar for at least a Moon cycle, letting the scents and oils mix and mingle to create a more consistent burn.

Abundance Incense

    2 tablespoons cinnamon

    2 tablespoons clove

    2 tablespoons nutmeg

    1 tablespoon ginger

    1 tablespoon orange peel

    1 pinch coffee

    6 drops orange oil

    4 drops cinnamon oil

    4 parts honey

Mix all the herbs and oils together, and then add the honey to bind it. Let it air-dry a bit, and then break it apart before you store it in a jar. The honey will add to the richness and aid in the blending of scents. If the mix is too "wet" for you, let it air-dry more until it reaches a dry, chunky consistency. The coffee might seem incongruent with the rest of the recipe, but a small amount of coffee can be used to speed up any magick, making this a "fast" abundance incense. For those who dislike coffee, another trick to speed up magick is to add a pinch of rabbit hair from a live and shedding rabbit. Such hair can be used in both speeding up magick and adding luck to the blend. Modern Wiccans generally do not use rabbit's feet or kill any animals for spell ingredients, though you will find such practices in older forms of both folk magick and medieval ceremonial magick. Cayenne pepper can also be used to speed up spells, but it is generally avoided in incense blends because the fumes that are released when it is burned are rather noxious if inhaled.

Money Attraction Incense

2 parts lavender
1 part pine needles
3 parts white sandalwood
½ part fenugreek seeds
½ part basil
½ part cinquefoil
3 parts red wine
1 cut-up dollar bill
Turquoise chips or ground pyrite

Rather than promoting new abundance and growth, this incense helps you go out and get what you want, and command enough authority or power to be successful. Some of the best money incense I know requires the shredding of a dollar bill and mixing the pieces in with the incense. The smell of the incense is not always great because of it, but it is very effective. I was first taught this technique by a very wonderful witch who made an amazingly complex money incense with the dollar bill. Although I never got the formula, I used his idea of the dollar bill.

If you are uncomfortable doing such a thing, you can use any foreign currency you have, or game money. I also like to store a turquoise stone in with the incense. It can be taken out after the first month, but turquoise has a great blend of both Venusian and Jupiterian powers that lends itself well to this mix. The wine helps add to the richness and power, though it will yield a different consistency than the previous honey formula. Again, air-dry for a bit before you break it apart and place it into the jar.

WHO'S-THE-BOSS POWDER

Sometimes dealing with your employer can be quite difficult, and a little magick can help deal with difficult situations in the workplace. The following two spells are not substitutes for actually communicating and dealing with issues in a healthy manner, but they can energetically set the stage for your direct work.

If you seek to smooth over issues with your boss in a noncombative manner, simply letting go of problems and moving forward, mix equal parts of these ingredients:

Fennel seeds
Gravel root
Frankincense
Lavender
Brown sugar

Grind all of the combined ingredients to a fine powder, and sprinkle traces at the threshold of your boss's office, your office, and wherever you might meet. Make sure the powder is fine enough to be almost invisible. Someone finding strange powder or seeing you spread it will not add to the likelihood of an easy resolution.

If you are fed up with your boss and desire a confrontation, and you want to put yourself in a position of power or control, mix the following herbs together and place them in a small red bag with a High John root or Solomon's Seal root, consecrated with oil:

1 part fennel seeds
1 part gravel root
1 part bay leaves
¼ part tobacco

Sprinkle the powder around the office as you would with the first mix. Realize that while you might be able to say what you need to say to your boss, using this mix and engaging in a confrontation might end with you getting fired. Sometimes losing a bad job is an important step to finding out what is right for you, but you are responsible for the consequences of all your actions, magickal and mundane.

BATHING IN BLESSINGS

Magickal baths are another traditional form of magick. Most of us think of using bath magick to cleanse ourselves of unwanted energy. We use ritual baths before larger rituals, or as part of uncrossing magick, to clear ourselves and our bodies from unwanted power directed at us.

Another form of bathing magick that is not as well known is to use baths to instill blessings. Sacred waters are bathed in and then not washed off for a period of time, usually twelve to twenty-four hours, to integrate the blessings of the substances in the bath. You can air-dry, or gently towel off by patting down. Don't vigorously rub yourself with a towel or you'll be rubbing away the blessings.

New Year Blessing Bath

One bath used either on the first day of the new year—be it secular January 1 or, for witches, November 1—or on your birthday is a bath of alcohol. Each of these days states a time of new beginnings. While you are in a filled bathtub, pour a bottle of either fine wine or champagne over your head, letting the alcohol flow into the bath water. Then bathe in the mix of alcohol and water. Come out of the bath without really washing it off, and let it dry on your skin for a few hours. Then you can take another bath or shower and wash up completely. Wine is said to be the "waters of life," and it will grant you a year of health, wealth, and blessings. Champagne is more specifically for financial success in the coming year.

Milk and Honey Bath

In paganism, the summerlands of the ancestors are described as the land of milk and honey, meaning that everything is sweet, abundant, and nourishing. All is provided for, as our ancient ancestors saw the Otherworld as a place of continual feasting and merrymaking, for physical life in our world could be difficult and filled with ills. The afterlife has all the blessings of our physical life with none of the sorrows. Those two ingredients, milk for nourishment and honey for sweetness and blessings, are used in money and love magick. This bath can be used for love or money, and you can steep herbs that are appropriate for either intention in the warm milk to lean the energies one way or the other.

> 3 cups milk
> 1 cup honey

Warm the milk in a saucepan, and dissolve the honey into it. You might add a little powdered cinnamon or nutmeg for a Jupiterian influence. Then add the milk/honey mixture to a warm bath. When you get out, do not wash your hair or skin. Let the milk and honey stay on your body at least for a few hours before you wash up again.

Basil Bath

Another powerful and simple magickal bath involves making an infusion of fresh or dried basil leaves and adding them to your bath water. Fresh, chopped leaves are said to be better because they resemble cash floating in the water. Mix the leaves with hot water to make a basil tea. Add the tea to the bath water. For a cleaner bath, you can choose to strain out the leaves before adding the tea, though some prefer the experience of green cashlike leaves floating in the bathtub with them.

Not only can this liquid be used in a bath, but it can be used as a floor wash to attract money and success to your business or home. It helps create a sympathy with others who will now be more likely to aid you, spend money in your establishment, or offer you good terms in a business deal. If you are lacking basil herb, you can use a few drops of basil essential oil in warm water for a similar magickal effect.

Money Bath

Mix the following herbs together and put them in a muslin or cheese-cloth bag. Soak the bag in the bath water to create an abundance and money bath. Such baths are best when they are done repeatedly. Folk tradition would suggest doing this bath either on Thursday or Friday, for four, seven, or nine consecutive weeks, or starting on a Sunday and doing it for seven days in a row, using fresh herbs each time if possible.

1 part sage
1 part ginger
1 part red clover
2 parts orange peel
2 parts lemon peel

MONEY MAGICK FLOWER ESSENCE

The flower essence of money plant (*Lunaria annua*), also known as silver dollar plant, can be used to understand why we have blocks to receiving wealth and abundance in our lives. Money plant's purple flowers eventually form seed pods that can be peeled back, resembling silver paper coins. It's used in feng shui as a prosperity remedy because it resembles money.

The simplest way to make a basic flower essence is to get a clear glass bowl or chalice and fill it with pure water. Pick the blooming flowers of the money plant and float them on the top of the water. Put it out in the Sun for three hours minimum, and if the day is partly cloudy, five or six hours. I've found mixing lunar and solar energies to be quite beneficial with flower essences, so if the Moon is near full, you can leave the vessel out all day and all night under the moonlight. You must take it in before the Sun rises again. In a ritualized manner, or sacred space, drink the water, and ask for your issues with money and prosperity to be revealed and then healed.

The therapeutic technique of flower essences would instead be to fill a quarter of a bottle with a preservative, such as brandy, rum, vodka, apple-cider vinegar, or vegetable glycerin, and then fill the rest of the bottle with the water from the vessel. This is now called the *mother essence*, and it should be dated and labeled. Next, fill a small dropper bottle, combining three parts pure water with one part preservative and anywhere from three to ten drops of the mother essence, depending on the size of the dropper bottle. Shake up the dropper bottle to activate the vibrational energy of the plant. This new bottle is called a *stock bottle*. Although flower essences are usually described scientifically, much like magick, there is an art to them as well, and not a lot of hard rules. The process is repeated with a new bottle of three parts water to one part preservative and three to ten drops of the stock bottle. Shake this mixture, creating a *dosage bottle*. Although you can safely take the essence from the stock or dosage level of dilution, the dosage bottle is said to have the strongest mental / emotional / spiritual healing effects, and several different stock essences can be mixed into one dosage bottle, creating a unique blend for an individual.

If you are diluting the essence and taking it at the stock or dosage level, you should take three drops, three times a day, for at least a month. You will notice a subtle, and sometimes not so subtle, shift in your thoughts, feelings, and attitudes toward money, helping you to transform your relationship with money. The essence can also be used in other rituals, in water and wine chalices as part of your magick circle, or in your bath water.

Other flowers that can be made into essences to help us understand our issues with money, abundance, and financial self-esteem include buttercup, rain of gold, tree peony, cabbage tree, harebell, and red trillium. Many of these essences are also available commercially if the living plants are not available to you. You can also experiment with the abundance and prosperity herbs in the previous chapters, and see if such plants will yield aid in prosperity as flower essences in ways that have not been obvious to traditional flower-essence practitioners. Gem elixirs can be made from the stones listed in the previous chapter as well, in the same way that the flower essences are prepared.

CHAPTER 8

LIVING THE CHARMED LIFE

Magickal charms for abundance are found all over the world. Basically, a charm is any physical object that is used for magick and held, carried, or kept in a special place. The creation of charms is an excellent way for nonpractitioners of magick to benefit from it. This is because a magick worker will make charms for individuals, and their use of the charms brings them the benefit.

Charm is a generic term for any magickal object linked to a specific spell intention. Traditionally charms come in two categories: Those that ward off unwanted forces, such as protection charms that ward off harm and misfortune, are known as *amulets*. Charms that draw blessings to you, such as love charms, are known as *talismans*. Most prosperity charms are considered to be talismans.

Charms can consist of many things. Some charms are made from simple pendants and jewelry. Others are made from paper, wood, stone, or clay. My favorite charms are small bags or bundles filled with herbs, stones, and other objects. They are referred to as a *mojo* or *gris gris* bags in Southern folk traditions. Charms work by combining the natural vibration, the virtue, of several different ingredients. The ingredients catalyze and react with each other, making more powerful magick, though some also consider objects made from a single substance to be charms.

MONEY MOJO

Here is an herbal charm that will aid in the expansion of good fortune and money in all that you do. Start with a royal blue bag, or a square of cloth with corners you can pull up and tie into a bag.

Gold, silver, yellow, or white thread
1 lapis lazuli stone
2 parts pine needles
3 parts cedar
1 part juniper berries
½ part oak bark
½ part sarsaparilla
9 drops jasmine oil
9 grains of corn (maize) or wheat

While you are in a magick circle, charge each ingredient and place it in the bag. Tie nine knots in the thread you have chosen, and then tie the knotted thread around the bag, sealing the charm together. Carry it with you on your nondominant side. If you are right-handed, carry it in your left pocket, or keep with your wallet or purse.

RIGHT PLACE, RIGHT TIME, RIGHT THING RING

I love to do ring magick because I love to wear rings. You can enchant something you would wear anyway to carry a bit of magickal intention with you and improve your life, even if you don't have the time to focus on your intention continuously.

One of my favorite affirmations from when I started in the Craft is "I am in the right place, at the right time, doing the right thing." Although I didn't know it at the time, it's really a call to manifest our True Will, our dharma, which is the essence of our prosperity magick in this book. If you are fulfilling your soul's purpose in every moment, you will have every resource you need. But life is tough, and the path to manifesting your True Will is hard. We can't keep focused on the right place, right time, right thing in our daily lives when we don't know these things with conscious certainty. Using an affirmation in daily meditation can help us, but infusing that intention into a charm can also be incredibly beneficial.

Ideally, you should use a gold ring that has no other magickal intention infused in it as the foundation piece of this spell. Gold is the metal of success, and in alchemical magick, it is the metal of the Philosopher's Stone, the metal of self-realization and enlightenment. If you don't or can't wear gold, as many witches feel much more comfortable with silver jewelry, you can use silver, but it's less effective. White gold would still work very well, if the color of yellow gold is your impediment. If the ring features any stone associated with prosperity or success, the stone will help to enhance the ring's effectiveness. I think ruby is ideal, but the ring can contain any prosperity stone that you feel comfortable using. See chapter 6 for more stones that could be used for the ring.

Create a magick circle and pass the ring through a purifying incense, or anoint it with salt and water to cleanse it. Then pass it through the smoke of a prosperity incense or herb to empower it with the energy of success. You can also anoint it with the oil of a prosperity plant or a mixed potion for prosperity and success. Charge the ring by reciting the affirmation "I am in the right place, at the right time, doing the right thing" over and over again. Borrowing from the Eastern traditions, I suggest doing this spell 108 times, as that number of repetitions is said to be the most successful, permeating a mantra throughout your energy body. Because 108 mantras or affirmations can be hard to count, you can use a set of beads. Traditional mala beads, available at many metaphysical and Eastern cultural shops, have 108 beads, with a larger starting "head" bead, to help you keep count. They are used much like a Christian rosary, though the single mantra is repeated. Many industrious witches make their own set of beads or knotted threads to keep count of affirmations and spoken spells. Make sure you are holding both the ring and the beads.

When you are done, say, "So mote it be." I also add, "I fix this charm so that none may remove it, unless it is for the highest good." This way, any of your doubts, or any other magick, won't interfere with your intention. Wear the ring regularly. See if you feel in greater alignment with your purpose and will. If you keep a magickal journal, note the days you wear it and the days you don't. Can you tell the difference? I usually can. Serious magickal practitioners eventually get to a point in their practice where they do feel their default state is to be in the right place, at the right time, and doing the right thing, rather than flowing against the tides of True Will. At that point, you don't need the ring as much, but it doesn't hurt to keep it around for those days when you are having difficulties.

COIN MAGICK

If one of the basic principles of magick is "like attracts like," we can literally use money to attract money. Coins make powerful talismans for money and wealth. There is a strong tradition of using coins in folk magick. You can use modern coins quite well, though magickally, you might be better off tracking down some older coins. In the United States, there are a variety of older coins still available from coin collector's shops and online that are more significant in doing magick, due to their imagery and the fact that older coins have a higher chance of being made of the metal they appear to be. Pennies dating after 1982 are zinc with a coating of copper, while those dated before 1982 are actually mostly copper. If you have access to old and/or foreign coins, you can also turn them into talismans for magick. Work with the images and designs on the coins to taylor your magickal intention to suit them.

Silver Dimes

Silver dimes, popularly referred to as Mercury dimes, are used in all forms of gambling and prosperity magick. Although they appear to depict the figure of Mercury/Hermes (patron of gamblers, commerce, and the crossroads) with his winged helmet, they actually are supposed to depict a female winged liberty image. Although some people still use the modern dimes for prosperity magick, many practitioners of Hoodoo and American folk magick believe that the older Mercury dimes are more powerful for this work.

Mojo Ingredient: Dimes are used in mojo charm bags. Single dimes or nine dimes together are common ingredients in gambling and money charms.

Leap Year: Mercury dimes from a leap year (e.g., 1940) are considered particularly lucky and potent.

Turning Silver: In some forms of folk magick and witchcraft, silver coins are "turned" or flipped over to increase wealth. One folk charm has you lay out three silver coins on the windowsill to absorb the moonlight on the night of the full Moon. Then at midnight, you turn over the coins, like pages in a book, to increase your prosperity, and so your silver will grow as the moonlight did. Then you would carry the silver coins in your pocket. Other variations have you do the same thing on New Year's Eve, or simply turn the coins in your pocket on the full Moon, or when the first crescent of the new Moon appears. The coins, once turned, can also be buried at a crossroads or under your front step, to bring you more prosperity.

Curse Breaking: To break a curse, particularly a curse that comes from the Hoodoo tradition, you can boil a silver dime in water or milk for short period of time, allow the liquid to cool to a safe temperature, and carefully drink it in order to break the curse's "poison." (Do not swallow the dime.) Dimes were used to test curse powders to see if they contained sulfur. If they did, the dimes would tarnish quickly, thus giving their power a scientific basis. Magickally, dimes are still potent in blessing and breaking curses, even if sulfur has not been used. Whenever I feel as though more things have gone wrong than usual, I drink silvered milk, just to make sure there is nothing "on" me. Silvered water can also be put in your bath to break curses and confer blessings, as silvered water is sacred to the faery folk, and it can disrupt malign magicks of human or otherworldly origin.

Wheat Pennies

The Lincoln Wheat Ear Cent, usually referred to as a wheat penny, was minted from 1909 to 1958, and it is a very magickal coin. Made from copper, it resonates with the power of Venus and, because of its image of wheat, with the power of the Goddess. It is used as a magickal talisman to provide money for hearth and home, food on the table, and all the necessities of life. I equate it with our pagan FFFF wisdom. I like to use three wheat pennies for the three forms of the Wiccan Goddess, and I carry them in a small green charm bag, charged for blessings and prosperity.

Buffalo Nickel

Known as the Indian Head nickel or buffalo nickel, this coin depicts a composite portrait of several different Native American chiefs on one side, and an American bison on the other. I've used this coin in work-related magick where tenacity and groundedness is required. I relate the bison to the astrological associations of Taurus, of fixed earth, so when those qualities are needed, I obtain a buffalo nickel and enchant it for my magickal purpose.

Birth Year Talisman

A coin from your birth year is another powerful good-luck and blessing talisman. Carry it with you as a charm, or add it to a talisman pouch. If you have a witch bag/medicine pouch of sacred objects, it can be carried in there, or made into a specific blessing pouch with other herbs and minerals associated with good fortune.

The Dime Prosperity Spell

One of the simplest spells for increasing in your financial status is to take a roll of dimes and enchant them for wealth. A roll of dimes is five dollars, equaling fifty dimes. Unwrap the dimes if they are rolled, and cleanse them of all unwanted energies. Smudge them in the smoke of a cleansing incense, such as sage, frankincense, lavender, or cinnamon. Or sprinkle them with salt water. In a magick circle, anoint each dime with a money potion or oil. Charge each one with the blessing of prosperity, making each one a talisman of good fortune and money. Then leave them out in public, one by one. Use them in shopping. Give them away. Put them into circulation. The more people who handle them and have blessings, the more blessings will return for you.

Foreign Coins

Foreign coins can be used as talismans, in charm bags, or as a substitute for many of the spells given previously. They particularly attract money from afar.

AID FROM THE ANCESTORS

In many magickal cultures, both Eastern and Western, it is believed that the dead help their loved ones from beyond the grave. They are our first magickal contacts, because they have a personal connection to us, they know what it's like to be human, and we carry on their energy in the form of our genetics, our family. They have an interest on many levels in seeing us succeed and prosper. Through our prosperity, they prosper too.

Offerings are made to the ancestors to strengthen them in the afterlife. Pagans often see the realm of the peaceful dead as part of the Underworld or Otherworld. Many simply refer to it as the summerlands. Ancestors are said to enjoy an afterlife of perpetual indulgence in earthly delights. Today we think of it as a metaphor, but I'm not so sure that our pagan ancestors did.

In Chinese traditions, there is a similar concept of the dead residing in an afterworld and living a very similar life to what they had on Earth. And like on Earth, they need some sort of economic credit, some resources. The living burn "hell money"—paper notes similar to monopoly money—as offerings, to send the essence of the money to their ancestors in the Otherworld. If you look at many Asian businesses and restaurants, you can find an ancestor altar for the prosperity of the family business.

There is a connection between the well-being of our dead and our own earthly prosperity. The Greeks and Romans saw the Lord of the Underworld as the Lord of Riches as well, because the dead were interred into the land, and from the land we find precious metals and gems.

Although the focus of my own spiritual work is not heavily centered on continual ancestor reverence, it does play a part in my craft. The following is a spell that I used with a friend to help him gain better direction regarding his life, his fortunes, and his career path.

TREE OF LIFE ANCESTOR SPELL

10 dimes

Bread or family pastry—ideally something you baked yourself

Wine or alcoholic beverage favored by family ancestors or the family as
   a whole

Since you are working with the ancestors, if you can purchase an alcoholic beverage that your family would generally drink, or a favorite of one of your ancestors, do so. On the Italian side of my family, red wine was the favorite choice, though they also liked their cheap beer. If the family has any special recipe for bread or pastry, use it. If not, a general good-quality bread, either baked or bought, will do.

Go to the graveyard where your ancestors are buried. If your ancestors are not buried near you, go to any graveyard in an area where your people have lived, though ideally you would want one where your own flesh and blood, or adopted family, have been interred. First, go to the highest point in the graveyard and ask the guardian, the spirit or entity that protects the graveyard, for permission to do this magick. If there is no high monument or statue in the graveyard and everything is of generally equal height, go to the main gate. Explain why you are here and what you hope to do with your ancestors. Make an offering to the guardian. Eat a small piece of bread or cake, and leave a piece of bread or cake at the foot of the guardian's space. Drink a small bit of alcohol, and pour some on the bread or cake at the foot of the space. Wait a few minutes. Intuit if the offering was accepted, or use an oracle device you are familiar with, such as the runes or tarot, to see if you get a "positive" response and receive permission. An upright rune or card can equate yes, or the meaning of the divinatory symbol can give you the indication.

If the offering is accepted, then go to the gravesite of your ancestors. If you have no family buried in the graveyard, continue your work at the site of the guardian. Call upon your ancestors. Knock on the gravestone three times and ask them to be present. If you have specific ancestors in mind, call them by name. If not, simply ask for your ancestors. Explain to them your situation, as you would if they were alive. Ask them for their help. Place the ten dimes (true silver dimes are ideal) on the grave in the shape of the Tree of Life. This is also the image found in the classic image of the Ten of Pentacles in the tarot (see chapter 3). Because the Ten of Pentacles signifies true wealth and the abundance of good family and home, it keys into the energy of the ancestors. Aligned with the tarot, it helps build momentum to work with your family spirits. Make your offering of cake and alcohol as you did before. Have a piece of the cake and then put a piece on the gravesite. Have a small drink and pour the rest out on the cake. Thank your ancestors and say farewell.

In a short time, you will notice a change in your fortune, a guidance from the other world to help you find the right job and obtain the right resources. Look for the blessings and influence of your family from the other side.

PROSPERITY RUNES

The Norse runes constitute a complete and complex system of magick that has grown in popularity in the modern occult community. Many witches have replaced the more traditional Theban script in their Book of Shadows with the rune set known as the Elder Futhark. Each rune contains its own magickal power, resonating with the archetypal forces of the universe, as the Norse saw them. Most people know the runes as a system of divination, like tarot cards, but they are used quite prominently in magick. They can be etched into magickal tools and talismans to confer their power to those objects, and grant blessings to the owner or user of the items. Because runes have such a rich history and strong link to universal forces, many witches and magicians favor them. They are not just symbolic of forces; not only do they need to be wholly empowered by the magician, like many modern symbols, but they carry with them their own inherent magickal virtue, making runic spells very powerful.

Runes are typically carved on wood to make a magickal charm, then reddened, often with red ochre, to bring out the design. Ash or yew wood is traditionally used for rune magick, because the Norse World Tree, where the god Odin hung to receive the mystery of the runes, is said to be an ash tree, or a yew, which is also known as needle ash. The charms can be individual runes carved on a wooden disc or section from a branch, or they can be long pieces of wood with several runes written from left to right, combining their powers. Runes can also be inked together graphically, to create one symbol known as a bindrune, which combines the virtues and blessings of several runes (see fig. 11). Modern rune magicians might use other forms of wood, clay, or stone, and use ink or paint to make their charms. Runes can also be carved on candles, sketched in the dirt, or drawn in the air to evoke their power.

Fehu

Fehu is the first rune of the Elder Futhark and is translated as "cattle." The cattle is representative of resources in the Norse world. Those who owned cattle had food and materials to both survive and thrive. Fehu is used today for any magick where you wish to increase your wealth and resources, including money magick, job promotions, business success, and entrepreneurial endeavors.

Uruz

Uruz follows Fehu in the Elder Futhark, and has a similar image, but rather than being the domesticated cattle, Uruz is the wild ox. Having less to do with societal wealth, Uruz can be used in magick where your will needs to be strengthened, so you are strong and healthy enough to get what you want and to succeed in your goals.

Kenaz

Kenaz is a rune associated with the torch and the fire and light of the torch. For prosperity magick, Kenaz can be used to increase anything, as the light increases. It also brings the power of inspiration in new projects.

Gebo

Gebo means gift, and while it also has many different associations with partnership and love, it is also quite literally a gift, an unexpected blessing, or the act of receiving something of value.

Jera

Jera is the rune of the year and the cycle of the harvest. In magick, it can be used for fertility, increase, and growth, as well as reaping the rewards of your hard work, just as the farmer reaps the harvest. Unlike Gebo, Jera is not an unexpected windfall of good bounty, but the expected reward of hard work.

Sowelo

As the rune of the Sun, Sowelo is a power of success and fertility in all workings. It adds power and light to all things.

Inguz

Named for the god Ing, with associations to the fertility land god Freyr, Inguz is used for the bounty that is connected to the land and growing things. It is the power of our concepts of prosperity that are the most pagan, our relationship with the life force of the land, and the blessings that come when we are in a balanced relationship with the land.

Othila

Othila is the rune of inheritance and ancestral lands. It should be used with caution in money magick, for it represents inheriting money, possessions, or lands from family members. While someone can give you something before dying, usually such inheritances occur post mortem.

Figure 11: Example of a Bindrune

THE SEALS OF JUPITER

In medieval ceremonial magick, talismans based on the seven planets were constructed. These were known as the seals or pentacles of the planet, even though the seals were not necessarily based on five-pointed stars. Each planet has several seals, and the traditional instructions and information for them can be found in a classic book known as the *Clavicula Salomonis*, or *The Key of Solomon*, first brought to the mainstream occult world's attention through a translation by the founder of the Hermetic Order of the Golden Dawn, Samuel Liddell MacGregor Mathers.

While the book is written for medieval Judeo-Christian magicians, with rituals using the Hebrew names of God and the traditional archangels, the lore within it has influenced modern witches, particularly Gerald Gardner, and it crept into Wicca. Modern witches have adapted the material to suit their own pagan system of magick. When created, consecrated, and carried by the recipient of the magick, these seals are said to change the fortune of the bearer, attracting blessings, banishing ills, and bestowing magickal powers, all depending upon the nature of the individual talisman.

The two seals that have the strongest bearing on prosperity magick naturally come from the Jupiter section. The Second Pentacle of Jupiter (fig. 12) is used to get "glory, honor, dignity, riches, and all kinds of good" as well as a peaceful mind, and it is also used to find treasure. Traditionally it should be made on virgin parchment, "with the pen of the swallow and the blood of a screech-owl," though honestly I don't know anybody who has done that specifically. Paper and ink has worked well for me, though I know those who have done well with a photocopy or computer printout.

The next pentacle of use to us here is the Fourth Pentacle of Jupiter (fig. 13). It is used for receiving riches, honor, and wealth in general. Sacred to the angel Bariel, this seal should be engraved upon silver on a Thursday, in one of the planetary hours of Jupiter, ideally when Jupiter is in the sign of Cancer. Since Jupiter is on approximately a twelve-year cycle, it can be a long time to wait until Jupiter is in Cancer.

Figure 12: Second Pentacle of Jupiter

Figure 13: Fourth Pentacle of Jupiter

While there are specific medieval instructions for their consecration as well as specific rituals, most witches I know use the seals much like runes, symbols that have an inherent divine power and historic practice, and can be adapted to modern needs. They can be written on paper/parchment and carried in a wallet or burned like a petition spell, made out of blue wax, etched into metal (tin or silver are ideal), or carved into candles. Some jewelry companies manufacture commercial talismans from medieval grimoires, including the Solomanic seals, making them available at occult shops and online.

Another kind of Jupiter talisman involves using the Magick Square of Jupiter (fig. 14). Planetary magick squares, or *Kameas*, are numeric patterns aligned with the energy of a planet. You would create a geometric sigil based on the patterns of the Jupiter Square by taking a simple intention and reducing it to its numeric pattern. For example, to make a Jupiterian talisman for wealth, you would take the word *wealth* and convert it to numbers:

1	2	3	4	5	6	7	8	9
A	B	C	D	E	F	G	H	I
J	K	L	M	N	O	P	Q	R
S	T	U	V	W	X	Y	Z	

4	14	15	1
9	7	6	12
5	11	10	8
16	2	3	13

Figure 14: Magick Square of Jupiter

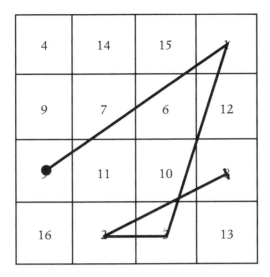

Figure 15: Wealth Sigil on Jupiter Square

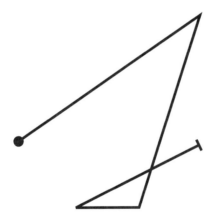

Figure 16: Wealth Sigil

Wealth would be 5-5-1-3-2-8. Plot out a line drawing using those numbers, omitting the repeated five, and you have a wealth sigil.

Traditionally, this sigil could be made into a paper talisman. In Qabalistic magick, Jupiter's number is four, so its shape is four sided, a square, and its primary color is blue, while its complementary color, the opposite color on the color wheel, is orange. You would cut out two paper squares, connected with a link like paper dolls, and put a different Jupiterian symbol for your intention on each, ideally writing in blue on orange paper or writing in orange on blue paper. Jupiter has a traditional seal association with the planet (fig. 17), along with sigils of the Planetary Intelligence and Planetary Spirit (figs. 18 and 19), which can also be used for one side. You could also use one of the pentacles of Jupiter. The talisman is then folded over. Something appropriate to the intention, such as a bit of herb, oil, or a mixture known as a fluid condenser, can be added to the middle of the talisman before it is folded over and

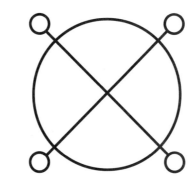

Figure 17: Jupiter's Planetary Seal

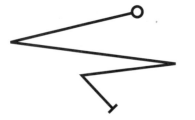

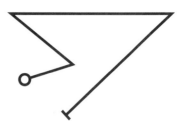

Figure 18: Planetary Intelligence Sigil   *Figure 19: Planetary Spirit Sigil*

sealed with glue. For this work, a bit of cotton with four drops of cedar or cinnamon oil would work very well for the center of the amulet. The connecting paper tab is now a loop where a string can be put through and worn like a necklace (fig. 20). Such talismans are often kept under clothing, hidden from prying eyes.

ANGELIC SEALS FOR ABUNDANCE

Many modern magicians feel more comfortable working with angelic forces than with the traditions of folk magick or more ceremonial forms of witchcraft. The angelic forces minister divine will, and can only truly work on humanity's behalf when we use our will to consciously invite them into our lives to work with us. When we do invite them, the angels are more than amiable in helping us in all our goals, including financial ones. Some people believe that financial magick is beneath the notice of the angelic forces, but I've found them to be quite beneficial in performing prosperity magick. They can be wonderful for simple boons, or for long-term help and guidance in careers and investments. Ideally, in helping us financially, they are helping us find our True Will in all areas of life.

Several archangels are appropriate to call upon in money magick. They have elemental or planetary correspondences that suit the intention of money magick.

Tzadkiel

Archangel of Jupiter. Tzadkiel is considered the archangel of righteousness, and he can be called upon to expand any good fortune and blessings you have. He is also associated with the Violet Flame, the energy that dissolves away all unwanted forces. Tzadkiel can aid you in removing blocks to prosperity. His day is Thursday, the day of Jupiter.

Haniel

Archangel of Venus. Her name translates to the "Grace of God," and she is the archangel of beauty and love. Being associated with the magnetic power of Venus, Haniel can be called upon for gifts, for blessings, for luxury and comforts of the home. Haniel's day is Friday, the day of Venus.

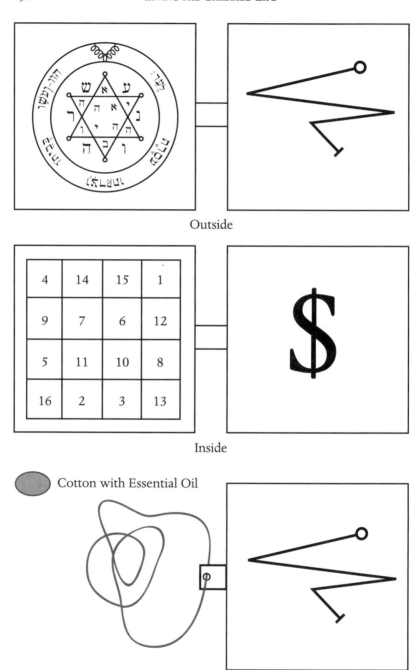

Figure 20: Jupiter Talisman
Outside (Seal and Sigil) and Inside (Magick Square and Dollar Sign)

Uriel

Archangel of the elemental earth. Uriel has dual associations, as both the archangel of the element of earth and the archangel of the "new" planet of Uranus. Uriel is known as the "Light of God" because this being sheds light upon the mysteries and shares knowledge of the unseen. In the earthy manifestation, Uriel holds the keys to the riches of the deep Earth, and he can be called upon for all prosperity magick. Uriel and Uranus have no traditional day, though Uranus is thought to be energetically the upper octave of Mercury, so Wednesday, Mercury's day, can be used.

Michael

Archangel of fire and the Sun. Michael's name means "he who is like God." Although he is more of a protection figure than a prosperity angel, his association with the Sun lends him the ability to create success, and his elemental association with fire aids with passion and enjoyment of your job. Some traditions list Michael as the archangel of Mercury, with Raphael as the archangel of the Sun. As a Mercurial figure, Michael can also play a role in money magick, as Mercurial god figures are associated with commerce, trade, communication, and gambling. Michael's day when he is associated with the Sun is Sunday, but when he is associated with Mercury, it's Wednesday.

Figure 21: Seal of Tzadkiel

Figure 22: Seal of Haniel

Figure 23: Seal of Uriel

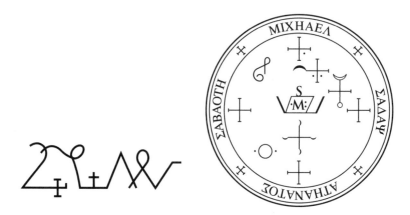

Figure 24: Sigil and Seal of Michael

The archangels associated with the seven classic planets have angelic seals that can be used in magick to commune more effectively with them. Uriel, being associated with an outer planet, does not have one of these classic sigils. The pentacle, alchemical earth triangle, or planetary earth symbol could be used for Uriel.

Choose which angel you want to work with for your prosperity. On the day of the angel, take a piece of paper and draw the sigil of the angel at the top of it. Ideally, match either the paper color or the ink to the angel in question. Tzadkiel uses blue and purple. Haniel is green and pink. Michael is yellow, gold, and red. Uriel is all earth tones of brown, black, and green. Then write your petition to the angel. What do you want the angel to do for you? What is your goal in working with the angel? Burn the petition in a cauldron or other flameproof container and scatter the ashes. Look for the angel's influence in your life, and work with the angel to manifest your dreams together.

GAMBLING CHARM

Gambling charms, used to influence the odds in your favor when playing games of chance and skill, are quite common in folk magick. American folk magick uses the imagery of grasping to get more money in such charms, as the winner grabs the pot and leaves. Ingredients such as lucky hand root (which is shaped like a hand), cinquefoil, and five-finger grass are used. High John the Conqueror root is used to show rulership and dominion over the situation. Lodestones are used to attract wealth, and Mercury dimes—in honor of the god of chance and gambling—are also popular in gambling magick.

To make a folk gambling charm, put the following in a red or green bag:

Lucky hand root
High John the Conqueror root
Cinquefoil leaf
Nutmeg, whole or powdered
Silver dime

You can periodically anoint the roots and the nutmeg, if it's whole, with High John oil, or with any fast-cash money oil you have, to "feed" it and extend its powers.

MORE PROSPERITY MAGICK

Some prosperity magick doesn't fall into a neat category of candle magick, talismans, potions, or baths. It may combine many of these forms of magick together, or use other techniques that are just as powerful. Some of these spells are traditional, or at least they have strong traditional elements, while others are modern. But all have had reported results, succeeding in what they set out to do.

Pot of Gold Spell

The Pot of Gold spell was first introduced to me in the book *A Spiritual Worker's Spell Book* by Draja Mickaharic, though I've seen a few variations of the principle before, as it uses lodestones to attract prosperity. Basically it's a charm to attract wealth by creating a magickal pot. Pots are sometimes created specifically to house a spirit, but this charm is designed to house the spirit of prosperity, so it can confer its blessings upon the owner or household. This is my own variation of the spell.

> 2 lodestones that magnetize together
> Iron filings (lodestone food)
> Gold and silver glitter (or crushed pyrite)
> Wheat grains or 3 wheat stalk heads
> Grains of dried corn (maize)
> Copper ingot, copper shavings, or a real copper coin
> 5 dimes (they do not have to be silver/Mercury dimes)
> 1 shredded five-dollar bill
> Several straight pins
> 1 small mirror
> 3 pieces of red or white coral
> 1 blue stone, such as turquoise, azurite, or lapis
> Pinch of nutmeg

Although this form of magick doesn't require a witch's magick circle, I assembled my own Pot of Gold in the sacred space of a circle and found it quite effective. The general instructions are to put all the listed items into a bowl, so make sure you have enough room in the bowl for everything. There are not precise instructions for the amounts of everything, such as the grains or glitter or how many pins, so use your best judgment and intuition. Then you should pray over the bowl, or pot. This spell prayer specifically names you as the person for whom the pot is intended, and it states that with this charm, you will have all the money you need, as well as excess money for recreation, pleasure, and retirement. As a witch, I cleansed and consecrated each item in the pot, but it is not considered traditional or necessary for this spell.

As the person who is benefiting from this charm, you must hide the pot away unseen, in a safe place. It should not be viewed by others or shown to anybody. The charm must be "fed" only when you are alone. The influence of another individual who might be jealous (consciously or unconsciously), or even unexpressed envy from a mate or partner, is said to make the pot vulnerable or even destroy it, so it is never shown to anyone else.

Every Tuesday, you should take out the two lodestones and put them in a glass of water with a teaspoon of whiskey in it. Keep them in the glass for a half hour, and then take them out. Put them back into the pot, and ask the lodestones for the money you will need for the coming week—including money for all bills, food, recreation, and savings. Add about a quarter teaspoon of iron filings to the lodestones. The lodestones will eventually grow over time with the addition of the filings. You can then slowly and carefully drink the glass of water and/or sprinkle it around the house to bless yourself and the entire house. If you do drink it, be sure not to consume any iron filings that might have flaked off the lodestones.

Spare Change Money Jar

One of the ways we mismanage our capital involves our utilization of all our extra assets. One symbol for the "extra" we have is our spare change. We lose and waste so much of our spare change, and that is symbolic of many other resources in our lives. One way to turn this around for you, literally and figuratively, is through the use of a money jar. Many of us collect our spare change at the end of the day, but this allows us to work magick with it, every day.

Get a large jar for spare change. If you can get it made of colored glass, such as green or blue glass, all the better. On the waxing Moon, ideally just after the new Moon, cleanse and consecrate the jar for prosperity. Add a few pinches of the following ingredients to the jar:

Powdered cinnamon
Yellow dock seeds
Juniper berries

If you like to count your change with a machine rather than roll it yourself, you might find that the bits of herbs will get in the way, so you can put them in a pouch and put the pouch into the jar. Then put in your spare change from the day. Hold the intention that whatever you put into the jar expands and multiplies in your life. Ask for the blessings of the universe for the highest good, harming none.

Place the jar in a position where you will see it daily, and get into the habit of putting your spare change into it. If you have an altar or shrine to your home spirit, the *Genus Loci* of your dwelling, you can put the jar there. Get the whole family to put their spare change into it. When it is full, count and deposit the money and start again. With this spell, you can literally see the assets building, but it will have a sympathetic effect in your life. I have a green jar on my altar, and after initiating this tradition, I found that my saving accounts went up quite considerably, and I began to learn more about investments and investment management.

Poetic Prosperity Spell

This spell was originally designed with Qabalistic magick in mind. It uses four coins to align with the fourth sephira of the Qabalistic Tree of Life, Chesed. Chesed's traditional planet is Jupiter, so while it rules over spirituality, it also rules over abundance and riches.

Cast a magick circle. Consecrate any four coins for prosperity, and place them around a blue candle charged for abundance. You can waft the coins and candle in cinnamon or cedar incense to further align them with Chesed, or anoint them with cinnamon and cedar oils. (Caution: cinnamon can be caustic on the skin and should be diluted with a base oil.) Call upon archangel Tzadkiel, the Archangel of Mercy, but also the

ruling archangel of Chesed. Ask for the riches you want. Then speak
this charm four times:

I ask for prosperity
By the power of four,
Material riches
To be at my door.
An increase in money,
Freely given.
An increase of money,
Easily earned.
I ask for this abundance
For the highest good,
In no way malign
Shall this spell turn.
[and after the fourth time]:
So mote it be.

Release the circle as you normally would. Now you have two options:
you can carry the four coins in a special pouch and "jingle" them every
day as a part of your call to the universe for more prosperity, or you
can bury them in a line, in front of your house, where you walk every
day. When you either jingle them or walk by them, make your wish for
prosperity, and if you have a specific need, think about it at that time.
The resources you need and want will come to you.

Italian Lemon Blessing Spell

The following is a prosperity and home-blessing spell from the Italian
Strega tradition of witchcraft, from the classic text *Aradia, or the Gospel
of the Witches*. It involves a lemon and a series of straight pins with colored tops. You can use any combination of colored pins except black,
which will bring trouble with your good fortune. Traditionally, it is said
that the lemon should be a green one, not yet ripe, but for those of us
who do not have access to a lemon tree where we can pick an unripe

lemon, the ripe lemons of the market will do. I've had success with a yellow lemon.

On the full Moon, with a prayer of good fortune to Diana, the Goddess of Witches, stick a lemon with as many of the pins as you can, as far in as the lemon rind will allow. Then hang the lemon by string or hemp cord in a corner of the home, purposely in a place where it will not attract too much attention. The lemon will bring good fortune and blessing in Diana's name to you and your family.

Walking Your Way to Wealth

A traditional witchcraft charm is to put herbs, or the infusions of herbs, into your shoes. As you walk, you invoke prosperity. The idea behind this magick actually comes from cursing and compelling magick. When someone's name or photo is placed in your shoe, you are "stepping" on that person, performing a ritual where you have power over him or her. By putting herbs that have the power of prosperity in your shoe, you are commanding those herbs to do what you want.

Some modern witches don't like this idea, feeling that it's malicious magick, but I've known quite a few who didn't know the concept behind stepping on the herbs and simply thought it was a way to get closer with the plant spirits, and they had great success. I personally believe intention rules most magick, and if you don't have the intent to cause harm, but you do have the intent of growing more close and intimate, for feet are intimate, then that is the effect it will have. When in doubt, ask the plant spirits.

Powders and teas of cinnamon, mustard, or nutmeg are the most common for this shoe spell, though I've found traditions using fumitory. Traditionally fumitory is an Underworld herb. Initially I thought it was strange that it would be used as a prosperity herb, but as we have learned, many Underworld deities are also accustomed to prosperity prayers and magick.

Balancing the Checkbook

Paying the bills causes a certain amount of stress for many people. Our fears manifest most strongly when we are watching our accounts shrink. When I first had a mortgage, my hand shook every time I wrote the check. Even though I could afford it, the idea of paying that much was staggering for me, and it brought up a lot of fear around money and scarcity.

When paying your bills and balancing your checkbook, ritualize the process in a very simple way. Put a simmering pot of water on the stove and throw in a few dashes of Jupiterian spices—cinnamon, clove, nutmeg...anything rich and spicy. If the simmering pot doesn't work for you, burn cinnamon incense. Let the smell permeate the home while you deal with money issues. This helps you relax and expand your consciousness, rather than contract in fear and tension. Take the residue of the water, or the cooled ash, and rub it into the edge of your checkbook and on the edges of the envelopes on the bills you mail out. You will be sending blessings of money as you pay your bills, and therefore you receive even greater blessings. If you use the simmering pot and any water remains, it can be added to a floor wash, or used to anoint the door frames and window frames, to attract prosperity to all those who reside in your home.

If you pay your bills online, you'll have to find a cyber-magick version of this spell that suits your practice. Perhaps simply having the pot simmering as you're online will aid your finances.

Spinning the Wheel of Fortune Spell

Generally in a tarot reading, the Wheel of Fortune indicates good luck, blessings, or a general windfall of good finances, prosperity, or opportunity. In ceremonial magick, the planet Jupiter is associated with the Wheel of Fortune, indicating beneficence and expansion. Most people looking for a "fortune-telling" reading instead of a reading on the greater spiritual issues are already having problems, so the change of fortune indicated by the spinning of the wheel is usually considered good, unless the reader uses inverted (upside-down) card positions and the card appears reversed.

While we know that the Wheel of Fortune has a much broader and deeper meaning, this spell uses the general meaning in divination to change your fate and bring prosperity. The spell is best for long-term projects and financial goals.

Wheel of Fortune tarot card
Turquoise stone
Petition spell paper

Write out your spell intention to be used with the wheel. What are your long-term goals?

Get out the Wheel of Fortune card from the tarot deck. If you read cards for yourself or other people often, you may need two decks. One deck is for readings, and the other is for spellwork. This spell requires you to leave the card on the altar for a short time.

While you are in a magick circle, hold the spell petition in one hand and the Wheel of Fortune tarot card in the other hand. Read your spell, but do not burn it or raise the cone of power. Fold up your spell paper in a way that covers all of your writing. Look at the card. Imagine that the card is a gateway, and you are standing before the Wheel of Fortune. Imagine the wheel spinning, and as it spins, your desired goals and intentions are moving toward you. Some imagine that the wheel is actually bringing the outcome, as if the entire image of successfully fulfilled goals comes up and over the wheel. Others imagine that the wheel is like a loom, and the strands coming off of it weave together to form the image of your successful goals.

Place the card down on your altar, and place the spell paper on top of it. Charge the turquoise crystal to manifest the energy of Jupiter and bring your intention into the physical realm. Then put the turquoise on top of the paper and card. Raise the cone of power to send forth the intention. Release the circle as you normally would, returning to ordinary consciousness.

Keep the stone, paper, and card on your altar to remind you that the power is building upon the cosmic wheel and things will be going your way very shortly. Results may be slow, but they usually end up as a long-term accumulation of what you desire. When you feel that your intentions have started to manifest, acknowledge this and carry the stone with you in order to continue to draw the intentions to you. You can burn the paper and scatter the ashes, and return the Wheel of Fortune card to your deck.

Banish Debt

While so much of our prosperity magick involves the powers of attraction and expansion, little has been said about the powers of reduction and contraction. There are always at least two ways to approach spellcraft. You can increase the things you want, or you can decrease the obstacles that prevent you from getting what you want.

Most people who have money problems often have issues of debt. They get indebted beyond what is reasonable. If you are investing in something over the long term, such as a home, which will appreciate in value, you are getting into reasonable debt, assuming you can afford the payment. Spending for education, while costly, is another long-term investment with future payback, ideally earning you better wages and a good career. While a car might not appreciate in value unless it's a collector model, you may find that it's a necessary expense, so such a debt can be considered reasonable. If you charge food, bills, gas, travel, or your entertainment expenses, and you can't afford to pay off the credit card bill every month, you are living beyond your means. You are accruing unreasonable debt. We get into this rut when learning how to handle our own finances, and hopefully we learn to dig ourselves out of debt and be more balanced in our financial approach. We can use magick to help us banish our debt, so we can naturally grow our assets without feeling strangled by our past mistakes.

Saturn is both the planet of karma and the planet of contraction. In astrological magick, it makes a nice partner with Jupiter. While Jupiter expands and blesses, Saturn contracts and binds. It is the taskmaster of the planets, forcing us to take responsibility for our past actions, be it in this life or a past life. That is the essence of the teaching of karma in modern metaphysics. Karma simply refers to "action," and it is the learning we experience from our actions. Doing Saturn magick can help us with our debts.

4	9	2
3	5	7
8	1	6

Figure 25: Magick Square of Saturn

$1,456.93 debt

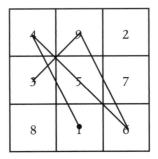

Figure 26: Sigil Construction

Black candle
White paper
Scissors
Patchouli oil

This spell is done best on a Saturday (which is Saturn's day), when the Moon is waning in light, to remove debt from your life. Add up your current amount of debt. Be sure to include any outstanding bills and payments, in order to get as close to a complete total as you can. Using the Magick Square of Saturn (fig. 25), make a sigil of the amount of debt (fig. 26). As Jupiter's number in Qabalistic magick is four, Saturn's number is three, so cut out a three-sided figure, an equilateral triangle, from white paper. On this triangle, draw the sigil you have constructed in black ink.

Cast your magick circle. Focus on your sigil. Imprint its image in your mind. Place it down on your altar. Then take your black candle, cleanse it, and anoint it with patchouli oil. Although patchouli oil is associated with money because of its earthy qualities, it is also a plant of Saturn and an essential oil that is relatively cheap, even when you're in debt. Charge the black candle to reduce your debt. As it burns, your debt burns away, until there is nothing left. Light the candle, put it in its holder, and place it on top of the sigil triangle. Release the circle as you normally would.

Financial management requires vigilance, and so does this spell. Watch until the candle is almost burned out, and from the last fires, burn the sigil and throw it in a cauldron or other flameproof container. Snuff out the candle, and take the remaining wax and ashes and bury them in the Earth. Such care shows to the powers of the universe that you are ready to be vigilant in your own finances, and together you can release the burden of debt.

Make sure you follow up this spell with real-world action. Speak to your creditors and see if a payment plan can be agreed upon. Look for debt-consolidation services. Seek out consolidation loans. The spell will aid in your debt reduction, but it won't make your past mistakes go away without any responsibility. Saturn is the planet of karma, of responsibility to your past, but the burden of your past can be eased considerably. You might find yourself receiving a windfall of cash that should be applied to your current debt.

Obtaining a New Job

Part of a successful prosperity plan is to have a job that you like and that earns you the money you need. Magick can be used to find a new job when you have one that is all right but not perfect, or to help you find what you need when you are unemployed and more desperate.

Make a list, in blue ink, of all the things you would want in the new job. What are the qualities the job will have? What are your requirements? Focus on what you want, not on what you don't want. If there is something you really don't want, focus on the opposite quality.

Make a perfumed water with the following formula:

1 ounce rubbing alcohol

5 drops orange essential oil

9 drops lavender essential oil

4 drops vanilla extract

Mix these ingredients, shake well, and sprinkle on your spell paper. Crumble up the paper, and burn it in a cauldron on the waxing Moon. The rubbing alcohol will lend a blue flame to the burning process, and the scents will bring richness to the magick. Expect the job fulfilling your listed requirements to come to you soon.

Charm for Success in Legal Matters

Success in court cases, legal matters, and all manner of justice, particularly justice that involves financial compensation, is also ruled by Jupiter. While some magicians will take a martial approach to court, invoking the power of war gods to have victory over the enemy, the Jupiterian approach grants natural regalness and power, where the outcome naturally goes your way rather than having to be forced your way.

Make a powder out of equal portions of the following herbs:

Frankincense

Lovage

Fennel seed

Marigold (or calendula) flowers

Sarsaparilla root

Galangal root

Add sumac berries if you know you are wrong or guilty and are simply trying to mitigate the verdict against you. Grind the herbs together to make a powder. Now either fill a purple bag with the powder, adding a High John root to the amulet, or create a Second Pentacle of Jupiter on paper, and take the powder, burn it on charcoal to make it an incense, and consecrate the pentacle of Jupiter in the smoke for success in your court case. Carry either charm with you the entire time you are in the court room, and ideally the entire time you are in dispute. When the court case is decided, burn the talismans completely and bury the ashes.

Protection against Theft

To protect your home, business, or vehicle from thieves, make this charm in a black bag just before the dark of the Moon. Choose one stone that you feel the strongest connection to—jade, garnet, amethyst, or tiger's-eye. Cleanse and charge it for protection.

Mix equal parts of the following herbs with one part of any spiked or thorned plant, such as rose thorns, whitethorn, burdock burs, thorn apple pods, or any type of thistle:[1]

Rosemary
Juniper
Agrimony
Cinquefoil
Fennel
Patchouli

Hang the pouch wherever you desire to cast your zone of protection. Ideally, remake the charm every year, burying the previous one.

---

1. If such thorns are not available, use three iron nails. Most nails today are steel, and while they can be used, iron carries a greater magickal charge. Iron nails can be obtained in hobby shops.

CHAPTER 9

MAGICK AND BUSINESS

Combining magick and money is a sticky proposition, even though they have quite a bit of history together. A book looking at the ways to make money through magick would not be complete without talking about the most obvious way of making money with magick, offering your services for hire. As someone who makes his living writing, lecturing, and performing magickal services, I've given this area a lot of thought because it attracts a lot of criticism from the pagan community.

The modern neopagan community has the most difficulty with the concepts of money and magick going together. We have a big backlash from making a break with conventional religious institutions and hierarchies. Very few of us were raised pagan or raised in a pagan community. Even if we were, it was not the dominant paradigm of our overall society. Because of this, we spend a lot of time thinking about ourselves in contrast to others, particularly those of other religions. We like to define ourselves by what we are not as much as by what we are.

When we look at an institution that is surrounded in opulence and still takes weekly collections from its congregation for its services, we can see hypocrisy. Institutions, such as the Catholic Church, are devoted to the ideals of Jesus Christ to minister to the poor, the sick, and the outcasts, and they do have many organizations in place that they fund to do just that. Yet they have incredible resources in precious metals, gems, artifacts, and artwork, and one wonders how much more they could do. Some religions take a donation at every service, while others tithe church members a certain percentage of their income. Many temples require a simple but steep annual membership fee in lieu of donation or tithing. Churches in America are tax exempt, meaning that they pay no local, state, or federal taxes because they are performing social services for the community. Those who left such religions, or felt rejected by them, particularly have problems with the financial transactions. We say things like, "Religion should be free," or "Religion should be available to all, not just those with the money." When we go to a new religion, we seek out one that shares our ideals regarding money, or we put our ideals into our new religion.

Gerald Gardner, whose work led to the rebirth of witchcraft, revealed to his coven his Ardanes, or old laws of the Craft, which included the following:

119. Never accept money for the use of the art, for money ever smeareth the taker. 'Tis sorcerers and conjurers and the priests of the Christians who ever accept money for the use of their arts. And they sell pardons to let men escape from their sins.

120. Be not as these. If you accept no money, you will be free from temptation to use the art for evil causes.

So in these simple lines we have a sense of separation from the Christian priests and "sorcerers and conjurers." In an effort to make witchcraft seen, at least among it adherents, as a tradition of priestesses and priests, it was divided from the conjure folk and sorcerers, the cunning men and women who helped the people with illness, love, finding lost objects, and cursing. Gardner's craft is more of a temple tradition devoted to the gods of nature and life, yet that is only one aspect of the Craft. Gardner's witches were not those who were dedicated to helping others in community, performing a vocation, but generally those who practiced under secrecy, ideally with no one knowing that they were anything but "normal" Christians, at least before Gardner's publicity campaigns. These were the days before "pagan pride," and most Gardnerians were in the "broom closet."

Gardner's laws are controversial for several reasons. They initially "popped up" in his teachings only when Doreen Valiente and other members proposed their own set of rules of behavior, aimed at preventing Gardner from being so public if witchcraft was to be kept secret. He basically stated, "We need no other laws; we have laws" and revealed the Ardanes. Many people believe he made up the Ardanes in an attempt to keep control over his coven and its more outspoken and independent members.

If you read all of the Ardanes, there is a strange, almost Christian quality to many of the laws, much more in alignment with the Judeo-Christian commandments of "Thou shall not" than the simplicity and beauty of the Wiccan Rede and Threefold Law. In Ardane 120, we are introduced to the idea that money tempts us into evil, and that perhaps it is something evil in itself. This is not particularly a pagan stance in any other time or place. It harkens back to the phrase "money is the root of all evil." While scholars believe it first appeared in English near 1000 AD,[1] the whole phrase comes from the Christian Bible, 1 Timothy 6:10.

For the love of money is the root of all evil: which while some coveted after, they have erred from the faith, and pierced themselves through with many sorrows.

While the idea could have gotten into English folklore and eventually Gardnerian Wicca because Christian ideas were mixed with pagan lore, it's really not a pagan idea. It's a Christian idea. Remember, this is the same philosophy that also tells us that snakes, fruit, and women are

---

1. Gregory Y. Titelman. *The Random House Dictionary of Popular Proverbs and Sayings* (New York: Random House, 1996).

the source of all our problems. The Bible takes the approach that it is better to seek riches in heaven and be meek and humble in the world, because seeking money is a block to seeking God. An ironic sentiment if you look at some churches, though philosophically, I'm fine with the idea if you come from a religion that believes you are separate from "God" and must seek out the divine, rather than the divine being all around you, in you, and a part of you always. It's just not my own way.

I find it even more interesting that, as priests and priestesses, we are separated from the conjurers and sorcerers, seen as something low in Gardner's day, yet these words were synonymous with our concept of the folk witch. Cultures that have surviving magickal traditions that were allowed to thrive (or at least were not completely suppressed) and then overrun by modern industrialization and reductionism are the cultures that are perfectly fine with the mixing of magick and money. Gardner might identify many of their practitioners of the art as conjurers and sorcerers.

You can find surviving magickal practices in the African diasporic traditions of Voodou, Santeria, and Ifa and their influence in American Hoodoo. While we'd like to think of Eastern traditions as being exclusively focused on enlightenment and spiritual evolution, you find the cultural equivalents to these magickal traditions in India and the Far East, in places where medicine, magick, and philosophy have not been separated. A Vedic astrologer will not only look at your natal chart, but also craft an amulet to overcome any misfortune predicted by your chart. A Taoist wizard practicing the old ways could give you a paper amulet to burn to bring healing as well as, or instead of, administering herbs or acupuncture. To those inclined to think of themselves solely as priests or priestesses of a temple, the practitioners of the magick arts in both the rural and urban areas, dealing directly with the community, would seem like charlatans or tricksters, deceiving as much as helping because they need to make a living. Thus arises the idea of the conjurer or sorcerer as something negative. But magickal practitioners can be, and, in fact, most often are, just as legitimate as any other tradespeople working in the same area. While esoteric, their results are tangible. If they weren't, people would eventually stop seeking them out and their trade would die off, as it would not be needed.

Such practitioners would be very similar to our idea of the European cunning folk or village witches. They are not necessarily priestesses or priests in a temple tradition (though some are, such as many Voodou hoguns and mambos), but they are performing a trade, just as the baker, butcher, or blacksmith is performing a trade. By doing their job, and doing it well, they would naturally be expected to be paid for such services. Cunning folks all across England were paid for their work.

Modern witches are in a strange situation. Eclectics draw not just from one tradition, but from many, including the world's traditions of Africa and the East, and those of the cunning folk of Europe. Yet, it is impossible to dismiss the influence the Gardnerian tradition, including the influence of its "laws," has had on our developing community. Many see these laws as one of the only "real" parts of the Gardnerian Book of Shadows that predates Gardner, even if it does have a Christian influence. Much of our rural folk magick does have a Christian influence. The laws and their sentiments have stuck, even though they have a Christian bias, because most of us are coming out of a Christian past. Yet we unconsciously think that by denying money, we are aspiring to the true spirituality espoused in Christianity and being better than the institutional forms of the religions that only pay lip service to the teachings. We believe we have found a place where religion is finally free and available to all.

Religion is free—or at least personal, mystical religion is free. Yet if you want to belong to a specific organization, that organization might have its own requirements and commitments to keep itself running, which can include a financial commitment. Anybody can follow the teachings of Christ and be a Christian, and not necessarily belong to a church and pay a donation or tithe. Anybody can choose witchcraft or paganism, and learn to listen to the spirits of nature and the gods. But if you want specific teachings, teachers, experiences, tools, books, or other services, an exchange of some sort usually occurs. The religion doesn't cost anything, but the experts' time or their products and services does. Part of the criticism comes from the idea that we shouldn't have paid priest/esses or any professional clergy, as we are all priests and priestesses. But some of us are full-time, public ministers to the greater community and outer world, while others are only ministers to themselves.

THE BUSINESS OF MAGICK

The more we become a part of the overall community, being open and honest about our craft, the more we are called upon for our services, to use our unique perspectives and talents to help in situations where we are needed. For many people, witches are the torchbearers, the psychopomp guides into the unknown. We fulfill this function, emulating our gods, such as Hecate or Hermes. Those seeking to explore the unknown need a hand to hold.

Many would suggest that we do this pro bono, for the love of doing it. Many of us do, particularly when it's seldom needed and only a part of our lives. Many of us start out this way.

And while most of us want to share openly and freely with all, there comes a transition point where the demand for our magickal services becomes overwhelming in the face of a regular career and the obligations of family and friends. Our time is limited and our time is valuable, just like everybody else's. The more we do for others, particularly when we refuse to turn others away, the more our time is devoured and we find ourselves empty and devoid of any ambition in our own life and spiritual practice. We've given it all away and not received anything tangible or lasting for it. While it is always magickal and an honor to perform a service for another, when our services prevent us from keeping balanced at our job or in our family, the magick begins to wear on us.

Some of us, willingly or unwillingly, are called to a magickal vocation. Much like the cunning folk whose primary job was to help others, we too are called in a similar capacity. Like the cunning folk, some of us have other jobs but know what our true vocation is, and still others among us are busy enough with our clientele that our magickal vocation is our only source of income. Like any other professionals, those of us who are full-time magickal professionals must make sure we have the education, experience, and success rate to legitimately work in these areas publicly. Professionals must continue to expand their education and training, learning new areas and diving deep into the classic material to truly justify their full-time work in a magickal vocation. If it is a career, treat it like a career, with the same seriousness and devotion that all other craftspeople have for their art.

While such a move to a full-time vocation is often criticized in the modern pagan community, it is an age-old vocation found in all other times and lands, and there has been a call, a need, to restore it to our modern society. Here are some "job descriptions" that fall under magickal vocations. Most full-time practitioners have a combination of several of these jobs in order to make a full-time practice.

Reader

Those with knowledge of a divination system or pure psychic skill can work as readers. All readers have their own style and technique. I prefer using the tarot cards because they can provide specific information and a system in which to work. If I have a client who doesn't understand something I am saying, I can then show that person the card, providing a visual image to work with and understand. Other divination systems that are traditionally used by public readers include runes, ogham sticks, palm reading, and tea leaf or coffee reading. More complex systems can also be used, such as astrology and numerology. Pure psychic readers can use a divination system, but typically they are simply going into a deeper trance state to get information directly for the client. Some use mediumship or channeling skills to draw messages not just from a generalized divine intelligence bank, which is referred to as the Akashic Records, but also from specific spirits, ranging from deceased relatives to angels or spirit guides.

Healer

Someone involved in the healing magickal arts has a wide range of modalities to work from and a wide range of descriptions that can portray the healer. Although I favor intuitive and traditional ritual and healing folk magick, many people today prefer to go to an alternative health care practitioner. Being trained in arts that are very magickal yet recognized as holistic health can be vital in making a healing practice commercially viable. Witches know how to heal with light and energy, but training in Reiki, therapeutic touch, or pranic healing makes it more accessible to the mainstream, rather than simply labeling it witchcraft healing. Most witches learn the magickal uses of herbs, but learning how to make herbal medicines is just as important, as many ailments can be healed with simple teas and tinctures.

Aromatherapy, flower essences, and homeopathic remedies are all very complementary to a magickal practice, yet they all require some advanced training and study to be used safely and effectively, particularly if a client is also using pharmaceuticals. Working with crystal healing, or laying-on of stones, is another powerful method of healing, though with much less potential of conflicting with conventional medicines. More esoteric forms of healing include the practice of shamanic healing, or using your relationship with the spirits and spirit world to create health and transformation in another person. Many psychic readers find that their work crosses over in healing, as they perform spiritual counseling and give advice of a healing and transformative nature to those who come to see them for a reading.

Magick Worker

Magick workers are those who use their knowledge and ability to cast spells for others. This is the most controversial of these vocations among modern practitioners, but the most traditional vocation among old-world practitioners. Magickal practitioners use their skills and offer their service to the community. If you need a love spell, healing, a hex, hex breaking, or a fertility spell, you go to the local conjure man or cunning woman, just as when you need bread, you go to the baker. Many modern pagans are aghast that someone's magick could be for sale, and argue that it's unethical. Many traditional communities with magick workers have the belief that the client, the one with the intention, is the one responsible for the ethics of the magick, and the magick worker's hands are clean. Some magick workers set their own ethics of what kind of magick they will or will not do.

As a modern magick worker, my own personal ethic is that I'll do spells *with* people, but not *for* people. I will teach them how to form an intent and put together the materials, but the final action to set it in motion—be it knotting a thread, lighting a candle, or reading a petition—must be done by them.

Teacher

Another controversial magickal vocation is that of magickal teacher. In some traditions of witchcraft, initiates take vows of not teaching outside of the coven structure, or not teaching in exchange for any compensation. I've known quite a few witches who have taken vows against teaching a particular tradition publicly. Instead, they teach publicly known material, or they specifically teach magick and not witchcraft. As someone who didn't take such vows, and started my training in public classes and workshops, I have found that having professional teachers is very helpful. When we restrict our teachers, it leads to teachers who don't have the time or opportunity to teach regularly and improve their skills. When someone is publicly active as a teacher, that individual hopefully gains enough private and informal teaching experience to be a more professional teacher, with a wide range of experience, knowledge, and talent. If you take a class taught by a public teacher, you are still entering a sacred contract with him or her, and the teacher is still responsible for presenting the material promised in the class, and you, as a student, are still responsible to learn it to the best of your ability. Sometimes these arrangements can be more professional if stronger boundaries are established, as this spares the students the drama of the teacher's personal life and coven.

Craftsperson

While the mass-market industry has grown for metaphysical products, nothing can replace the handmade crafts for ritual tools and charms. Witchcraft is regarded as a craft, and much of its arts have been intertwined with the work of artisans. Many new witches are attracted to the arts of woodworking, pottery, stained glass, sculpture, leatherwork, jewelry making, and metalworking. Finding artisans who can infuse true magick into their art is quite an amazing thing, and such tools are highly valued by practitioners of the Craft.

When approaching any of these roles as a paid vocation, you must negotiate the difficult terrain of setting prices for your service. Having no standardized guild or guidelines, all practitioners set their own prices. Generally my guideline has been to recommend having a realistic understanding of your skills, and those of other similar practitioners in your area. Set a price that you would be willing to pay for your services. Practitioners who are closer to larger cities and more liberal areas receive much more for their services than those in the rural and remote areas. Some witches offer their services through donation. Although this is altruistic, it can often leave you frustrated. People may pay far more than you think your services were worth, because they don't know the going rate, and you're not giving them any guidelines—yet their high donations make you uncomfortable. Or, you receive far less than what you think your services were worth, and you soon grow disenchanted and feel unappreciated. Traditionally, one is not to bargain over Craft tools, but pay whatever price is set if one feels called to purchase a tool. This is another of the Gardnerian Ardanes:

125. Never bargain or cheapen anything whilst you buy by the art. So be it ordained.

Those who reject the Ardanes often reject this bit of advice as well, though I disagree. I believe in paying our artisans and craftspeople, our tool makers, what they feel their creations are worth. If I can't afford it, then that particular tool is not for me.

Many suggest doing work for trade, and although many trades are mutually beneficial, many are not. We have a romantic image of the cunning folk receiving bread, cheese, or meat, the necessities of life, instead of a little coin when the country folk come calling. While that can work well in a society that is less dependent on currency, in our modern society it's hard to pay your mortgage or credit card bill with a chicken or loaf of bread. If you do decide to do trades for your services, make sure the trade is beneficial for you. The classic trade suggested by many witchcraft authors is having someone do your yard work or weed your garden. I actually like to do that myself, for it's some downtime in touch with the Earth, and while offers to do it are nice, they are actually detrimental to me. I try to do trades with other skilled practitioners and craftspeople so that one valuable service is traded for another.

If you are publicly doing work involving the magickal arts, it is important to research the local and state laws of your area. Many have laws restricting psychics and readers from taking money, or labeling it as a "love donation" as opposed to a fee, or not clearly advertising that their services are for entertainment purposes only. Others have restrictions on touch that prohibit hands-on healing, unless you have a medical or cosmetic license that permits you to touch others. Sometimes these restrictions can be circumvented by becoming an ordained minister and offering spiritual counsel or spiritual healing to those of the same faith, but if so, you must make the religious nature of your services apparent. No one must mistake your spiritual healing for practicing medicine without a license.

THE MAGICKAL BUSINESS

I've found that those who run successful businesses, or those who are generally successful in their chosen career, even if they are working for someone else, use magickal principles. They might not know these are magickal principles—and in reality, they are universal principles, for magick is the birthright of all—but they are still using ideas and practices that are common among magicians, witches, and sorcerers.

Those who own or run successful businesses refer to their business as if it were an entity. Legally, we set up businesses as corporations to give them the legal status of a person, but most people don't look at businesses that way. In talking to those who have had unsuccessful, or marginally successful, ventures or shops, I have noted that they see the business as an extension of themselves, of their energy and their will. Such owners have tight control over the business, but when their personal life or health suffers, the business takes a corresponding "hit" as well. When the business suffers, then the owner's personal life is affected.

In magickal reality, any business has the potential to be a spirit, to be its own entity, and that entity has its own life. But by understanding the business entity's unique needs and talents, based upon how it was created, you can guide its successful development.

In the terms of a magician, the business entity is a semi-permanent thoughtform, or a magickal construct. Other traditions could refer to it as an artificial elemental, golem, or created fetch or familiar. It is not a naturally occurring spiritual entity, guiding the development of something found in nature, but a human-created entity, guiding the development of something found in the human world, and in this case, the business world.

Such magickal constructs have certain characteristics that make them successful constructs, and when you review the following list, you'll find that most successful businesses have the same characteristics.

Name

Magickal constructs must each have an individual name to identify them and a name that resonates with their nature, with the purpose and function they serve.

Sigil

A graphic symbol or charm is used to embody the name and energy of the construct. In magick, sometimes this is a geometric sigil, and other times it is something akin to the Djinn's magick lamp or bottle. In business, it's the corporate logo.

Location

The construct is tied to a physical object or location. A protection construct will be tied to the location it is intended to protect. Other times the entity will be tied to a particular object, such as a statue. For a business, this is the business headquarters that maintains the bulk of the spirit's energy, but that energy extends out to wherever its business is being held. If the headquarters is relocated, ideally rituals should be performed to "take" the entity to the new location, along with its sigil or vessel.

Feeding

The construct must be "fed" for it to continue to be effective. The birthing ritual only gives it so much energy, and to continue its work indefinitely, it must be fed with energy that is compatible to its nature. In magick, some constructs are offered coins, burnt incense, lit candles, or bodily fluids. Sometimes just the acknowledgement of success gives a construct the psychic attention it needs in order to be sustained. In business, the entity is usually fed psychically with attention rather than ritual offerings. The more time, effort, and love you put into the business, the more you feed it.

Magicians believe that powerful and long-lived constructs can develop into more permanent and somewhat independent entities known as *egregores*. I think we can look at many of the big corporations that have outlived their original owners and founders and see potential egregores.

One of the major mistakes business owners make is not learning to feed the entity somehow, or taking more from the entity of the business than they are giving back to it. Sometimes an entity gains so much for others in the business, and the owners can take a lot, in terms of financial reward and benefit, but in many small business, the business owner expects the entity to be working for him or her, like another employee, rather than the entity holding the business together. I've seen many owners drain their own company just as it was beginning. You have to find a way to get what you need from the company, yet sustain it.

I saw owners of a previously successful metaphysical store get frustrated because they no longer wanted to put the energy into the shop, and they didn't set up a structure where others could truly care for the business. They took and took from the shop financially and didn't give it the time and effort as they once did, as they believed that after a twenty-five year investment of time, the shop "owed them." While that might be true, they didn't set up a system to keep it self-maintaining, so it didn't maintain itself, and eventually they drove the business into the ground and had to close. No one was interested in buying it.

Others learned to acknowledge their companies, and such metaphysical companies did blessing ceremonies for the business itself, smudging the building with sage, but also invoking the spirits of the business to partner with them in good fortune. If you have a metaphysical background, and particularly if you have a metaphysical business, use the principles of magick and mysticism in your work. To forget your magickal thinking at work is just foolish.

Those working for others can still have a successful career by acknowledging the entity of the business they work with. Realize that along with the people in the company who are driving it, there is an entity involved that can be acknowledged, fed, and partnered with to make your own work successful. Simply acknowledging and "feeding" the entity with a good thought, a blessing, and a candle, if possible, smooths your relationship with the entity and strengthens your bond with it, increasing your success.

The business entity, like a person, has more than one self. There is the core "construct" self, and there is also a higher, more divine self guiding the company's purpose in the greater world.

In some modern New Age teachings, there is a concept of a deva ruling everything natural and man-made. *Deva* originally referred to a bright and shining spirit, thought of as a little god in the Hindu traditions. Every blade of grass has its own deva, and there is a larger, overarching deva of all grass. Modern practitioners compare it to angels and archangels, only ruling over material things. In the modern teaching, there is not only an overarching deva (also called the overlighting deva) of a forest or mountain range, but also an overarching deva of the shopping mall or the corporation. It's like the higher self or divine consciousness of both natural and manmade entities. Occultists would think of it as the *spiritus loci*, the spirit of a place, but our modern definition of the deva goes beyond the spirit of a natural place to include all things.

If you are having a hard time at a job, or with a boss or co-worker, one of the magickal ways you can work out this issue is by communing with the overlighting deva of the company, and through the deva, the higher selves of those involved.

EXERCISE 10: COMMUNING WITH THE BUSINESS DEVA

1. Decide what deva you wish to commune with, and find appropriate images and symbols that will help you connect to it, including things such as the name of the busi-

ness, the main address, and perhaps a logo or letterhead. The logo can be used much like a traditional medieval sigil or symbol to attune to this spirit. If you are very familiar with the business, if you've been working there or even if you founded the company, you might not need anything.

2. You can be as ritualistic or as simple as you want. If you have never done this exercise before, get into a quiet space with your materials, light a candle, and have a notebook and pen by you to take quick notes during the exercise or when you are done. If you have had experience with spirit contact before, you can do this exercise almost anywhere, under any circumstance.

3. Perform steps 1–6 from Exercise 5: Reprogramming Consciousness.

4. Ask to speak with the overlighting deva of [*name the company*], either silently in your mind, or out loud. Wait. Listen and feel with your psychic senses. Let whatever impressions, visions, voices, and feelings that come to you manifest, and go with your first impression. The business spirit might be very different than what you are expecting.

5. Speak to the spirit as you would a person, even if you are not hearing a psychic response from it in words. Explain your problem or issue with the business, employees, or structure, and explain your wishes to resolve the situation in a manner that is for the highest good of everyone involved, including the spirit of the company.

6. Ask the deva if there is anything you can do to resolve the situation. Open yourself to your intuition and follow your first instincts. If the business is "your" business, ask the deva if there is anything that should or could be done to "feed" the spirit of the business, to make it healthy and strong.

7. Thank and release the overlighting deva.

8. Perform steps 8–10 from Exercise 5: Reprogramming Consciousness to end the vision work.

After this exercise, wait and see how the situation changes. You might notice a small, slow improvement or a major shift in the experience, based upon your direct communication with the deva.

I've known people who were toxic for their company (including the person who spoke to the deva) who were fired almost immediately, because it wasn't in everybody's best interest for those individuals to remain. Be careful what you wish for, or what you agree to, because the guiding deva will put forces into motion to change the situation, but remember that the deva's sole job is to really watch out for its own area. If you are the force not serving the highest good, it will release you as much as anyone or anything else.

LIFE PLANNING

We can also have success by looking at our lives like a business. I know that sounds depressing. Few people want to plan out life like a business, and you don't have to. Many people have quite successful and happy lives with no plan or forethought, but many other people feel unfulfilled and directionless, and they don't know how to find direction. I had a good author friend and mentor share with me a technique for achieving success not only in one's vocation, but in one's entire life.

This technique is really an expansion of Exercise 3: Goal List. That exercise helped shape overall goals based on the five elements, and this exercise helps you refine them. You must look at your life like a company, with many departments. They are departments of home, family, rest, spirituality, and recreation, and you run the different areas of your life, making sure that no part of your business gets neglected. You must create a business model, a business plan for your life. You can still be open to new opportunities, unforeseen blessings, and higher guidance, and still respond to unforeseen difficulties, but a plan gives you a starting place. The plan can always change, but if you don't have a plan, you have no place to begin to make the changes. Making a plan sets an intention for your life, and the biggest part of magick is setting an intention. Without it, nothing else moves.

1. Start by crafting a mission statement for your life. If you had to articulate your overall purpose, what would it be? Think of it as the mission statement of your life's business. You might have several smaller objectives in life, but the overall theme should be reflected in the mission statement. Magicians talk about knowing your True Will or Mystic Will. If you had to sum that up into a small statement with an overall theme, what would it be?

2. What are your goals? What benchmarks must you meet for you to be successful? Are your goals reasonable? What are the objective benchmarks that you use to measure your success? Your goal might be financial solvency. What does financial solvency look like? How much would it be in the bank, or how little debt would you have? Happiness is a goal, but what does happiness look like to you, day to day? Make a list of your goals, like you did in the previous exercise. Include not just financial goals, but your personal, emotional, and spiritual goals. They are all a part of your True Will. Set benchmarks for those goals, so you know when you've reached them.

3. What are your departments for the business of your life? What is your main work? What is your day-to-day work? What are the different parts of your life that require attention? If you are running a company or particularly if you are self-employed, what do you need to have done but can't do yourself and need help with? Departments can include such nonbusiness things as home, family, and rest. Anything that is important to you needs to have its own department, gaining a part of your intention. If you think you are automatically going to take time out to rest, build friendships, and spend time with family, you might be wrong, particularly if you are focusing on your success. Make rest, magick, exercise, and anything else you need to have a well-balanced life a part of your business plans.

4. Make a list of your assets. What are the things you have that are a benefit for you? Include both material/financial assets and your personal, spiritual, and artistic resources. Resources include all the things that help you do what you want to do in the world, and they are not always listed in terms of monetary worth.

5. Make a list of your detriments. What are the things you need to be successful in your life goals, but are lacking? Include not only financial issues, but personal, spiritual, and emotional issues as well. Are there things you can do to improve, or to get help from those who have the resources you need?

6. What are your sources of income? Like the previous questions, income is anything of value that comes into your life business, not just financial income, though of course it includes the money you earn. What are the actions you take that you feel fill you up and rejuvenate you? What are the things you are excited to do?

7. What are your expenses? Like income, expenses go beyond money, and include not only bills and debts, but things that you dislike doing, or actions you take that you feel drain your personal resources. This can include any worries and fears that actively drain you, as well as imbalanced relationships that drain you.

With all of this information now before you, revise your goals. What things do you need to achieve to accomplish your goals? How would you divide your goals in terms of a timeline? I make a list of one-year goals that are more specific, with benchmarks, and then less formed three-year goals, and then even less formed five-year goals, marking general trends that I want to move toward. As you adapt your plan each year, you can adjust your goals and flesh out your benchmarks to make the plan sensible and successful for you.

To ritualize my life plan, I read it in the magick circle once I've created it, and revise it at least once every year, usually right after the "new year" of Samhain. I have my business-plan goal list on my altar and read it as a part of my daily altar devotionals. I've fused the business idea of making a plan of action with the ritual action of sacred space and affirmations.

EXERCISE 11: LIFE PLAN

Get into a quiet space and answer the preceding questions, creating your current life plan. Take your time to meditate and reflect upon them. While you shouldn't procrastinate from doing this exercise, you don't have to rush into it either. I've taken several weeks to refine and redefine my goals until I'm satisfied. I usually give myself the time from Samhain to Yule as a "between" time to sort out my life, and by the waxing of the Sun, I implement my new life plan for the year. Taking your time, but having a deadline in mind, can be very motivating to help you focus on your goals and needs.

Once you have the draft completed, write it out as you would a petition spell, with fine penmanship on special paper, perhaps light-purple paper for success and spirituality with Jupiterian qualities. Keep the list somewhere important, so that you will see it regularly. I put my life plan on my altar, folding the 8.5" × 11" pages in half, and gently sliding the folded paper into the edge of a mirror frame that is a part of my altar. That way I can take it out easily and review it, but I also see it every day, even on the days when I don't review it specifically. It becomes a part of my overall magickal practice.

At the end of the year, review what you have accomplished and the areas of life where you were not so successful in achieving your goals. Determine if your goals were appropriate and if continuing on this path is still appropriate. Or, with the wisdom you have gained over the year, have your views and future goals changed?

CHAPTER 10

CREDIT IN THE REAL WORLD

While all this prosperity magick and money magick is wonderful, what does it get you if you don't know how to use your money in the "real" world? I've been blessed to know some amazing witches who taught me the art. They could conjure great sums of cash when needed and have moments of great success in business. Yet they couldn't hold on to it or take it the next step. They didn't know how to apply their magickal success to the reality of daily economics.

One of the first lessons we learn as spellcasters is that we must follow up our magick with real-world intention. If we do a spell for a new job, we must send out our resumé, answer ads, and fill out applications. The job offer could be a mysterious knock on the door out of the blue, but our magick usually aligns the perfect possibilities so we can take advantage of them. If we don't follow up the esoteric actions with real-world action, those possibilities don't align very easily.

If we want to change our relationship with prosperity, with the financial component of our lives, we must follow up that intention, and all of our magick, with real-world action. We must educate ourselves in the reality of the economic world that we live in. While this is primarily a magick book and not a guide to financial planning, here are some grounded, real-world things you should be thinking about if you are serious in transforming your relationship with money. Witches always follow up their magick with real-world action, to support the magick on all levels.

FINANCIAL WORTH

What is your financial worth? Your financial worth is really a look at the ratio of your assets to your debt. Have you ever made a list of your assets and calculated them to a numeric value? Count the assets that you can sell today if you needed money. While we have all sorts of assets with personal or emotional value, be ruthless and consider street market value. Main assets include bank accounts (both savings and checking), investments, real estate, and any collectors items or expensive jewelry you have. Now add up all of your debts, including mortgages, credit card bills, and other outstanding payments and loans. What is your overall financial health? I know it's a really hard thing to do the first time, but if you don't know where you are, you can't possibly change your relationship with money.

BUDGET

Do you have a budget? If not, why not? Make a list of all your monthly expenses, and if you have yearly or biannual expenses that are not monthly, such as some types of insurance, pro-rate them to their monthly expense. Make sure you allow for "fun" money or things not on the budget, as you know you'll spend money on things that are not absolutely essential. Do your monthly expenses exceed your monthly earnings? If so, how can you transform this relationship so your earnings are more than your expenses? If you don't know the amount you need to adjust, you can't attempt to make a change and be successful.

For those of us who are self-employed and never know how much money we will make in a month, budgeting is hard. I avoided it for years because I didn't want to worry about how much money I was or was not making. I suggest keeping a monthly tally of all your bills and expenses. Then you can compare that to your monthly income and see what the averages are over six months or a year. Such records will help you plan and realize when you are going over or under budget and when you need to make changes.

SAVINGS

Does your budget include savings? Savings are key to future investment. Only those who can gather enough capital for future projects can really be successful. Otherwise, you are just treading water month-to-month, with no backup or future. Even if you can only save a small amount each week or each month, do so. It's better than nothing. We spend money mindlessly on little things, when we could forego a few of those mindless purchases and start building a savings account.

PAYING BILLS

While it should go without saying, pay your bills on time. We tend to avoid the things we don't like, or that depress us, but if you feel your finances are out of control, one thing you *can* control is when you make your payments. If you can consolidate your bills through one company, particularly your phone, Internet, and cable services, you will often get a discount, and only have one bill and less postage. Always check your bills. These days, we tend to get "accidentally" charged for things we've already declined, be it on credit cards, utilities, or other services. Don't pay for something you are not receiving, even if the charge is small, because it will accrue over time. If you are not getting satisfaction when you call to get a charge removed, don't be afraid to ask for a supervisor. Don't be afraid to write a letter of complaint when necessary. Likewise, don't be lazy when receiving outstanding service. Write a letter of praise to the corporate office and name the person who helped you, along with the date and time you were helped.

CREDIT

Modern society encourages us to live on credit, making us think that if we can pay something off in the future, we can afford it. Large debt should only be carried over for long-term investments that will grow in value over time, such as a mortgage or education. If you cannot pay off your credit cards every month, then you are spending more money than you can afford. Living off your future potential is not a pagan ideal, and is a sure way to destroy yourself in the long term. If you want to use credit for a splurge or a vacation, take the time to save up the money for it, so you are not in debt and accruing interest, a payment that has no value to it.

Many of us may have a month or two where we go over budget and can't make full payments for our credit card debt, but if we have more than one month a year where we can't, there is a long-term problem. If you are failing to pay off your monthly bills on credit regularly, you have a bigger problem. If you have accrued credit card debt, you must make following a strict budget to get out of debt your priority if you want to transform your relationship with finance and prosperity.

If you are dealing with credit card problems, there are many clever ways to deal with them. I've found starting with a prayer to Hermes or Ganesha to be the best magickal advice, but then look for credit card offers. Transfer your largest debt on to any cards that offer zero interest for a long period of time, and make sure you pay it off before the period is over and the interest kicks in. When this is done, cancel the card. Make sure you read the fine print before contracting a new card, as some have penalties that don't make such tricky moves worthwhile. Contact your credit card companies. Threatening to end your account can often lead to renegotiating your terms and interest rates. Also, look for cards that offer some benefits, such as frequent flyer miles or hotel discounts if you travel. There is probably a card out there with benefits that suit you. If you are going to use credit cards at all, you might as well get some benefits from them.

CASH

When beginning my own business, I had a financial advisor tell me, "Cash is king." I believe he meant this more in terms of cash being hard to trace if it is not claimed for taxes, yet there is more truth to his words. People generally find that when they budget out and prepare to have cash on hand at the start of the week, rather than relying on credit or going to ATMs regularly and often incurring user fees, they spend less and save more. If you don't have the cash on hand for something, then don't buy it. Carry some extra cash for the unforeseen events and simple pleasures of life, but if you are shopping and see something that is a large purchase, and if its price doesn't fit into weekly cash allowance, don't buy it. Think about it. Plan for it. We spend the most when being spontaneous and frivolous, rather than looking at what we can really afford. Plan out your cash at the start of the week, and stick to it, rather than using credit cards regularly. When you look back over the month, you'll be surprised at how much less you've spent.

INVESTMENT

Once you have control over your debt and have accrued savings, think about investing for the future. If your employer does not have a retirement plan for you, it is your responsibility to save for your retirement. Many pagans, particularly pagan elders who have selflessly dedicated their lives to the work of the gods, do not take this into consideration. While I believe in trusting the gods, I also believe that the gods help those who help themselves. Such elders sometimes look to the community to support them. As a part of my own ethics in magickal business, I believe that you should be paid for the work you do, and unlike the clergy of other religions, you should not expect people to support you unless you work in a church or other structure than has a program built into it to support elder teachers and ministers. It seems that only those groups on the Left Hand Path, particularly the Temple of Set, openly encourage their initiates to plan for retirement in order to make sure they are not burdens to others, and also to know that they have enough money to enjoy their later years doing the things they love and traveling wherever they want. Planning for the future is part of following up our intentions with real-world action.

INSURANCE

Some investment guides will tell you not to have insurance if you are not absolutely required to have it because you most likely won't need it, but lack of insurance in a situation when you need it can create an unrecoverable financial catastrophe. As a self-employed worker, I've found that having a variety of insurance is an essential safeguard just in case something goes wrong. You don't have to have five-star insurance to cover every detail, but you have to have enough to cover a catastrophe, be it homeowner's insurance, disaster insurance, life insurance, health insurance, liability insurance, or disability insurance. Each of us will have different needs depending on our work and living situation, but make sure you are protected in an appropriate manner.

TAX EXPENSES

If you are self-employed or have a part-time business, make sure you document every expense itemized, and deduct it. Talk to an accountant or business planner if you are unsure what is considered an expense for your business, but you can deduct for a variety of expenses that you would be getting for your home office anyway. If you have a dedicated area for your business, portions of utilities and rent or mortgage might also be considered a business expense. I deduct for travel, car mileage, office supplies, research books, herbal ingredients, crystals, and magickal tools, as they are all essential for my job. Often home businesses are also a great way to pay for expensive hobbies.

FINDING GOOD ADVICE

There are many financial books, classes, and advisors available to those who are seeking information. Look at people in your life who are financially successful, and don't be afraid to ask them where they get their advice or education. They could recommend a resource or a reputable planner. Get several points of view, and make the best decision for you and your family.

While all of this might seem like common economic sense to many people, I've found that as I've helped pagans with prosperity magick, many have needed to learn these basic lessons. Most of us never learn financial common sense in school, and if we don't have good financial role models in our home to educate us, or the desire to learn in our adult life, we are missing a big part of our life education in terms of stability and security. Our culture has such a strange shame around financial education. Many people feel like they should already know about finances, so they don't ask questions or seek out education. Instead, they simply muddle along as best they can. Part of the magician's call to "know thyself" is to know where your strengths and weaknesses are, and work on transforming your weaknesses for your greater good.

With this education in real-world economics, and our education in the spiritual principles of success, we can grow our prosperous life. Prosperity truly is growing a healthy, full life at all levels, fulfilling your soul's purpose, not just getting money. Like my very talented teachers and peers have shown me, getting money is not that hard. Keeping money, growing money, and more importantly, growing happiness is the hard part.

When I first became a self-employed witch, I constantly worried about having enough money, even though I was repeatedly told in meditation by my Goddess not to worry, to have no fear. I was starting my writing career, and teaching more, but also seeing clients for tarot readings and healing sessions. I made a prosperity charm to alleviate my fear and carried it with me every day. It worked well. I got more and more clients, which at the time was the easiest and quickest way for me to make the most money. I had so many clients that it ate up my time for writing and teaching, so the writing and teaching got pushed into my home and family time. I had a constant flow of a small amount of cash, so I never felt like I would run out, but I was working so hard that I didn't have the time to fulfill any other plans or enjoy my life. I later learned to earn larger sums of cash in more spread-out intervals, giving me the time to do my other work and enjoy life. Although it wasn't ideal for a Sun sign Taurus who wants financial security, I found my security in myself and in my relationship with the gods. In nature, we have times of bounty and times of scarcity, times of growing and times of fallow. The plants and animals all trust that they will have what they need, knowing that spring follows the scarcity of winter, and the abundance of summer follows the new growth of spring. I too had to trust in my own prosperity cycles. Like a spiral, the goal was to ever expand outward, but just as the wheel turns, our fortune goes up and down.

When we identify spiritually with the archetype of the witch, we also get some unexpected baggage. Another strong identifying point of the pagan mystic is a sense of rural poorness. We also seem to embrace, consciously or not, the energy of poverty consciousness when we embrace the witch within. The image of the poor witch was reinforced through the Inquisition. While we can debate who was really a witch among those killed during the Burning Times and how many were actually killed, those who were killed were often the elderly widows and widowers. They needed financial support and lived in a community where church support ended or was restricted, and the previous pagan society was transformed from a tribal way of living to the start of our modern lifestyle, which emphasizes the needs of the individual and immediate household, rather than those of the entire community and tribe. Those who lived on the edge—financially, mentally, politically, and spiritually—were the ones most likely to be persecuted. The image of the witch as the beautiful enchantress has utterly changed to the elderly hag.

Even in early times pictured as idyllic by modern neopagans, the magickal traditions were divided between the more modern and financially savvy temple traditions of the urban areas and those of the rural peasant folk with their illicit religions at the crossroads. While as a modern witch I feel that both are my spiritual ancestors, it is really the rural folk magicians at the crossroads whom we would identify as the classic witch archetype. Their practices, which some modern scholars label *witchcraft*, survived when the temples were torn down or transformed and dedicated to new gods. These pagans were considered poor even by the standards of the day, yet they were prosperous and rich in many ways that we ignore today, when we use the bank account as our only measure of success. As modern practitioners, we must learn to embrace both archetypes, the temple priest/ess and the rural sorcerers, in our new definition of the witch. We can be rural or urban, wealthy in spirit and in the material world. We can be anything we choose to be, but first we need to open up to a wider self-definition that allows us, as witches, to be anything we want. With a new self-image, we can have the riches of the heavens, Earth, and all realms in between.

APPENDIX: ASTROLOGY

Planets			
Planet	Sign(s) Ruled	Day of the Week	Description
Sun	Leo	Sunday	Sense of Self, Ego, Identity, Core Energy
Moon	Cancer	Monday	Emotional Self, Hidden Self, Psychic Ability, Feelings
Mercury	Gemini, Virgo	Wednesday	Mind, Thought, Memory
Venus	Taurus, Libra	Friday	Attraction, Relationships, Love, Romance, Friendship
Mars	Aries (secondary: Scorpio)	Tuesday	Will, Action, Drive

Planet	Sign(s) Ruled	Day of the Week	Description
Jupiter	Sagittarius	Thursday	Higher Self, Blessings, Inner Teaching, Wisdom, Mercy
Saturn	Capricorn	Saturday	Responsibility, Guilt, Consequences, Lessons Learned, Manifestation
Uranus	Aquarius	—	Higher Mind, Intuition, Insight, Social Consciousness
Neptune	Pisces	—	Inspiration, Dreams, Delusions, Psychic Power, Creativity
Pluto	Scorpio	—	Higher Will, Creation through Destruction

Zodiac

Sign	Ruling Planet	Quality	Element	Gender	Color	Statement	Body Part	Keywords
Aries	Mars	Cardinal	Fire	Male	Red	I Am	Head	Leadership, Identity, Will, Action, Aggression
Taurus	Venus	Fixed	Earth	Female	Green	I Have	Throat	Security, Comfort, Luxury, Materialism, Stubborness
Gemini	Mercury	Mutable	Air	Male	Multicolored	I Think	Arms	Communication, Speaking, Writing, Socialization
Cancer	Moon	Cardinal	Water	Female	White, Pearl	I Feel	Stomach	Family Caregiving, Breasts, Boundaries, Empathy, Mothering
Leo	Sun	Fixed	Fire	Male	Yellow, Gold	I Create, I Perform	Back, Heart	Creativity, Charisma, Entertaining, Recognition
Virgo	Mercury	Mutable	Earth	Female	Brown, Green	I Analyze	Intestines	Service, Analysis, Discernment, Perfectionism

Zodiac

Sign	Ruling Planet	Quality	Element	Gender	Color	Statement	Body Part	Keywords
Libra	Venus	Cardinal	Air	Male	Pink, Pastel Colors	I Balance	Kidneys	Balance, Relationship, Artistic Ideals, Justice
Scorpio	Pluto	Fixed	Water	Female	Scarlet	I Transform	Reproductive Organs	Mystery, Sex, Death, Mars, Secretive, Powerful, Obsessive
Sagittarius	Jupiter	Mutable	Fire	Male	Purple, Blue	I Understand	Thighs	Exploration, Freedom, Searching, Administration
Capricorn	Saturn	Cardinal	Earth	Female	Black	I Use	Knees	Responsibility, Bones, Stature, Structure
Aquarius	Uranus	Fixed	Air	Male	Electric Blue	I Know	Ankles, Nervous System	Individuality, Equality, Innovative, Eccentric
Pisces	Neptune	Mutable	Water	Female	Sea Green	I Believe	Feet, Endocrine System	Inspired, Idealistic, Mystical, Addictive, Delusion, Romantic, Creative

Houses

House	Natural Ruler	Sphere	World	Keywords
First House	Aries	Personal	Identity	House of Identity, How People Perceive You
Second House	Taurus	Personal	Material	House of Resources, Possession, Money
Third House	Gemini	Personal	Connective	House of Learning, Communication, Siblings
Fourth House	Cancer	Personal	Conductive	House of Home, Domesticity, Family
Fifth House	Leo	Interpersonal	Identity	House of Children and Lovers, Ego, Creativity
Sixth House	Virgo	Interpersonal	Material	House of Service, Day-to-Day Work, Health
Seventh House	Libra	Interpersonal	Connective	House of Partnership, Marriage, Public Romance
Eighth House	Scorpio	Interpersonal	Conductive	House of Transformation, Letting Go, Mysteries
Ninth House	Sagittarius	Transpersonal	Identity	House of Higher Education, Philosophy, Religion
Tenth House	Capricorn	Transpersonal	Material	House of Career, Vocation, Purpose
Eleventh House	Aquarius	Transpersonal	Connective	House of Social Consciousness, Friendship
Twelfth House	Pisces	Transpersonal	Conductive	House of Merging, Mysticism, Delusion

BIBLIOGRAPHY

Beyerl, Paul. *A Compendium of Herbal Magick*. Custer, WA: Phoenix Publishing, 1998.

———. *The Master Book of Herbalism*. Custer, WA: Phoenix Publishing, 1984.

Cabot, Laurie, with Tom Cowan. *Power of the Witch: The Earth, the Moon, and the Magical Path to Enlightenment*. New York: Dell Publishing, 1989.

Conway, D. J. *The Ancient & Shining Ones: World Myth, Magick & Religion*. St. Paul, MN: Llewellyn Publications, 1993.

Cooper, Phillip. *Basic Magick: A Practical Guide*. York Beach, ME: Samuel Weiser, 1996.

Cunningham, Scott. *The Complete Book of Incense, Oils & Brews*. St. Paul, MN: Llewellyn Publications, 1989.

———. *Cunningham's Encyclopedia of Crystal, Gem & Metal Magic*. St. Paul, MN: Llewellyn Publications, 1992.

————. *Cunningham's Encyclopedia of Magical Herbs.* St. Paul, MN: Llewellyn Publications, 1985.

Dyer, Wayne W. *Real Magic: Creating Miracles in Everyday Life.* Audio cassette. New York: Harper Audio/HarperCollins Publishers, 1992.

Fairfield, Gail. *Everyday Tarot.* Boston, MA: Red Wheel/Weiser, 2002.

Flowers, Stephen Edred. *Hermetic Magic: The Postmodern Magical Papyrus of Abaris.* York Beach, ME: Weiser Books, 1995.

Gaiman, Neil. *The Sandman: Brief Lives.* Trade paperback. New York: Vertigo Comics/DC Comics, 1984.

Gifford, Jane. *The Wisdom of Trees.* New York: Sterling Publishing, 2001.

Goddard, David. *Sacred Magic of the Angels.* York Beach, ME: Samuel Weiser Books, 1996.

Greer, John Michael. *The New Encyclopedia of the Occult.* St. Paul, MN: Llewellyn Publications, 2003.

Grimassi, Raven. *Encyclopedia of Wicca & Witchcraft.* St. Paul, MN: Llewellyn Publications, 2000.

————. *Spirit of the Witch: Religion & Spirituality in Contemporary Witchcraft.* St. Paul, MN: Llewellyn Publications, 2003.

————. *The Witches' Craft: The Roots of Witchcraft & Magical Transformation.* St. Paul, MN: Llewellyn Publications, 2002.

Guiley, Rosemary Ellen. *The Encyclopedia of Witches and Witchcraft.* New York: Checkmark Books, 1999.

————. *Harper's Encyclopedia of Mystical & Paranormal Experience.* New York: HarperCollins Publishers, 1991.

Heath, Maya. *Ceridwen's Handbook of Incense, Oils, and Candles.* San Antonio, TX: Words of Wizdom International, 1996.

Illes, Judika. *The Element Encyclopedia of 5,000 Spells: The Ultimate Reference Book for the Magical Arts.* London, England: Element Books, 2004.

————. *The Element Encyclopedia of Witchcraft: The Complete A–Z for the Entire Magical World.* London, England: Element Books, 2005.

————. *Emergency Magic! 150 Spells for Surviving the Worst-Case Scenario.* Beverly, MA: Fair Winds Press, 2002.

————. *Pure Magic: A Complete Course in Spellcasting.* San Francisco, CA: Weiser Books, 2007.

Kaminski, Patricia, and Richard Katz. *Flower Essence Repertory: A Comprehensive Guide to North American and English Flower Essences for Emotional and Spiritual Well-Being.* Nevada City, CA: Flower Essence Society, a division of Earth Spirit, 1994.

Mickaharic, Draja. *A Spiritual Worker's Spell Book.* Bloomington, IN: Xlibris Corporation, 2003.

Morgan, Diane. *The Charmed Garden: Sacred and Enchanting Plants for the Magically Inclined Herbalist.* Scotland, UK: Findhorn Press, 2004.

Morrison, Dorothy. *Everyday Magic: Spells & Rituals for Modern Living.* St. Paul, MN: Llewellyn Publications, 2002.

———. *Utterly Wicked: Curses, Hexes & Other Unsavory Notions.* St. Louis, MO: WillowTree Press, 2007.

Moura, Ann. *Green Witchcraft II: Balancing Light & Shadow.* St. Paul, MN: Llewellyn Publications, 1999.

———. *Green Witchcraft III: The Manual.* St. Paul, MN: Llewellyn, 2000.

Passion, Lady, and *Diuvei, Coven Oldenwilde. *The Goodly Spellbook: Olde Spells for Modern Problems.* New York: Sterling Publishing, 2004.

Penczak, Christopher. *The Outer Temple of Witchcraft: Circles, Spells, and Rituals.* St. Paul, MN: Llewellyn Publications, 2004.

Pendell, Dale. *Pharmako/gnosis: Plant Teachers and the Poison Path.* San Francisco, CA: Mercury House, 2005

Sawyer, Pat Kirven. *Ancient Wisdom: The Master Grimoire: Herbs, Oils, and Incenses; Their Magickal Uses and Formulas.* The Woodlands, TX: Seventh House Publishing, 2005.

Shulke, Daniel A. *Viridarium Umbris: The Pleasure Garden of Shadow.* United Kingdom: Xoanon, 2005.

Skelton, Robin. *The Practice of Witchcraft Today: An Introduction to Beliefs and Rituals.* New York: Citidel Press, 1990.

Slater, Herman. *The Magickal Formulary Spellbook, Book I.* New York: Magickal Childe, 1987.

Valiente, Doreen. *An ABC of Witchcraft Past and Present.* New York: St. Martin's Press, 1973.

———. *Witchcraft for Tomorrow.* Blaine, WA: Phoenix Publishing, 1978.

Webb, Don. *Uncle Setnakt's Essential Guide to the Left Hand Path.* Smithville, TX: Runa-Raven Press, 1999.

Webster, Richard. *Feng Shui for Beginners: Successful Living by Design.* St. Paul, MN: Llewellyn Publications, 1992.

Whitcomb, Bill. *The Magician's Companion: A Practical & Encyclopedic Guide to Magical & Religious Symbolism.* St. Paul, MN: Llewellyn Publications, 1993.

Yronwode, Catherine. *Hoodoo Herb and Root Magic: A Materia Magica of African-American Conjure.* Forestville, CA: The Lucky Mojo Curio Co., 2002.

Online Resources

Alchemy Works: The Materials of Magic. http://www.alchemy-works .com (accessed May 15, 2008).

Leland, Charles Godfrey. *Aradia, or the Gospel of the Witches.* http:// www.sacred-texts.com/pag/aradia/index.htm (accessed August 23, 2008).

Vampyress. "Herbal Magick," *Vampyress Grimoire.* http://www.geocities .com/vampyressgrimoire/Herbal.htm (accessed June 14, 2008).

Yronwode, Catherine. *Lucky Mojo.* http://www.luckymojo.com (accessed June 1, 2008).

INDEX

TO WRITE TO THE AUTHOR

If you wish to contact the author or would like more information about this book, please write to the author in care of Llewellyn Worldwide and we will forward your request. Both the author and publisher appreciate hearing from you and learning of your enjoyment of this book and how it has helped you. Llewellyn Worldwide cannot guarantee that every letter written to the author can be answered, but all will be forwarded. Please write to:

Christopher Penczak
℅ Llewellyn Worldwide
2143 Wooddale Drive, Dept. 978-0-7387-1587-2
Woodbury, Minnesota 55125-2989, U.S.A.

Please enclose a self-addressed stamped envelope for reply,
or $1.00 to cover costs. If outside the U.S.A., enclose an
international postal reply coupon.

Many of Llewellyn's authors have websites with additional information and resources. For more information, please visit our website at http://www.llewellyn.com

The Witch's Shield

Protection Magick and Psychic Self-Defense

CHRISTOPHER PENCZAK

An intelligent and ethical guide to protection magick.

Is it possible to gain spiritual enlightenment even in difficult or threatening situations? In this thorough and thoughtful handbook, readers are urged to take responsibility for their own actions, ask what the situation might be teaching them, and hold compassion for those viewed as doing the harm.

Popular Wiccan author and teacher Christopher Penczak takes a threefold approach to protection magick in this guide for witches, pagans, shamans, and psychics. First, find out how to protect yourself using personal energy, will, and intent. Next, discover how to connect with your guardian spirits, angels, and patron deities. Finally, learn how to use traditional spellcraft and ritual for protection.

978-0-7387-0542-2, 216 pp., 6 x 9, includes CD   **$19.95**

The Outer Temple of Witchcraft

Circles, Spells, and Rituals

CHRISTOPHER PENCZAK

As you enter the heart of witchcraft, you find at its core the power of sacred space. In Christopher Penczak's first book of this series, *The Inner Temple of Witchcraft*, you found the sacred space within yourself. Now *The Outer Temple of Witchcraft* helps you manifest the sacred in the outer world through ritual and spellwork. The book's twelve lessons, with exercises, rituals, and homework, follow the traditional Wiccan one-year-and-a-day training period. It culminates in a self-test and self-initiation ritual to the second degree of witchcraft—the arena of the priestess and priest.

978-0-7387-0531-6, 448 pp., 7½ x 9⅛   **$19.95**

CD Companion

CHRISTOPHER PENCZAK

Reading meditations from a book is one thing, but when you can relax to the author's voice and appropriate background music, it is much easier to immerse yourself in the elemental realms and build a personal relationship with the goddess and god. This four-CD set leads you through many of the exercises in the book *The Outer Temple of Witchcraft*. It guides you through the meditations, the journeys to the elemental realms, and the casting of a magick circle. It even includes chants for celebrating the seasons and raising power, along with ritual music (without words) for setting the tone of your ceremonies.

978-0-7387-0532-3, set includes four CDs, 5¼ x 7½ Amaray DVD case $26.95

Magick of Reiki

Focused Energy for Healing, Ritual & Spiritual Development

CHRISTOPHER PENCZAK

What is Reiki? How has this Japanese healing tradition evolved over the years? How are modern magick practitioners using Reiki energy in their spells and rituals?

Christopher Penczak answers these questions and more in his groundbreaking examination of Reiki from a magickal perspective. The history, mythos, variations, and three degrees of Reiki are discussed in depth. Penczak also suggests way to integrate Reiki and magickal practice, such as using Reiki energy for psychic development and with candle magick, crystals, herbs, charms, and talismans.

978-0-7387-0573-6, 288 pp., 7½ x 9⅛   **$18.95**

Instant Magick

Ancient Wisdom, Modern Spellcraft

CHRISTOPHER PENCZAK

What if you could practice magick anytime, without the use of ceremonial spells, altars, or magickal tools? Items such as candles, special ingredients, and exotic symbols are necessary to perform many types of magick, but these items aren't always feasible, attainable, or even available. The purest form of magick—tapping into your own energetic awareness to create change—is accessible simply through the power of your will.

Popular author Christopher Penczak explains how to weave natural energies into every facet of life by inspiring readers to explore their own individual willpower. This book features personalized techniques used to weed out any unwanted, unhealthy, or unnecessary desires to find a true, balanced magickal being. Penczak's innovative, modern spellcasting techniques utilize meditation, visualization, words, and intent in any situation, at any time. The results can seem instantaneous, and the potential limitless.

978-0-7387-0859-1, 216 pp., 6 x 9 **$13.95**

Silver's Spells for Abundance

SILVER RAVENWOLF

Take charge of your finances the Silver way! One of the most famous Witches in the world today shows you how to get the upper hand on your cash flow with techniques personally designed and tested by the author herself. She will show you how to banish those awful old debts without heartache, get money back from someone who owes you, and transform your money energy so it flows in the right direction—toward you!

An abundance of spells can aid you in everything from winning a court case to getting creditors off your back. You'll also find a wealth of historical and practical information on spell elements and ingredients. *Silver's Spells for Abundance* is the first in a new series of five books by best-selling Wiccan author Silver RavenWolf.

978-0-7387-0525-5, 192 pp., 5³⁄₁₆ x 8 $12.95

Spirit of the Witch

Religion & Spirituality in Contemporary Witchcraft

Raven Grimassi

Find peace and happiness in the spiritual teachings of the Craft

What is in the spirit of the Witch? What empowers Witches in their daily and spiritual lives? How does a person become a Witch?

In *Spirit of the Witch*, Raven Grimassi, an initiate of several Wiccan traditions, reveals the Witch as a citizen living and working like all others—and as a spiritual being who seeks alignment with the natural world. He provides an overview of the Witch's view of deity and how it manifests in the cycles of nature. Seasonal rituals, tools, magic, and beliefs are all addressed in view of their spiritual underpinnings. Additionally, he shows the relationship among elements of pre-Christian European religion and modern Witchcraft beliefs, customs, and practices.

978-0-7387-0338-1, 264 pp., 6 x 9   **$12.95**

Mapping Your Money

Understanding Your Financial Potential

KRIS BRANDT RISKE

(Includes CD-ROM to calculate and interpret your financial picture.)

Whether we are filthy rich or impoverished, money plays an important role in all our lives. Getting a grasp on finances can be as simple as consulting the stars. Whether you're a pinchpenny or a spendthrift, *Mapping Your Money* can help you understand your money mindset and financial outlook.

How can I become more wealthy? Why is my sister so frugal? Is it too late to change my spending habits? These and other financial questions can be answered with this valuable astrological tool. No previous astrological knowledge is needed. A birth date and time is all that's required to astrologically analyze financial traits for yourself and others.

978-0-7387-0672-6, 240 pp., 7½ x 9⅛, CD-ROM for PC format with Windows 95/98/ME/XP **$19.95**

To order, call 1-877-NEW-WRLD
Prices subject to change without notice
Order at Llewellyn.com 24 hours a day, 7 days a week!